Caribbean Cruising

First Edition

Published by The Nazca Plains Corporation
Las Vegas, Nevada
2009

ISBN: 978-1-934625-99-6

Published by

The Nazca Plains Corporation ®
4640 Paradise Rd, Suite 141
Las Vegas NV 89109-8000

PUBLISHER'S NOTE
Caribbean Cruising is a work of fiction created wholly by *Lew Bull's* imagination.
All characters are fictional and any resemblance to any persons living or deceased is
purely by accident. No portion of this book reflects any real person or events.

Cover Photos, IStockPhoto
Art Director, Blake Stephens

Dedication

To my mother, Frances,
For 91 years you have lived your life with fun and laughter
And I'm grateful for instilling that fun in me.

Caribbean Cruising

First Edition

Lew Bull

Chapter 1

It was a very ordinary day, except that a gentle drizzle fell and the sun had been blocked out by a low cloud, and those attending Margaret Withers's funeral were all standing, huddled together under somber black umbrellas next to the open grave. The drone of the priest's voice was matched only by the squishing sound as people adjusted their standing positions on the wet ground. Myra Bloomberg stood passively listening to the priest's incantations, and slowly became lulled by his monotone voice. The sudden ringing of a mobile phone shattered the tranquility and solemnity of the occasion. What made this occurrence even more startling and controversial was the tune that the phone was playing: *When the Saints go marching in.* Heads turned in all directions to identify the location of the disturbance, but the priest was not about to be outdone by a polyphonic version of an old hit song. The melody continued while everyone became more and more frustrated by the sound, until eventually, a lady standing next to Myra nudged her.

"Dear, I think it's yours," she whispered.

"Is it?" queried Myra and then realized that in fact the melodious disruption was coming from her handbag. She grinned at the priest, apologized for the disruption, opened her bag, which brought out a louder version of the tune and switched on the phone.

"Hello," she answered, whispering so as not to disrupt the funeral service any more.

"Hi Mum, why are you whispering?" asked Michael, her only son.

"Hello darling. I'm whispering because I'm at a funeral… no don't hang up; I can talk … what's the problem? …It's Mrs. Withers… I don't know if you knew her… many years ago she used to live next door to us … long before your father died…"

1

"Excuse me," interrupted the priest, glaring at Myra as she smiled back at him.

"It's my son," she innocently replied, and carried on her conversation.

"Now where was I? ... Oh yes... she was our next door neighbor and she had a daughter ... Chrissie, Chrassie, or something like that; I'm not sure what her name was, but you and she never seemed to get along... well any rate Mrs. Withers died so I thought I should attend her funeral... hm? ...No problem, talk... Oh, I'd love to come for dinner. What time? ... 7:00 sounds fine to me and then I'll fill you in on the entire goings on that are happening here. Is Selwyn cooking as usual or are we eating take-away? ... Good...Take care love. Bye."

Myra switched off her phone and turned smiling to the woman next to her.

"My son," she grinned.

"May we now continue?" asked the priest, sounded exasperated.

"Yes, please do," replied Myra.

The service continued uninterrupted and Mrs. Withers was eventually laid to rest in the damp ground. Possibly as a result of the embarrassing phone conversation, after the funeral everyone seemed to avoid Myra, much to her consternation, but she put it down to their anti-social upbringing that they wouldn't speak to her, so she climbed in her car and headed home.

On arriving home she took off her wide-brimmed black hat with a peacock feather festooned on its crown, kicked off her black high-heel shoes, took off her somber black funereal dress, that never got worn other than to funerals, and changed into something more comfortable and more Myra – bright and colorful.

She dialed a number and waited for the phone to ring.

"Rob Clayton, Private Investigator. How may I help you?" came the sweet sounding voice.

"Hello, is that you Selwyn? It's Myra."

"Oh hi Myra, how are you?"

"Fine thanks. I just wanted to know if I must bring anything tonight."

"Oh, did Michael get hold of you?"

"Yes and he told me to be at your place at 7:00, but I just wanted to know whether you needed anything."

"I don't think so, just you."

"So tell me, sweetie, how's the job going and how's Rob?"

"He's fine and we're actually quite busy at the moment."

"Oh good, that means you've got lots of cases to tell me about."

"Myra, you know we're not supposed to discuss our cases; they're confidential."

"Please, Selwyn, you're family. If my son-in-law can't keep me up to date with the latest scandal, then what good is he in the family?"

"You know you drive a hard bargain, Myra. But listen I must go and do some work. We'll see you tonight, then."

"Bye my darling."

"Cheers, Myra."

Selwyn replaced the phone and shouted through to Rob's adjoining office, "Myra sends love."

"How's the old bird?" shouted Rob back.

"She's fine. She's coming to dinner at our place tonight, so she just phoned to find out if she must bring anything."

"She really is a sweet and caring mother. Mike's lucky to have her."

"We're all lucky to have her because she treats both me and you as though we are her other sons."

"You're right, Selwyn. If it weren't for her sense of humor and caring nature, I don't know what I would have done after the incident with Greg and the murder of his son's boyfriend. Come to think of it, I don't know what I would have done without you and Mike. You really supported me throughout that time."

Two years had gone by since Greg was arrested and charged with the murder of Byron Browning in Miami and still Rob had not made any contact with his old friend. He knew that Greg still had another four years of his sentence to serve, but didn't know whether Greg would come back and try to make a life with Rob again or not. Rob had managed, through the friendship with Michael and Selwyn, to forget about Greg and to try and get on with his life. The two young men had often taken Rob away for weekends and Myra, bless her, had tried to introduce Rob to many eligible young men, but without much success. Ever since the murder trial two years previously, she had constantly pestered Rob by giving him the names and details of these young men, who ranged from doctors to lawyers and accountants to professional businessmen.

It was also coming up to two years that Michael and Selwyn had been together and their relationship seemed to be growing stronger and stronger. In fact the dinner party that Myra had been invited to was to celebrate their second anniversary of being in a relationship, but they hadn't told her.

"I hope you're also coming tonight for dinner?" asked Selwyn as he marched into Rob's office, "or have you got a date?"

"No such luck, buddy. I'll be there for dinner, so long as you're cooking."

"Oh yes, I'm slaving away in the kitchen tonight," replied Selwyn.

"Selwyn, on a more serious note, I need you to go on a stakeout from tomorrow."

"Where to?"

"I've taken on a case that involves fraud and theft and I need you to infiltrate an organization in order to find out who's carrying out these deeds. The CEO has approached me so he knows of my plans to put you in among the workers. You'll be a new employee, learning the ropes of the business and should you find out anything about what's going on there, you report directly to me and I'll pass it on to the CEO. We don't want you associating with or speaking to the CEO, because none of the workers do that and if you did speak to him, it might blow your cover."

"Is it dangerous?" enquired Selwyn.

"No more dangerous than any of the jobs we do. I'm not expecting guns being fired or anything like that, if that's what you mean."

"So where is it?"

"It's a clothing store in Main Street. You're going to meet the CEO who will employ you and tell you in which department he wants you to work; after that, you're on your own. Any questions?"

"Sounds simple enough. I think it should be OK."

"Oh, and one other thing, you'll need to make sure that you dress accordingly; nothing casual."

"You mean tie, jacket and all that crap."

"Afraid so."

After their conversation, Selwyn returned to his office and continued with his admin and letter writing until it was time to head home and start preparing dinner for the guests.

Chapter 2

Michael and Selwyn busied themselves in their kitchen preparing for Michael's mother and Rob's visit. They had decided to make Chinese for a change and the rice and various other dishes were steaming beautifully on the stove. The beers were chilling in the fridge and Myra's whiskey was ready for her.

At precisely 7:00, there was a knock on the front door of Michael and Selwyn's apartment.

"That'll be Mum," said Michael going to open the door for her.

Myra was immaculately dressed as usual, with not a hair out of place. One thing about Michael's mother, she was the epitome of fashion and always looked smart no matter where she went; even if it was to have tea with a friend, Myra looked as though she was off to a wedding or some such event.

"Hi Mum, come in," said Michael giving his mother a welcoming kiss.

"Hello my boykie. How are you?"

"Fine thanks Mum, and you?"

"Couldn't be better."

"Where's by beautiful son-in-law?"

"Busy in the kitchen, as usual."

"And tell me, what are we having for dinner tonight?"

"Chinese."

"Oh, God, not take-away!"

"No, the chef's been busy at it since he got home from work."

They both wandered through to the kitchen where Selwyn, with oriental apron on, was busily slaving over the stove.

"Wow, you look smart, Myra. Are you going out after dinner?" asked Selwyn, giving her a peck on the cheek while he continued to stir the ingredients of a

5

large saucepan.

"No such luck, my boy, but you know me. I always like to dress up when I go out. And this apron?" asked Myra, pointing to Selwyn's oriental design apron.

"Rob gave it to me. It was given to him by a client and he thought it would make him look ridiculous wearing it so he offered it to me," replied Selwyn.

"Now tell me, what does the Chinese writing on it mean?"

"I haven't an idea, but I like the picture of the Great Wall."

Michael laughed and said, "But you must see Selwyn on informal occasions."

"Why? What do you mean?"

"Well the apron gets worn, but nothing else gets worn underneath it."

"Ooh! You saucy thing. So why aren't you giving me a treat tonight?" Chuckled Myra, patting Selwyn on his cute butt. "So when am I going to see it?"

"See what?" asked Selwyn, innocently.

"This cute naked butt of yours."

"You'll have to ask your son if he'll allow me to reveal that to you," joked Selwyn.

"You know him; he'll probably get embarrassed and say no. Never mind, Selwyn, we'll make a date one day when Michael's not around, then you can show it to me" she laughed.

"You know Mum, you're incorrigible; you'll never change," said Michael, almost with frustration in his voice.

"Michael, leave your Mum alone. That's what makes her so special, her willingness for fun," replied Selwyn.

"Come Mum, let's go into the lounge and get you a drink. The whiskey's waiting for you."

Michael and Myra made their way through to the lounge where he poured her a drink and they sat chatting while Selwyn finished off the meal in the kitchen.

"Mum, you should have cut me short when I phoned you while you were at the funeral. It's very impolite to do what you did."

"Rubbish! When my son calls me, I talk to him, and neither the living nor the dead is going to stop me. In any case, Mrs. Withers was dead; she was in no hurry to be buried!"

"Was it a big funeral?"

"Not really. I thought she had more friends than what turned up, but maybe it was because of the weather. That's the problem with funerals; you can't always arrange them to suit the weather. It also plays havoc with the outfits to wear on these occasions."

"But I'm sure that you looked lovely, as usual."

"Naturally, but I must tell you about Mrs. Liebewitz."

"Mum, I'm not really interested in your scandal, because that's all it is."

"No it's not. Well then tell me this, is Rob coming tonight?"

"Yes, why?"

"Well I'll wait for him and then I'll tell him about Mrs. Liebewitz."

"What does he need to know about Mrs. Liebewitz?"

"You said you weren't interested in what I had to say, so I'll stay shtum until Rob arrives!"

"Don't be silly, Mum."

"I'm not being silly. It's just that you're obviously not interested in my daily happenings, so I won't bore you."

Myra adopted a resolute expression and clammed up. She sat indulging in her whiskey, savoring each sip that she took. Just then, Selwyn emerged from the kitchen, sans his apron.

"Come and sit next to me, Selwyn, my darling son doesn't want to hear my stories, but I'm sure you'd like to hear them."

Selwyn flashed a glance towards Michael, not so much to reprimand him for not listening to his mother's stories, but more as a *help!* Sign, but Michael wasn't about to come to the aid of his partner. Fortunately for Selwyn, he was saved by the bell, or rather the knock on the front door. Both boys shot out of their seats and headed for the front door.

"Both of you to greet me! Wow, I've never had that before," said Rob in amazement.

"It's my Mum," whispered Michael. "She's driving us up the wall."

Rob chuckled at Michael's comment about his mother, walked past them and went into the lounge.

"Hi, Myra. Nice to see you," he said, kissing her on both cheeks.

"Hello Rob. Good to see you again. I'm well, but how are you?"

"Just great."

Rob seated himself alongside Myra on the couch and they started chatting casually to each other.

"Drink, Rob?"

"Beer please, Mike."

Michael headed off to the kitchen and soon returned with a cold beer for Rob, which he handed to him.

"Cheers," he said on receiving his beer. "By the way, are we toasting anything?"

Michael and Selwyn smiled to each other.

"Well if you must know, the reason we invited you both for dinner is that it's Michael and my second anniversary together."

"Oh great! Congratulations you guys," said Rob, rising from his seat and kissing each of the boys.

"Why didn't you tell me, Michael?"

"Because we didn't want a fuss."

"Well you've lasted two whole years," murmured Myra.

"Do you remember when you first met me, Myra?" asked Selwyn.

"Yes! You shocked me because I was expecting a nice Jewish boy whose

7

name was Selwyn, and instead, what did I get? A nice Black goy. Not that I'm complaining, because I know how you've looked after my Mikey for me."

"But he's also looked after me and been good to me," replied Selwyn.

"Well he had no choice, my boy," continued Myra. "If he hadn't, I would have given him a damn good hiding."

Michael laughed at the thought of his mother giving him a hiding.

"You laugh? You're not too old or big to put over my knee and smack that little ass of yours," she said.

"Myra, I wouldn't do that, if I were you," said Selwyn, "because he might enjoy it."

"Oh, is he into a little S & M?" enquired Myra, glee written across her face.

"What do you know about S & M, Mum?"

"You'd be surprised what I know. You think I'm some stupid Yiddisher mama, well let me tell you, I've been around and I know what goes on in life. Talking of life, that reminds me. Rob I wanted to tell Michael a story earlier, but he wasn't interested so I said I'd wait until you arrived."

"Mum, I'm sure that Rob doesn't want to hear, and in any case, he doesn't know who Mrs. Liebewitz is."

"Well I'll tell him."

Myra then turned her attention to Rob and proceeded to regale him with her story of Mrs. Liebewitz.

"Mona Liebewitz and I have been friends since I don't know when. We lived near each other many years ago and we saw our children growing up together. Well Mona was telling me the other day about her son Monty, such a nice boy. He's just turned forty-three and he's a gynecologist. Well at any rate, Monty seemed to be too preoccupied with his career to worry about anyone, but Mona tells me that he's met someone and they're getting married."

"Good for old Monty," said Michael, with a rather bored tone.

"He's a surgeon."

"Who's a surgeon, Mum?"

"Monty's partner that he's going to marry."

"But you said, 'he' didn't you?"

"That's right," glowed Myra. "After all these years it turns out that Monty's gay and Mona never knew. Of course I told her I had always had the idea that he was, but didn't want to say anything about it.'

Michael passed a tired look to Selwyn. It was amazing how much his mother knew about people and whether they were gay or not.

"So now he and his partner are going to get married?"

"Yes and Mona's so excited. She's giving them a really fancy wedding and they're going off to the Bahamas for their honeymoon."

"Are you hinting that Selwyn and I should now have a wedding after having spent two years together?"

"No, but I did get to thinking that it might be nice."

"You're only saying that because you don't want to be left behind as it were. Selwyn and Rob, you must understand that some Jewish mothers thrive on competing against each other. Anything you can do, I can do bigger and better. Not so, Mum?"

"That's not true, Michael, but I just thought it would be nice. Don't you agree Selwyn?"

"I'm very happy the way we are, Myra. I don't need some lavish affair, which is a waste of money, especially after we've already spent two of our years together as a couple. Of course the honeymoon part sounds nice."

"Oh," came a deflated and uninspiring reply from Myra. Obviously she was hoping to outdo Mona Liebewitz's wedding.

"Have you been invited to the wedding, Mum?"

"No, not yet, but they apparently haven't set a date yet."

"I wonder which of the two is the bride?" remarked Michael.

"Don't be facetious, Michael," said his mother.

"I like your thoughts on the honeymoon, Selwyn," said Michael having sat and cogitated. "Maybe we could go on a cruise and treat that as our belated honeymoon."

"That sounds like a really great idea. Why don't we look into that," suggested Selwyn, and then added, "There's just one problem."

"And what's that?" enquired Michael.

"It's easy for you to take leave, but I'll have to talk very nicely to my boss, who can be a bit of a shit sometimes."

Rob grinned at the thought of being called a 'shit', but didn't take offence as he knew it was all in jest. "Why don't you ask him, them?" said Rob, waiting to see if Selwyn would respond.

"I'll have to get him on his own when he's in a good mood and then seduce him; then maybe he might allow me to go."

"Lucky boss," chirped Rob.

"If you're going to seduce him," said Michael, continuing the banter, "the chances are he might like the seduction so much he might want to go on holiday with you."

"Hey, I never thought of that! That means I can leave you at home, can't I Michael."

"Not on your life!"

"What about me?" piped up a solitary voice.

"What about you?" asked Michael.

"I'm the mother of the groom. Shouldn't I be allowed to go as well?"

"Four is a clutter, Mum."

"Why four?"

"Well if the groom and the bride are there, and the best man is accompanying them, because he happens to be the bride's boss, and then we have the groom's mother tagging along, it becomes a clutter," said Michael, having worked everything out.

"Oh, so you don't want me there, that's fine. I know when I'm not wanted," bemoaned Myra, producing an Oscar award performance; the only thing missing were the tears.

"I'm sure we could make a plan," volunteered Rob.

"Hey, whose honeymoon is this anyway?" asked Selwyn beginning to get worried that between Rob and Myra, he and Michael could even find themselves left on shore.

Dinner was served and devoured, and dishes were washed and dried, then they all settled down to more drinking and talking. Eventually, at some late hour in the night, both Rob and Myra excused themselves and set off home, but before leaving, Rob reminded Selwyn of his 'new job' and to dress appropriately the following morning. Michael and Selwyn decided to have a nightcap and contemplate the idea of a honeymoon that had been put forward earlier, and then Selwyn went through his wardrobe to take out some clothes for the following morning.

"Where are you working tomorrow?"

"I don't know. All Rob's told me is that it's a clothing store and I must dress accordingly. I'm probably going to be a salesman."

"And what are you investigating?"

Apparently it's a fraud and theft case, but I don't have a specific person to watch, so I should imagine it's going to be quite difficult."

"Just be careful, Selwyn. Don't say too much and just keep your wits about you."

The two young men climbed into bed and soon were in dreamland, resting after a most entertaining evening.

Chapter 3

Michael was up first the following morning and started getting their breakfast ready. Once he had got everything ready he went into their bedroom and gently shook Selwyn to wake him up.

"Time to get up, Sleeping Beauty. You've got a new assignment starting today."

Selwyn yawned and pulled Michael down to him in order to give him a good morning kiss.

"Do you know how I feel like getting dressed up like some fancy Christmas tree? I hate wearing a tie."

"But you're now going to be a high-powered clothing salesman."

"Sure," came the disheartened reply.

Selwyn crawled from the bed and shuffled to the bathroom where he stood under the pouring water of the shower, allowing its freshness to wake him up properly. His light brown body glistened as the water ran over his smooth skin. He stood soaping his lithe body, wondering whether he should approach Michael for a little bit of early morning sex. The soap suds trickled down his long, flaccid cock and he began stroking his length in an effort to get an erection. Soon he had achieved it and he stood under the water admiring the thickness of his hardened cock, bringing himself closer to his climax.

After he had showered, shaved and checked for any blemishes on his skin, he wandered back into the bedroom and proceeded to get dressed. On completion, he went in the kitchen where Michael was and putting his arms around Michael, hugged him.

"What's that for?" asked Michael, a little surprised.

"I just felt like loving you, that's all."

"Wow, but you look smart. I don't think I've ever seen you so formally dressed." Michael laughed and added, "I'm used to seeing you either with nothing on or in drag."

"But you know that I haven't done any drag acts for about a year and a half. In fact it stopped just after I started working for Rob."

"You're right. It has been quite some time. Selwyn is Rob fetching you from here, or are you going into the office?"

"I've got to go to the office and then he's taking me to meet the CEO of this company."

"In that case, hurry up and I'll drop you off at the office."

They completed eating their breakfast and set off for Selwyn's office, where Rob was waiting when they arrived.

"Good luck, and I'll see you later," shouted Michael as he drove off.

Rob and Selwyn headed off to the clothing store, with Selwyn asking a thousand and one different questions.

"Just remember what I've taught you Selwyn, and remember that should you find anything out, it's to come directly to me. Don't mention any of your findings to anyone there, including the CEO. You'll meet him today and he knows the set-up we're doing, but you don't speak to him again, because apparently no-one in the company speaks to him, and here I'm referring to the sales staff."

They drove through the traffic for about a half hour and then pulled up outside an elegant building.

"This is it, Selwyn. DOC Fashions."

"What does the DOC stand for, Rob?"

"It's the initials of the CEO, Derek Oliver Campbell."

They parked and went in to the reception area and asked for the CEO. While they waited, Rob and Selwyn admired the array of clothing on sale. Although it was an eclectic mix of styles, they all looked smart, whether it be casual wear or formal. A tall, elegantly dressed man approached them. He had slicked back dark hair, was slim and had piercing blue eyes. When he reached Rob, he extended a broad but long-fingered hand, which Rob took and shook.

"Derek, this is Selwyn. Selwyn, this is Mr. Campbell."

"How do you do, sir," said Selwyn extending his hand, but didn't receive a reciprocal hand to shake.

"You'll be working in the casual department to begin with and then we'll move you around. Your hours are 9:00 until 17:00. You will have a forty-five minute lunch break, a morning and afternoon tea break of ten minutes each, and no smoking in the building. Any questions? No? Good."

Selwyn never even had a chance to open his mouth should he have wanted to ask a question. Mr. Campbell seemed excessively formal. In fact, Selwyn considered him incredibly cold and aloof, but, he had a job of work to do for Rob.

"I'll pick you up at 17:00 this afternoon and take you home, Selwyn. Take care," said Rob and he left the confines of elegance to return to his uninteresting office.

Mr. Campbell had an assistant who took Selwyn to the casual clothing section and introduced him to the staff there. There was to be Selwyn and three other salesmen, Brent, an African-American of about twenty-one, with a shaved head, who seemed friendly enough, Chris, a tall, slim, rather camp individual with fairly longish dark hair and a smiling open face, and Bobby, who was a typical jock. Bobby intrigued Selwyn as he looked decidedly masculine, yet Selwyn sensed an underlining fallibility in the man. Bobby was like a cross between Rob, who was a giant of a man, and Michael, who was muscular but not as defined as Rob was. Bobby strutted when he walked and Selwyn liked the look that this gave Bobby. Instinctively, Selwyn attached himself to Bobby and made sure that any questions that needed to be asked, he would ask Bobby.

Bobby explained various necessary pieces of information to Selwyn, such as how the credit card system worked and how they dealt with alterations to clothing should the client require it, down to how to use the cash register. Selwyn hung on every word that Bobby said.

"How long have you been working here, Bobby?"

"Two years."

"And the others here?"

"I've been here the longest and then Chris, but Brent only started about a month ago. I tend to stick to myself most of the time. And you, what were you doing before you came here?"

Selwyn had a panic attack. He couldn't say that he worked for a P.I. nor was he willing to say that he was a part-time drag artiste par excellence.

"I was studying," came the reply, "but I decided to drop out. I found it boring."

"I wanted to go to college to play sport," said Bobby, after hearing the word 'study', "but my folks couldn't afford sending me there and I couldn't get a scholarship."

"That's sad because you look like you've got quite a good body."

Selwyn was back to his old tricks. Although he and Michael had been happily together for two years, Selwyn still suffered from his over-active libido and had this constant desire to bed any man he saw. Of course he knew that Michael was well aware of this problem and should he meet a man that he liked, he would always try to involve Michael as well. Bobby seemed different, though. Somehow Selwyn wasn't entirely sure that Bobby would even consider going with another man.

"Thanks for the compliment, Selwyn. I think it's because of my going to gym that my body's as developed as it is."

"Have you ever thought of modeling?" asked Selwyn, and then quickly added, "What I mean is that with your body, you could get plenty of work; photo shoots for example."

"Actually, I've never given it much thought, but you might have a good point there," said Bobby, admiring himself in one of the many mirrors scattered around the store.

Much of the rest of the day was spent with Selwyn following either Bobby or one of the other salesmen around, watching what they did and trying to learn what was required to be a successful salesman. At lunchtime Selwyn went off to the store's canteen and sat down to have something to eat. While he was sitting there, Chris came up to him and asked if he could sit with him.

"Sure, Chris, grab a chair."

The tall man slinked off to find a chair and then returned with it, placed it at the table and sat down, his long legs, seemingly slid under him as he lowered himself into the chair.

"Do you mind if I give you some advice?" asked Chris, leaning across the table and using a sotto voce voice to speak to Selwyn.

Selwyn was a little mystified by this approach.

"Sure," he answered, also leaning in towards Chris.

"I'd be very careful of the boss, you know Mr. Campbell."

"Oh really. Why?" asked an intrigued Selwyn.

"He's very haughty and spies on all the staff."

"But why would he do that?"

"I don't know, but I've often caught him watching me, and it worries me."

"Does he sneak around to watch you, Chris, or is he constantly in the casual section watching you, openly?"

"Sometimes he comes and stands and watches, without saying a word, and other times I catch him sneaking a look from behind one of the other counters. It's actually very worrying."

Selwyn wondered if Chris might be his target regarding the fraud and theft, so decided he'd make a point of watching out for Chris.

"Has he ever spoken to you when he's been watching you?" asked Selwyn.

"Not really. He might come and ask how I am, but nothing about the actual sales transactions."

"Maybe he's just trying to be friendly towards you."

Chris flicked a lock of hair that had fallen across his brow and over one eye. "Once he came up behind me and placed a hand on my shoulder," remarked Chris, fear written across his face.

"What's wrong with that?" asked Selwyn.

"It seemed so strange. In fact, you know what, now that I think about it, that day was the only time I've ever seen him smile."

"Oh well that's a good sign. I thought he was incapable of smiling. When I was introduced to him this morning I found him intimidating."

"Exactly! That's what I mean. And did he look at you in a funny sort of way?"

"Hm, not really. He just looked at me as though I was a piece of dirt to be trampled all over."

"Ah!" exclaimed Chris. "I like you. You see him exactly the same way that

I do. For a moment I thought I was paranoid and it was only me who saw him in that light."

"Chris, I don't think you need worry about him. I'm sure that he's harmless. What I mean is that I don't think he's a Hannibal Lector type person."

Chris gave a nervous laugh. "I hope not, but tell me about you."

"Well what do you want to know?"

"Are you married or single; do you live alone or not? Those sorts of things."

Selwyn's mind flashed. Does he divulge his real life-style to Chris or does he fabricate it?

"I share an apartment with a friend."

"Oh that's fabulous. I live alone. And your friend, what does she do?"

Selwyn wanted to laugh, but bit his tongue and kept a straight face.

"Actually Chris, I share a place with a male friend."

His eyes lit up.

"Oh, that's fabulous, and what does he do?"

"He's in the property business."

"Fabulous. And tell me, how long have you been staying with him?"

"Two years."

"So long! That's fabulous."

Selwyn was beginning to tire of hearing Chris's 'Fabulous' to everything and thought he'd scream if he heard it once more.

"What about you, Chris. Have you never thought of sharing a place with someone? It does cut costs you know."

"I have, but I don't know who'd want to share with me?"

"Have you ever asked anyone?"

"Not really. I did ask someone many years ago, but they declined," he replied, looking sad as he said it. "But I'm happy on my own. I've got my cat, Charlie, to keep me company, so it's not so bad."

"What type of cat is Charlie, Chris?" asked Selwyn, trying to show interest.

"He's a Siamese."

"Oh that's terrific."

"But tell me Selwyn, do you and your friend ever go out together?"

"Yes, but sometimes he has appointments so I just stay at home while he goes out on them."

"Oh. And what do you do when you're on your own. You know, when he's not there?"

"Nothing much.

"Do you ever watch videos?"

Selwyn wondered where this conversation was heading.

"If I'm in the mood, yes."

"And what types do you like watching?"

Where on earth was this conversation heading, wondered Selwyn?

"Oh, I'm not fussy, I've got a pretty Catholic taste. I'll watch almost anything."

Chris smiled. "If your friend goes out one night, maybe we can watch a video together. You could always come round to my place, if you like."

"Thanks," replied Selwyn, who was now getting a little concerned about Chris's ulterior motives, if he had any; so he looked at his watch and decided that it was time to head back to the sales area.

Selwyn headed back, closely followed by Chris. When they returned, Bobby and Brent went for their lunch break.

While they were standing behind their counter, a customer came towards them.

"I'll get this," said Chris, smiling to the approaching man.

"Good afternoon sir, how may we help you?"

"I'm looking for beachwear."

"Right here, sir?"

"Could I have a look at your bathing costumes."

"Certainly sir. What type were you wanting; Speedo, board shorts?"

"Speedo please."

"If you'll come this way, I'll show you our stock."

Chris led the man a little distance from Selwyn and proceeded to show him a variety of Speedos.

"What size, sir?"

"I'm actually not sure."

Chris took hold of a tape measure and wrapped it around the customer's waist, read the measurement and trotted off to find the appropriate size.

"I've brought you two sizes, sir. Try these on and if they fit, we can then decide on colors and styles. Would you mind coming with me to the fitting room, sir."

Chris led his customer to the fitting room, opened the door for him and ushered him in, closing the door behind the customer. Chris stood outside the change room and waited while the customer tried on his Speedos. After a while, the customer opened the door and peered out. Selwyn could see that he had on a canary yellow Speedo and watched as Chris spoke to the man, then the door closed again. While Selwyn was standing watching Chris and the customer, he noticed, out the corner of his eye, that Mr. Campbell was also watching, but he wasn't sure whether the boss was watching him or Chris. The change room door opened once more and this time Selwyn could see the man wearing a black Speedo. This time, Chris went into the change room with the customer and closed the door behind him.

Selwyn surreptitiously watched to see if Mr. Campbell had seen Chris disappear into the change room, which he obviously had done, because he started moving towards the change room into which Chris had gone. Selwyn immediately picked up a Speedo costume and hurried towards the change room in the hopes of warning Chris before the boss got to him. Selwyn knocked on the change room door and opened it a little to warn Chris. When he glanced in he saw Chris in a compromising position on his knees in front of the customer. Immediately Chris rose to his feet and hustled out of the change room, just as Mr. Campbell arrived.

"What's going on here?" asked the intimidating CEO.

"The customer needed a size bigger, sir, so I brought it to give to Chris who was helping the customer."

Chris was the color of embarrassment. His face went puce. "Thank you for getting the bigger size, Selwyn," said Chris taking the Speedo from Selwyn, who returned to where he'd been standing before Mr. Campbell had made his advance. Mr. Campbell's eyes narrowed and he glared at Chris, but then turned and marched off.

"Thanks Selwyn, you saved me that time," said Chris, slowly returning to what might be considered a normal color.

"What were you doing?"

Chris once more blushed and tried to busy himself rather than answer Selwyn's question, but Selwyn was well aware what Chris had been doing.

"Please don't tell the others," pleaded Chris.

The customer emerged from the change room and walked with Chris to the cash register.

"I'll take this one, thanks, and thank you for your personal assistance," said the customer, smiling at Chris, but turning to Selwyn and giving him a wink.

Once the customer had left, nothing more about the incident was discussed and the rest of the afternoon passed by without any drama or excitement. At 17:00, Rob was waiting outside for Selwyn and the two drove back to Selwyn and Michael's apartment.

"How did it go today?" enquired Rob.

"I survived, but we had a bit of fun this afternoon."

"Why what happened?"

"A customer came in looking for a Speedo costume and one of the guys served him, but did so in more than one way."

"What do you mean?"

"Well, Mr. Campbell was watching and the guy went into the change room with the customer and I saw old Eagle Eye heading in his direction, so I grabbed a Speedo and rushed to the change room. When I got there, the salesman was on his knees giving the customer a blowjob…"

"…You're joking!" exclaimed Rob, bursting into laughter. "What did the boss say?"

"I managed to warn the guy and told the boss that they needed a larger size Speedo and I had taken it to the change room and the salesman was helping the customer."

"But did you find anything out about the thieving and fraud?"

"No, not yet, but give me time and I'll find out for you."

When they arrived at Selwyn and Michael's apartment, Rob went upstairs to have a drink with the boys, where Selwyn had to regale Michael with his story about Chris and the customer.

"Do you think the boss knew what was going on?" asked Michael, at the end of the story.

"I don't know, but Chris said an interesting thing to me. He said he'd noticed the boss watching him, but he didn't know why. Do you think he might be the guy who's stealing, Rob?"

"I don't know, but based on what you saw today and your story, I wouldn't think so. I think this Chris is probably just into a little excitement in his life."

"You mean hitting on customers," laughed Michael.

"Just keep your eyes open tomorrow, Selwyn, and if you have to, phone me the minute to see anything of importance."

"Sure, Rob. Does that include Chris getting it off with another customer?"

"Don't joke, I'm serious."

***

The following day Selwyn was back at work, with a more subdued Chris on hand.

"Selwyn, I must speak to you. Privately!"

Selwyn looked at Chris and realized that Brent was standing nearby so he agreed to move away with Chris.

"What's the problem, Chris?"

"It's about yesterday."

"Oh I wouldn't worry. I haven't said anything to anyone."

"I know you haven't, but I got called in when I arrived this morning."

"By whom?"

"Mr. Campbell. I had to go to his office. He sat very upright in his chair, looking very stern. I was really intimidated by his appearance. Then he asked me outright what I was doing with the customer."

"What did you say?"

"I told him I wasn't doing anything. Just in case he asks you, would you say the same?"

"OK. And then?"

"He did the strangest thing. He stood up and moved around his desk to where I was standing, rested both hands on my shoulders, looked me straight in the eyes and said that he hoped I wasn't lying. It was creepy."

"How so?"

"He had a slight smile on his face as he said it. I don't know if he's some sort of nut case."

Selwyn laughed. "Maybe he was just being friendly."

"Friendly!" exclaimed Chris, "I don't think so."

"Well then, maybe he likes you and doesn't want you to get into trouble."

Chris gave this second hypothesis of Selwyn's some thought.

"Do you really think so?"

"Why not? After all you're a good looking guy who does a good job, and here I mean sales job, and I'm sure that you bring in a fair amount of money for his company."

"If you put it like that, then maybe you're right."

"Chris, I wouldn't worry about it, if I were you."

"What are you two going on about?" interrupted Bobby, going over to where they were chatting.

"Nothing, just chatting," replied Selwyn.

At approximately 9:00 a.m., an attractive young woman came up to the counter where Bobby was standing. Chris sidled up to Selwyn and whispered in his ear, "That's Bobby's girlfriend."

"I never thought he had one," commented Selwyn.

"Well, so he says, but you never know, it might just be for show. You know you often get these sorts of people who can't really have a relationship so they pretend."

Selwyn watched with interest as Bobby 'charmed' the young lady. She said she was looking for some shirts for her boyfriend, so Bobby showed her a number of items.

"What size does your boyfriend wear?" asked Bobby.

"He's about your build," she replied.

Selwyn heard this and thought it strange for her to say these things, particularly if she was supposed to be Bobby's girlfriend.

The girl held five shirts in her hand and asked Bobby which ones he liked. He told her and of the five, there was only one that he didn't like, so she placed it back on the rack and took another in its place.

"I think I'll take these," she said, handing them over to Bobby.

Selwyn watched as Bobby folded them and placed all five in a store carrier bag and then took the girl's credit card. He entered a figure in the machine and swiped the card. A slip was spat out and the girl signed the slip, thanked Bobby and left with her parcel. Bobby placed the store's copy of the credit card slip in the cash register and then he strolled off to talk to Brent. Selwyn couldn't resist the temptation to open the cash register and look inside. Once he had opened it and looked at the slip inside, he was convinced that Bobby must be the guy they were after.

"Chris, I'm just going to the toilet quickly, in case anyone is looking for me. I won't be long."

Selwyn hurried to the privacy of the toilet, dialed Rob's number on his mobile phone and waited.

"Hi Rob," he whispered. "Can't talk loud but I think I might have something. A credit card was used for a sale right now and five shirts were bought, but when I checked on the slip that's in the cash register, only one shirt was charged for and it was the cheapest. What do I do?"

"Nothing. I'll contact Derek, but you don't say a word to anyone. Who took the sale?"

"Bobby, the jock. I believe it was his girlfriend who bought the shirts, so they're probably for him."

"Thanks Selwyn, now get back to work."

The phone went dead and Selwyn returned to his counter.

Half an hour later, Mr. Campbell wandered through the store, inspecting merchandise. He reached their section and chatted quietly to Chris, who once more blushed, but seemed more relaxed with the boss after his morning talk. He then went to the cash register and, loud enough for all to hear, asked Bobby if they had any sales this morning. Bobby said that they had and he opened the cash register, whereupon Mr. Campbell took out the credit card slips that lay there. He peered at them, noted the one for the shirts and then wandered over to the shirt rack where he studied his stock. One thing about Mr. Campbell, he knew what was in his store. If a belt was missing he knew; if the suits were in the incorrect size racks, he knew. Unbeknown to the staff, he was mentally counting the number of shirts on the rack, and then he disappeared to his office.

At 14:00 in the afternoon, two police officers walked into the casual clothing section, accompanied by Mr. Campbell, who pointed Bobby out to them. They spoke to Bobby and the policemen, along with Bobby, disappeared in the direction of Mr. Campbell's office. Chris and Selwyn threw glances at each other.

"What do you think is going on?" enquired Chris.

"I don't know," answered Selwyn.

That evening when Rob arrived to pick up Selwyn, he relayed what had happened. Rob had informed Derek Campbell who in turn had called the police after his little inspection and they had gone with Bobby to Bobby's place and found the stolen shirts there, whereupon he was arrested.

"Now what happens?" asked Selwyn.

"You stay there until the end of the week, and then you tell them that you're leaving because you don't think this is for you. That way, they won't suspect that you were in on the plot," said Rob. "Mr. Campbell, will obviously be aware of our plan and you'll be paid off."

During the rest of the week, Selwyn remained at the store, still under cover, but noticed that Mr. Campbell's attitude had changed towards both him and Chris.

"Good morning, gentlemen," said Mr. Campbell the day after Bobby's arrest. He smiled and walked on, but Chris noticed this change and his eyes lit up.

"Selwyn, did you hear, he greeted us."

"Oh Chris, could I see you in my office," commented Mr. Campbell after he had greeted them.

"Oh dear, what do you think he wants me for?"

"Well just go and see," replied Selwyn.

Chris trotted after Mr. Campbell, the camp one following the tall elegant one.

"I know it was you," Selwyn heard, breathed close to his ear. He spun around to face Brent.

"I beg your pardon?"

"You heard me. I know it was you who bust him."

Selwyn wasn't sure what the meaning of this statement was, but he certainly understood the tone of voice being used.

"I don't know what you're talking about."

"You were the fucker who split on Bobby."

"I still don't know what you're going on about," replied Selwyn maintaining his innocence and not wanting to blow his cover. It then dawned on Selwyn that nobody in the store had been told where Bobby was nor had they been told why he wasn't at work, so how did Brent know if he wasn't a friend of Bobby or in cahoots with him. The only event that they had seen was the two policemen who came into the store, and Bobby going off with them.

"I'll get you for that," hissed Brent, hate written across his face.

Selwyn shrugged it off and walked away. Quite some time later, Chris re-emerged, glowing to say the least. He looked excited and seemed to be walking tall, so to speak.

"You look bright-eyed and happy," commented Selwyn when Chris reached him.

Chris blushed but pretended to busy himself.

"I can see from your expression that you're not in trouble with the boss."

Chris smiled sweetly. "Not at all," he said. "On the contrary, I think I'm now in his good books."

"Oh! Why?"

"Selwyn I can't say."

"You can't or you won't?"

Once again Chris blushed, even a deeper red than before.

Selwyn was no slouch and had been working for Rob for two years, so he'd learnt to read people's reactions and thoughts.

"Is this something personal and private between you and Mr. Campbell?"

Chris was now getting more embarrassed.

"Something very personal and ... intimate, perhaps?"

Chris was fanning his face because he was getting so hot with embarrassment.

"Something ... intimate in his office, perhaps?"

By now Chris was beside himself and didn't know what to say or do.

"On his desk ... perhaps?"

Chris gushed and blushed. He squirmed to avoid saying anything but he knew that Selwyn was hot on the trail. Finally, Chris couldn't contain himself

"Yes," he whispered. "You know about my incident in the change room? Well he asked me to repeat what happened there."

"On him?"

Chris nodded.

"In his office?"

Again Chris nodded, beaming all the while.

"So you gave the boss a blow job in his office?"

"Yes!" exclaimed Chris triumphantly.

"What was he like?"

Soon the two men were huddled together as Chris gave Selwyn all the information. They giggled like two schoolgirls as Chris gave blow by blow, if you'll excuse the pun, descriptions of Mr. Campbell's desires and size of his appendage. This conversation instantly brought Chris and Selwyn closer together.

"Chris, on a more serious note, if you're now on speaking terms with Mr. Campbell, I don't know if you know why Bobby' not here…?"

"…Yes, I do, he told me."

"Well I think you ought to tell Mr. Campbell to watch Brent as well."

"Why?"

"He threatened me this morning while you were with the boss."

"What do you mean he threatened you?" said an alarmed Chris.

"He said I was responsible for Bobby being arrested and that he was going to get me."

"I'll go right now and tell him, but don't you think you should tell him?"

"You've become his best friend suddenly so I thought he'd listen to you. He's not going to listen to me."

"Don't say a word as to where I am, but I'll go and see him now."

Chris scuttled off in a hurry to Mr. Campbell's office and soon returned with the news that Selwyn wasn't to worry about a thing.

At the end of the day, Selwyn went to the bathroom before waiting for Rob to pick him up and take him home. He went in and was standing at the urinal, when Brent entered the bathroom. Both men stood side by side at the urinal, but neither spoke. Brent then went to a wash-hand basin and stood washing his hands. Selwyn then went to wash his hands, and it was while he was doing this, that Brent grabbed him by the arm, spun him around and punched him. Selwyn went flying to the floor, blood beginning to ooze from his nose. Although he was stunned by the attack, he quickly rose to his feet to defend himself, but another blow hit him, forcing him back to the ground. It was then that a barrage of kicks aimed at his upper body began raining down on him. Just then the bathroom door opened and Mr. Campbell walked in.

"Cut it out!" he shouted, giving Brent a fright.

Selwyn lay groveling on the cold floor, blood flowing freely.

"What's going on here?" commanded the boss, his voice trembling with anger. "Explain yourself, young man."

Brent stood heaving, trying to regain his breath.

"What is the reason for this?"

Brent never said a word, but stood staring at the boss and then at Selwyn. The bathroom door opened once more and Chris poked his head in and saw Selwyn.

He rushed to his friend and knelt down beside him.

"Ooh, you're bleeding," said Chris screwing up his face at the sight of all the blood.

"Chris help Selwyn there please, and you, young man, you come with me."

Mr. Campbell frog-marched Brent out of the bathroom and up to his office where he promptly telephoned the police. Within minutes they were there and took Brent away having had charges of assault laid against him on Selwyn's behalf by Mr. Campbell. Once the police had taken Brent away, Mr. Campbell returned to the bathroom to see how Selwyn was doing. Chris had helped clean him up and stop the bleeding.

"Selwyn, I've laid charges of assault against him on your behalf and I've also told the police to look into the possibility of him being an accomplice of Bobby's in the theft of goods from my store. Is Rob coming to fetch you from work?"

"Yes sir," mumbled Selwyn, obviously still in some pain.

"We'll stay with you until your lift arrives. Come Chris; let's help Selwyn to the street to wait for his lift."

Selwyn was helped to his feet and the three of them made their way out to the street to await Rob. It wasn't long before the vehicle pulled up and a shocked Rob saw a bruised and disheveled Selwyn. He leapt from his car and rushed to his young friend's assistance.

"What happened here?" asked Rob, anxiously.

"Rob, he's fine but a little shaken up," said Mr. Campbell. "I'm sure Selwyn will tell you everything, but I'll call you tomorrow after I've been down to the police station."

They loaded Selwyn into the vehicle and Rob drove straight back to drop Selwyn off at Michael's.

Michael was very perturbed when he saw Selwyn; after all he'd never seen his partner in such a state before. He comforted Selwyn and laid him on the couch and pampered him to the extent that Selwyn actually suggested that he should get beaten up more often.

While they were sitting there, Rob's phone rang. He answered it and it was Mr. Campbell, who told Rob to tell Selwyn not to bother going in to work any more and not to worry about working until the end of the week. Rob also told Selwyn that he didn't want to see him at the office for the rest of the week and to take things easy for a while, which pleased Selwyn enormously.

"Now you can stay home and rest," said Michael, giving Selwyn a kiss on the forehead.

"Thanks love, and thanks for your support, Rob."

Rob, having ascertained that Selwyn was in capable hands left and went to his apartment, leaving the two young men alone.

"How about if I stay home with you tomorrow?" asked Michael.

"That would be nice, but don't you have appointments tomorrow?"

"Nothing at the moment," replied Michael, "and even if I get a call now, I'll try to put them off."

"Maybe we can go to the pool tomorrow," suggested Selwyn.

"That's not a bad idea, but do you think you'll look OK to go in public tomorrow?"

"Let's play it by ear," replied Selwyn. "Who's really going to notice me? In any case, the only person I want noticing me is you."

Michael made dinner that night and the two spent a quiet evening together watching TV.

Chapter 4

By the end of the week, Selwyn's face was once again looking handsome and he and Michael had been able to spend quite a bit of quality time together. When Michael had told Myra of Selwyn's attack, she was not only horrified, but also rushed over to their apartment as soon as she could. She had cooked and looked after Selwyn on days when Michael was at work and treated him as though he were an invalid who was unable to take care of himself. It was during one of these times that she and Selwyn concocted their plan.

"Darling, I went to the travel agency yesterday and made enquiries about a holiday. Remember we had said it would be nice for you and Michael to have a honeymoon, seeing that you weren't about to have a formal wedding as such. Well, I've got all the info."

She and Selwyn sat on the couch with travel brochures scattered all around the lounge.

"I thought it would be lovely for the three of us to do a cruise together," said Myra, confidently.

"You mean the three of us; you me and Michael?"

"Did you have anyone else in mind?"

"I thought maybe Rob might like to join us, after all, I'd have to get his permission to take leave and it would be a lot easier if he came along."

"True, I didn't think of that, but that would mean we'd have to have a number of cabins, then."

"I'd speak to Michael, but I'm sure he wouldn't mind if Rob shared a cabin with us and then you have a single to yourself."

"And what if I want to take along a friend?"

"Well that's up to you Myra, but I thought we wanted to keep it sort of family, if you know what I mean?"

Myra, nodded her head as if to say she understood, but it wasn't going to stop her from planning everything. She was not only a matchmaker, but seemed also to be an organizer.

"I like these brochures," said Myra, thrusting about four brochures into Selwyn's hands. "They're all cruises."

"I don't have a problem with that. In fact I'd quite like to take a cruise, but where?"

Myra re-took the brochures that she had handed to Selwyn and proceeded to flip through the pages.

"How about this?" she said pointing to a page depicting a glorious white liner and pictures of tranquil aqua marine seas.

Selwyn looked at the pictures and then read the captions under them. He also read the itinerary and smiled. He liked what he read.

"Anything else?" he asked.

"Oh yes! There are these as well," she continued, turning to various other pages.

They looked, read, oohed and aahed until they had agreed on four different tours.

"Now what do we do?" asked Selwyn.

"Speak to Michael when he comes home and perhaps you could also speak to Rob and see what they think of the idea. In the meantime, my darling, I must away and get home."

Myra set off home leaving Selwyn surveying the brochures, after which he dialed Rob's number.

"Hi Rob, it's me. Are you doing anything tonight?"

"Why, have you got a date for me?"

"Yes, two."

"That sounds even better, who?"

"Michael and I want you to come round for dinner and drinks. Say seven or seven thirty, if that suits you."

"That sounds great. Must I bring anything with me?"

"No, just bring yourself."

Selwyn rang off and immediately phoned Michael.

"Hi babes, I'm sorry to worry you. I've had your mother round today and she's come up with a plan."

"That sounds dangerous," replied Michael, knowing how his mother could concoct plans.

"Listen, I just phoned to tell you that I've invited Rob around for drinks and dinner tonight. I hope you don't mind?"

"Mind? Of course I don't mind. In fact it'll be nice to have him round especially after he's been driving you to work every day; it can act as a small thank you."

Selwyn rang off after he'd completed talking to Michael and set to preparing something for them to eat later. He also hid the brochures. The kitchen was a hive of activity as he created something exotic to eat, perhaps in preparation for a cruise to some exotic place.

Michael arrived home to the smells of spices, fruit and a drink waiting for him.

"OK! When I come home and you have a drink in your hand for me, then I know something's wrong," said Michael, looking suspiciously at Selwyn.

"Nothing's wrong."

"Then what are you after?"

"Nothing."

"Nothing? You mean you're not hoping I'm going to whip you off to bed?"

"Well that would be nice, but perhaps later. No I just wanted to spoil you, especially as you've been spoiling me lately."

"Are you sure?"

"Yes."

Michael was still skeptical about Selwyn's behavior.

"You haven't broken something?"

"Michael, why won't you just trust me on this?"

"It's just I get a little worried when your behavior patterns change."

"Don't worry; I'll reveal all when Rob arrives."

"Is he in on whatever you're up to?"

"No. He has no idea."

Michael, realizing that he wasn't going to get any information from Selwyn, accepted the drink and went and relaxed on the couch.

At approximately 19:15, there was a rap on the front door and Michael opened to let Rob in.

"Hi Mike, what's the occasion?"

"Hi Rob, I'm afraid you're as much in the dark as I am. I know that Selwyn wanted to invite you round to say thanks for taking him to work everyday this week, but I know there's something brewing because when I got home I was handed a drink at the door."

"Is he looking for sex tonight?"

"I don't think so because he would have just asked, but I know something is afoot."

"Hi Rob," said Selwyn coming to the front door.

"How are you feeling?" asked Rob coming in and heading to the lounge.

"Much better thanks. I think you can even see the swelling has gone down and I'm looking much more handsome than I did a day or two ago."

"Absolutely. But tell me exactly why I have been invited here tonight. I also believe you're not telling Michael either, what's happening."

"Oh, all right. You know I can't keep secrets from you two. Michael, your

27

mother spent the day with me and she came up with a plan, as I told you…”

“… That’s what worries me; my mother’s plans.”

“She suggested that we all go on a cruise. Remember we’d spoken about not having a honeymoon when we’d gone into our relationship, well, I thought it a good idea, and so she brought around a whole wad of brochures.” Selwyn went to his hiding place and retrieved the brochures, which he placed on the couch next to Rob. “But Rob, we want you to come with us.”

“Gee thanks, I’d like that.”

“However, there is one other thing; your mother wants to tag along.”

All three burst out laughing.

“Can you imagine Myra on a ship full of sailors?” said Michael.

“Can you imagine Selwyn on a ship full of sailors?” joked Rob.

“Now listen,” said Selwyn, ignoring their jests. “Rob either you’ll have to take a single cabin, or if you’re willing I’m sure that you could share with us; or, third option, you might want to bring a friend. If you want to do that, you can still share with us and we could book a four-berth cabin, or we could both take double cabins. Whatever we choose, I’ve made it clear to Myra that she’s not sharing with us.”

Michael and Rob roared with laughter at the thought of Myra possibly sharing with them.

“Myra and I went through the brochures and we’ve isolated four tours and we need you two to decide what you’d like to do. We isolated two Western Caribbean and two Eastern Caribbean cruises. Have a look at these itineraries and make a choice.”

Rob and Michael sat together on the couch studying the various tours, while Selwyn set the table for their dinner.

After having studied the itineraries, Michael said, “If I look at these, I think I’d prefer to do the Eastern Caribbean cruise. What about you Rob?”

“Looks good to me, but I’m not fussy.”

“Selwyn,” shouted Michael through to the kitchen, “Which port were you thinking of for the departure?”

“Miami,” shouted back Selwyn.

Rob and Michael looked at each other.

“Why Miami?” shouted Michael.

“I like Miami.”

“How about you, Rob. Any bad memories or thoughts about Miami?”

“Mike, I don’t worry about the past. What has happened has happened. I know that Greg is there and so is my ex-wife, but that doesn’t worry me at all.”

It had been a long time since Rob gave a thought to Greg, but he wasn’t about to start now.

Selwyn came into the dining area and placed a piping hot plate of food on the table.

“Come and get it,” he shouted to the two men on the couch. “Chili Con Carne and salad at your service.”

Michael and Rob got up and went to the table to join Selwyn there.

"Have you two decided where you want to go?"

"We thought of the tour to Puerto Rico, St. Thomas, St. Maarten and the Bahamas," replied Rob. "How does that grab you?"

"It grabs me fine," answered Selwyn and it's funny you two chose that, because that was the one that Myra fancied."

"I think it'll be great fun because we'll have two days of sailing at sea and then on the other days, we'll dock at the various ports," said Michael, studying the brochure he had brought to the table.

"Now comes the clincher," said Selwyn smiling broadly. "How about us departing on the last Saturday in March?"

"Why?" questioned Michael.

"Because it'll be more interesting."

"No, seriously, why that date?"

"Because Myra and I found out that on that date, the tour is primarily a gay tour. Just think of all those men on board!"

Rob and Michael were aghast.

"No wonder Myra wanted to go," chuckled Michael. "Are you serious about this, Selwyn?"

"Very. There could be a few women on board, but it's going to be ninety percent men. Now, Rob, do you want to share a cabin with us, bring a friend, or find a friend on board?"

"What a choice," said Michael. "Do I get a choice too?"

"Sure," replied Selwyn, "you can either share a cabin with me, or with Myra."

"What about me finding a friend on board?" asked Michael, with a serious look on his face.

"If you really want a friend, I'm sure that we can find you one once we get on board, so long as I can also have one," remarked Selwyn.

In between eating and drinking, they poured over the brochures.

"If we go on the cruise we said we'd like to, to accommodate Rob sharing a cabin with us, that's if he's not taking a friend or wants to be on his own, then we'll have to book a balcony stateroom because I see they have a sofa bed, plus a queen-size bed," said Michael, pointing to a picture of a cabin.

"I don't have a problem, if you two don't have a problem about me sharing with you," replied Rob.

"We'd love you to share with us," said Selwyn, taking Rob's hand and squeezing it. "You might even get lucky and share the queen-size bed with us!"

Rob didn't even blush, but retorted, "I thought you were never going to offer!"

"Now what about Myra? Where do we put her?" asked Selwyn.

"Definitely not next door," replied Michael.

"Why not? It would be nice to have her close by," said Rob, feeling sorry for the old dear.

"Rob, have you ever been on a cruise before? Those cabin walls are usually paper-thin, so every cough or fart is heard through them."

"Including if you're having sex?" interjected Selwyn.

"That too, unless you keep the histrionics down to a minimum," continued Michael.

"In that case we'd better put her on another cruise liner all together because with all those men on board, she'll never sleep for the noise that will go on," chirped Selwyn.

"Are we decided then that this is what we'd like to do?" asked Michael, "because if we are then I think it's only fair that we chat to my Mum and see what she feels about our arrangements. How about us all meeting back here on Saturday, if you're not busy, Rob?"

"That'll be fine with me," he replied.

Michael immediately phoned his mother to tell her about Saturday evening, to which she was very excited and said that she couldn't wait.

***

"Michael, I've been meaning to tell you about Mrs. Jankowitz. Remember I told you a long time ago that she was having an affair with her pool man while her husband was at work, well they've upgraded, moved house and got a bigger one."

"Bigger house or pool?" asked Michael.

"No darling, bigger pool man. When they moved areas, she left her old pool man and found a new one. He's much bigger than the old one ..."

"...Bigger in what way?" interrupted Selwyn.

"In all ways, apparently," giggled Myra. "She says she can't get enough of him, so he has to come and clean their pool four days a week. I think it's a shame that they allow their pool to get so dirty!"

Rob, Selwyn and Michael, merely looked at each other without laughing at Myra's innocent comment.

"Rob, I've also thought about you. Why don't you take Marc my plumber with you? You dated him once didn't you?"

"Yes I did Myra, but I don't know."

"He's very good-looking especially when he takes off his shirt. I always tell him to take it off when he comes to mend my pipes," continued Myra. "I think you and he would make a fine pair, then at least you wouldn't be on your own on the ship."

"That's very thoughtful of you Myra. I'll tell you what, I'll think about it."

Neither Michael nor Selwyn commented on Myra's choice for Rob. They knew that Rob had agreed with Myra's description of Marc and Rob had enjoyed his date with him, but as Rob had said, 'there was nothing much upstairs in the brain.'

"Now listen Mum, we've agreed on the cruise we'd like to do, but we want to know whether you're bringing a friend along to share your cabin."

"I thought of asking Ethel Berkowitz because she can be fun sometimes, but I haven't decided. I also thought I might go on my own in the hopes of finding a man."

"Mum! How can you!"

"Life sometimes gets lonely, Michael, especially now that your father's gone, may his soul rest in peace, but I have to have some enjoyments in life. You know what I mean?"

Michael didn't react.

"I know what you mean Myra," said Selwyn leaning across and giving her a hug. "A girl needs to get pleasure sometimes."

"Precisely put. Thank you, Selwyn. Look, don't worry about me. You boys sort yourselves out and I'll just fit in."

"Do you want me to do the booking, Mum?"

"Would you mind?"

"Just let me know within the week if you're going to take someone along because we'd have to tell the travel agent their name. The same would apply to Rob."

"No problem," said Rob, then added, under his breath, "but I'm not sure about Marc the plumber."

Selwyn whispered back, "If you don't want him, bring him for me. You did say he was a big boy and you know I like big!"

Rob laughed at Selwyn's comment; "You're absolutely irrepressible."

Once the discussion on the cruise was over, they all settled in the lounge to enjoy each other's company and their drinks.

"What's happened about the episode in the store, Rob?" asked Michael.

"I heard on Friday that the one guy, Bobby, got a three year sentence, but the guy that attacked Selwyn was only sentenced to six months, suspended, so basically, he's free to roam around."

"That's what I like about our judicial system, the criminals wander around freely," said Michael with an element of venom in his voice.

"Do you know what I think?" interjected Myra.

"Here we go. Some earth-shattering theory coming forth," said Michael, still with a tinge of sarcasm in his voice.

"I think that if someone steals, then chop off a hand; if he rapes someone, chop off his …"

"…Yes Mum!"

"Well then he won't be able to do it again," she continued. "Then if he murders, put him out of his misery. Simple!"

"So you think that's going to solve all the problems of the world, Mum?"

"Sure."

"Myra, getting a suspended sentence means that if this Brent guy does anything serious within the six month period, he can be arrested again and charged not only for the new crime, but also for the previous crime of assaulting Selwyn," explained Rob.

"I understand Rob, but why wait for him to commit another crime before you deal with the first crime?"

"It's a bit more complicated than that. I think they try to give people a chance to right their wrongs, and also if they put everyone in jail, for their crimes, our jails would be overflowing," said Rob.

"Ooh! I've just had a thought!" exclaimed Myra, changing the topic. "Michael, you remember Mrs. Green don't you? She was your high school English teacher."

"Yes, what about her?"

"She's got a very eligible son. He's been living in England and he's just come back to the States."

"So, what about him?" enquired Michael.

"His name's Josh and I think he'd make good company for Rob. He's good-looking, very presentable with a fine body and he's intelligent. What more could you ask for?"

"How do you know this, Mum?"

"I make it my business to find out these things. If you weren't in a relationship with Selwyn, I would have matched him up with you. He's a lovely boy and so well-mannered."

"How old is he, Mum?"

"He's your age, going on twenty-seven."

"Well, it's up to Rob if he wants to meet him. Personally, I'd just go on the cruise Rob and take your luck there if you meet up with someone," suggested Michael.

"Mike, I'm willing to meet the guy, if it makes your Mum happy."

"There you go again just trying to keep her happy. It's you who has to be happy, not her."

"Don't be so harsh on your Mum. She's got a good, caring heart, and she's worrying about me as though I were also her son."

"You're right, Rob. I'm sorry. You make the decision."

"Myra, I'd like to meet Josh if he wants to meet me."

"Oh he does," replied Myra with enthusiasm.

"How do you know, Myra?" asked Selwyn.

"I've already spoken to him about Rob."

"There you go!" exploded Michael. "I told you Mum was a match-maker."

"When I told him that Rob was a private investigator," continued Myra, "he was so excited to meet you. He said it sounded such a romantic job to have. He said it conjured up visions of a very macho man and that's what he wanted to meet."

Selwyn and Michael both stared at Rob.

"Well, he's right about the macho part," said Selwyn, "but I'm not so sure about the romanticism in the job, especially not when you're being beaten up by strange men."

Myra ignored the comments flying from Michael and Selwyn.

"Rob would you be able to meet him on Monday night for drinks?"

"Sure, Myra, I'd be pleased to meet him, but where?"

"There's a little bar and restaurant near your office called *La Piccolo*; well I've booked you a table for 7:30 in your name, if that's OK with you."

All three men roared with laughter at this information. Myra had preempted the whole affair and had gone ahead and booked without so much as a by your leave. She was determined that Rob and Josh should get together. Myra was indeed in a class of her own when it came to matchmaking. When Rob was able to control his laughter at the thought of Myra's planning, he smiled sweetly at her and thanked her for her concern for him.

"I'd do it for any of you boys," was her reply. "And what's more, it'll make Mrs. Green a happy woman to know that her Josh has met someone nice for a change."

"Why, does he usually meet rubbish, Mum?"

"Apparently he had a sordid relationship while living in England. His partner used to beat him."

"Beat him!" exclaimed a startled Selwyn.

"Yes, dear, with whips! Must have been terribly painful. Michael I sincerely hope that you never do things like that to Selwyn."

"Not unless he asks me to do it," muttered Michael.

"What was that?" enquired his mother.

"Nothing, Mum."

"Perhaps he liked it," commented Selwyn in hushed tones to Michael.

"Don't worry Myra, I'd never whip Josh," said Rob, with sincerity, "or anyone else for that matter."

"I know you wouldn't, Rob. That's why I told him that you'd be good for him."

"Now tell me, Myra, if I'm to meet him at the restaurant, what do I look for? What does he look like?"

"He's about Michael's height, five foot eleven; thick-set, has very short dark brown hair, and has a small moustache."

"And does he wear leather, Mum?"

"Don't be silly. How would I know?"

"Sounds interesting to me," said Rob, almost in confidence to Selwyn.

Once Myra had made her conquest as it were and had managed to set up a date for Rob, she was happy to make her way home with clarity of mind, knowing that there might even be not only a honeymoon on the cruise, but also a 'wedding'.

Chapter 5

An element of excitement filled Rob as Monday evening drew nearer. Both Michael and Selwyn were as excited as Rob was.

"We want a full account when you get home after your date," instructed Selwyn. "Irrespective of the time, do you understand?"

Rob wasn't sure who was more intrigued by the date, him or Michael and Selwyn. Myra hadn't contacted him since their evening of planning the cruise, but Rob knew that she was probably going to get feedback from Mrs. Green. Rob showered after he returned home from the office, shaved and splashed some after-shave on, then pulled on his jeans and a casual shirt. He looked at himself in the mirror and saw the reflection of a large, masculine, good-looking man. His biceps bulged out of his short-sleeved shirt and his buffed chest was almost popping his shirt buttons in an effort to escape their confined space. Yes, he looked good and was ready to face his date.

Rob drove to the restaurant, found parking and went in to the restaurant. There were a number of people already eating while there were others seated at the bar counter. He wandered over to the bar, looking out for Josh, but didn't notice anyone fitting the description that Myra had given him. He ordered a beer and stood at the counter, sipping his drink, waiting.

As each person entered the building, Rob gazed in the direction of the door. Eventually, a man fitting Myra's description entered. Rob liked what he saw, certainly from a distance, so he waved in the direction of his date, who promptly made his way over to the counter and greeted Rob.

"Hi, you must be Rob. I'm Josh."

"Hi Josh. Pleased to meet you," replied Rob taking the man's hand and shaking it. He felt a firm grip on his as he gazed into the luminous green eyes. What beautiful eyes, thought Rob, they certainly pay tribute to his surname. "What can I get you to drink?"

"What are you having?"

"Beer," answered Rob.

"I'll have the same thanks."

Rob ordered a beer for Josh from the barman, who handed it to Josh.

"I don't know how you feel about blind dates?" asked Josh.

"To be honest, you're my second."

"Oh, who was your first?"

"A guy by the name of Marc. One of Myra, Mrs. Bloomberg's match-making dates."

"I take it the fact that you're here now, it didn't work out?"

"He was very nice, but we had very little in common."

Rob noted Josh's attire, which impressed him. Josh had on a tight-fitting shirt of a material similar to that of Lycra, except it wasn't Lycra, but its tightness enhanced his physique which impressed Rob. He also had on a pair of well-fitting leather jeans, but nothing that you would call cheap and nasty. The overall package exuded sexuality. What also impressed Rob, was Josh's accent. He had acquired a British accent, but not one of those 'hot potato' accents, which one associates with people from upper class schools. The accent, too, Rob found sexy to listen to. As they stood talking at the bar counter, Rob felt warmth emanating from Josh, both in personality and physicality. They sat at the bar counter for a while, drinking their beers and then Rob suggested they get a table and have dinner together.

"I believe you're a private investigator," said Josh with a sign of pleasure as he said it.

"Yes, I believe Myra told you."

"Yes, she did, but it sounds such an exciting type of job. Do you get to see much action?"

"Sometimes there's action like fights, but I see it just as any other job. I don't see the glamour in it like some people do."

"I bet you meet some interesting people, though."

"Oh yes, but then you also meet criminals."

"What was the most exciting or frightening experience that you've had, Rob?"

Rob thought for a while and then said, "I don't really know. I don't see this job as being exciting, not in the way I think you're looking at it. Frightening, is a different thing altogether. I've been shot at, stabbed once ..."

"...Stabbed! That must have been awful."

"Awful is not the word – painful!"

"Why what happened?"

"I'd been investigating a suspected drug dealer and was in a hotel room with this guy when he decided that perhaps I wasn't on his side and that I was trying to bust him, so he attacked. Normally I can defend myself, but it happened so quickly and unexpectedly, that he managed to stab me in the arm, but I finally wrestled him to the floor, disarmed him and took him off to the police."

"Do you still have a scar from your ordeal?"

"Sure," laughed Rob, pulling up his sleeve to divulge his muscular bicep with the scar clearly marked on his arm.

"Not bad!" said Josh.

"Not bad? The scar?"

"No, the bicep," replied Josh, giving Rob an ever so subtle smile. "Nice build you've got there."

"Thanks, but you're not so bad yourself. Obviously you work out a lot, because I can see from your shirt that you've got a well-defined body."

"I try to work out whenever I get the chance, but that's not often."

"What do you actually do, Josh?"

"At the moment, I'm just doing a part-time job for a friend of my Mum's. When I was in England, I was working as an architect. I'd gone to England to study at Oxford University, and after I'd qualified, I chose to stay there and work. I liked the people but not the weather, but I managed to get a couple of small jobs, including a modeling job, which had nothing to do with architecture, but I enjoyed the exposure. Obviously to make it in the modeling world, you've got to have the goods, so I made a point of developing my physique, which eventually paid off."

"Photographic or ramp modeling?" asked Rob.

"Both, but I found I made more money from the photographic modeling. Also if you were prepared to do certain things, you got paid extra."

"Like what?"

"Nude modeling, for example."

"You've done that?"

"Sure, quite often."

"For magazines?" queried Rob.

"Yes. I've done a couple of spreads for *Playgirl* and a couple of other mags."

"What other magazines are there that take nudes?" asked Rob, trying to play ignorant.

Josh smiled. "Gay mags. You get good money for that."

Rob's face lit up. He wondered whether Selwyn had any of those magazines to see if he could find pictures of Josh in them.

"Done any movies, Josh?"

Josh blushed.

"My Mum doesn't know about these, but yes," he whispered so that those around us didn't hear his information. "Some porno movies."

"Por...!" gasped Rob. "Wow!"

Dare he ask which ones in order to go and hire them or would that be too presumptuous of him?

"What sort?" whispered Rob, leaning across the table so as not to make his question too loud for others to hear.

Josh also leaned towards Rob until their faces were almost touching.

"Gay!" he whispered.

"Wow!

For Rob this was exciting because he'd never met, let alone known, a porn star.

"Tell me more," he said. "It sounds as though this job is far more exciting than mine."

"I just did a couple of movies. Both were about a bit of S & M you know. I had to wear leather and there was some whipping and chains, etc, but it was great fun."

Immediately Rob burst out laughing.

"Ha, Ha, Ha! I'm sorry Josh, it's just that certain things now make sense to me. Myra said to me that you had been in a relationship but had broken up because your partner used to beat you, with whips."

Josh joined in the laughter.

"That's what I told my Mum. I mean I couldn't tell her I was making porn movies. Yes I did get 'whipped', nothing serious though, during the making of the films, but my relationship as she calls it wasn't with anyone. I wasn't in a relationship."

"You mean there was nobody in your life?"

"Not a soul. It was my cover for doing the films, purely for my mother's sake."

"Did you enjoy making the movies?" enquired Rob, still leant over the table to be close to Josh's face.

"It was fun and I met some great guys. We were like a family."

"And you never had a relationship with any of them?"

"I just found it difficult to have a relationship because let's say that you and I were in a relationship but we were also making these movies together. There'd be times when I'd have to go with another guy in a movie scene, then how do you think you would have reacted, watching this other guy fuck me? I think the only way to have a relationship in that business, if you're going to have one, is to have someone who's actually out of the business; to have the motto of 'out of sight, out of mind.' If I think about it, none of the guys I worked with had partners in the business."

"And now that you're back in the States, are you going to get into the business here?"

"No, I don't think so. Look, it made me good money while I did it, but it's not a career job. If I can get a permanent job in an architectural firm, I might stick to what I'm qualified in."

Going through Rob's mind was the thought of asking Selwyn if he had any gay porno movies and if so which ones.

"What were the names of your movies, Josh?"

Again Josh laughed.

"Do you want to see me naked, is that it?"

Rob became embarrassed.

"No, no, nothing like that," he stammered.

"Come round to my place sometime and I'll show you the movies. Better still, if you play your cards right, you could see the real thing!"

Now Rob blushed profusely. Of course he would love to see the real thing. He had taken a liking to Josh, irrespective of the type of job he had done.

"But enough of me. Tell me all about you, Rob."

"I'm afraid I can't match your illustrious career. I'm just a simple P.I who lives alone, but has some very dear and good friends. I believe, according to Myra, that you and Mike, her son, grew up together."

"That's true, and I'll tell you something else that I don't think anyone knows; I always fancied him when we were growing up. He was in my Mum's English class so I often saw him, even though we didn't go to the same school."

"Are you serious?"

"I thought he was incredibly sexy and I thought he had the most beautiful body."

"You know that he's in a relationship now."

"I believe so. But tell me more about you."

Rob thought for a moment and then gave Josh an edited version of his life.

"I used to be married, I have a son who's living in California, I'm now divorced because of my interest in men, but still remain very good friends with my ex-wife, and I did have a short-tem relationship with a guy by the name of Greg. There, that's my life."

"What happened to Greg?"

"Josh I'd rather not talk about that, if you don't mind. That's part of my life that's behind me now."

"I'm sorry, Rob, I didn't mean to upset you."

"It's OK. You haven't upset me, it's just that he turned out to be not what I had expected, and that's all."

"Let's change the subject then," suggested Josh. "Where do you normally go for your holidays?"

"Anywhere, when I can get away…"

Suddenly Rob stopped talking and went into a deep thought mode.

"Josh, I know we've only just met each other tonight, but would you like to go for a holiday with me and a few others?"

"Sounds interesting. Where and when?"

"Well Michael and his partner, Selwyn, have decided, or should I say, Michael's mother has decided, that they want to have a honeymoon after two years of living together, so they're going on a cruise and I've been invited to go along. I've been given a choice of either sharing their cabin or if I can get a friend, I and the friend can share our own cabin. Would you like to come along with me?"

Josh fell silent. He thought for a moment and then replied, "I'd love to."

"Great. Then that's a deal. I'll tell them that I won't be sharing their cabin but I'll have my own."

"Where's the cruise going to, Rob?"

"Puerto Rico, a couple of the Caribbean islands and the Bahamas. It'll be a week, but the added fun is that it's going to be primarily a gay cruise."

"That should be fun!"

"Oh, and there's an added twist, Myra's coming along."

"I hope she's not inviting my mother to accompany her, because then I'm not going."

"Don't say that."

"What and have my mother cramping my style? Never!"

"Well, we'll see what we can do."

They ordered their meal and a bottle of wine; ate to their heart's content and after polishing off the wine, Josh suggested that they go back to his place for coffee.

"Then you can see the movies if you'd like."

"I'd forgotten about them," remarked Rob. "Sure, let's get moving then."

Rob called for the bill, paid and they both set off, Rob following Josh in his car.

Josh's apartment was very up-market; neatly, yet simply furnished and with a beautiful view of the city, with all its twinkling lights aglow.

"Coffee, Rob?"

"Thanks Josh. Black with one sugar, please, but can I help you?"

"You relax and I won't be a minute."

Josh hustled into the kitchen and soon the water was boiling for their coffee, while Rob sat in the minimalistic lounge admiring the lights outside.

Soon, Josh returned with two steaming cups of coffee. He placed them on the coffee table and sat down on the couch, next to Rob.

"OK, so where are the movies," said an excited Rob.

Josh rose and went into his bedroom, returning almost immediately with two movies.

"Take your pick," he said handing them to Rob.

Rob looked at the titles and the pictures that covered both the front and back of the containers. His face lit up when he noticed one of the photos on the back.

"That's you isn't it Josh?"

Josh smiled and nodded his head.

"Let's watch this one," said Rob, handing back the movie.

Josh placed it in the machine and very soon it started. The TV screen flickered momentarily and the titles suddenly appeared.

"Do you want me to fast-forward to my scene?"

"Please. I don't think I want to watch the others. I want to see what sort of an actor you are."

"Are you sure that's what you actually want to watch?"

Rob grinned broadly.

Josh found the scene and sat back.

Rob sat fascinated by what he was seeing. It wasn't that he'd never seen a porno film before, but he'd never sat next to one of its stars and watched it at the same time. The scenes changed and soon Josh was naked on the screen.

"Oh, wow!" whispered Rob.

"What?" enquired Josh.

"You're a big boy, aren't you?"

Josh chuckled at the compliment.

Rob sat watching intently, every move that Josh did. As he watched he could feel himself becoming aroused and he tried to adjust the way he was sitting. Josh noted this and smiled, because even though he was the star of the scene, both what he was watching on the TV and the fact that Rob was also becoming aroused too was arousing him. Rob made another move to adjust his awkward position.

"Problem Rob?"

"You could say that."

"Why don't you take them off, if you're finding them uncomfortable."

Without hesitation, Rob undid his belt, unzipped his jeans and shucked them to his ankles. His white briefs were tented and Josh could see the engorged outline of Rob's magnificent appendage. He was tempted to touch, but chose to refrain from that. He noticed a gentle throbbing movement coming from within Rob's brief and it was at this point that Josh couldn't control his actions. He stretched a hand across to Rob's bulge and gently squeezed the contents of his briefs. Rob let out a long, deep groan and to Josh this was the invitation to take charge. Josh sank his mouth over the cotton-covered package and began licking and kissing Rob's growing length.

A small wet patch began to appear on Rob's briefs as his pre-cum began to leak from the tip of his throbbing cock. Slowly, Josh, pulled down the waistband of Rob's briefs to allow the large mushroomed-shape cock-head to appear. Josh licked around the top of Rob's cock, taking in the oozing pre-cum and then licking his lips. Josh opened his throat and sank his mouth down the thick, long stem until his chin nudged Rob's balls.

"Aargh! Yes!" exclaimed Rob, as he remained focused on the screen.

Josh's mouth traversed the length of Rob's cock, lubricating it with his mouth and tongue, and then he went to work on Rob's pendulous balls that were waiting to be sucked into Josh's mouth. As Josh gave Rob's balls a tongue-wash, so Rob began to thrust gently upwards. He watched intently at the screen and saw in the movie how Josh positioned his tight ass over the other actor's waiting cock and sink slowly down till his ass rested on the actor's crotch.

"Ride me," whispered Rob. "I want to fuck you."

Josh raised his head and smiled at Rob, then turned to see what section of the film was now showing. When he saw the scene, he turned to Rob and said, "Is that what you'd like?"

"Ugh huh!" exclaimed Rob.

Josh got up, made his way to his bedroom and returned with a couple of condoms and some lube. He lubed up his ass and unrolled a condom down Rob's thick cock, then positioned himself astride Rob's cock and slowly sank down onto it.

Both men groaned as the massive muscle sank into Josh, but Josh never hesitated at any point. He continued to sink further down Rob's cock until his ass came to rest on Rob's balls.

"Fuck! That feels good and so tight," sighed Rob, as he held onto Josh's hips.

Rob began to slide Josh up and down along his slick cock and with each movement, Josh tightened his ass even more, almost strangling Rob's cock shaft. Rob was groaning and sighing with each thrust because Josh was tightening his vice-like grip on Rob's cock and bringing him closer to shooting his load.

"Josh, if you carry on like this, you're gonna make me shoot," cried Rob.

Josh increased the rhythm as he rode Rob's cock and as he did so, he took hold of his own cock and began stroking it furiously.

"Josh, I'm gonna shoot," cried Rob.

"Me too," responded Josh.

Their grunts and groans increased in volume as both men fired their respective loads, Josh's ass muscles clamping tightly around Rob's cock with each load that fired across Rob's chest, and with each tightening of his ass, milking Rob's cock of its juices.

That night, there was very little sleep found between Rob and Josh as the night progressed. In the early hours of the following morning, they both fell asleep and only woke when Josh's alarm clock brought them rapidly back to the real world. They lay in each other's arms, glowing, their lips touching gently, until it was time for them to get up and for Rob to head off to work.

Chapter 6

"You didn't phone last night when you got home to tell us how the evening went," said Selwyn, almost in a reprimanding tone.

Rob smiled at his friend.

"There's a simple answer to that; I didn't go home last night."

"You slut!" exploded Selwyn, but in jest. "How was it? Come on, tell all!"

"We both had a very good evening, that's all."

"No it's not. Come on, fill me in with all the details."

"We had drinks together, and then we sat down for dinner and then went back to his place for coffee…"

"…Until the early hours of this morning! Do you think I believe that?"

Rob just giggled. He was happy and it showed. Selwyn could see that his boss was not his usual self and that something exciting and special had happened.

"And the cruise? Have you decided to take Josh along?"

"I did ask him and he said yes he'd love to come along, so I think we'll have to book two separate cabins, oh, and one for Myra, but there's a condition."

"What condition?"

"Josh doesn't want Myra asking his mother to share a cabin with her. He'd rather not go on the cruise if his mother also goes along."

"You mean to cramp his style?"

"That's exactly what he said."

"So, are you happy, Rob."

Rob blushed. "Very."

"Now do you think you might change your views on relationships?"

"That I can't say just yet. Look, obviously people go on first appearances and that's the draw towards each other. Josh is very good-looking, has a nice body and is really great in bed, so who knows what it'll lead to. Physically I find him attractive and having spoken to him, he's got a brain, not that I want a relationship with an encyclopedia, but at least he can hold a conversation and he's articulate."

"Rob, I really hope things pan out for you and that you get happiness from this. In fact, I can't wait to tell Michael. He's going to be so pleased for you because he thinks a great deal of you."

"That's nice to know, but I never knew that he thought that highly of me, if you know what I mean."

"Don't you believe it, he thinks you're marvelous, and I'm sure that if I weren't around and in a relationship with him, he could quite easily go for you."

"Now you're joking with me."

"No I'm not. You ask him when you see him next. But more importantly, must we go ahead and book the cruise?"

"I would say definitely, but I'd also say book Myra's cabin as far away from ours in case she persuades Mrs. Green to join her. I wouldn't like to lose my new-found friend because his mother's watching his every move."

"Don't worry about a thing. I'll give Michael a call and perhaps he'll be able to book today. Do you want him to book your cabin next to ours, Rob?"

"Please if that's possible."

"We might even be able to get one with an inter-leading door."

"What and have you two barging in on me and Josh every five minutes. As much as I like you guys, no thanks."

Selwyn went into his office and dialed Michael's phone number.

"Michael, good news!"

"Don't you even say Hi before you start shouting down the line?"

"Hi, then. I've got great news; Rob's got someone to share a cabin."

"Who? Josh?"

"Yes. He didn't go home last night. Apparently he spent the night at Josh's apartment and had a ball! Probably more than just that! I've never seen him so happy and he says we can go ahead and book a separate cabin for him and Josh. I asked him if he wanted it next to ours and he agreed, but he suggested we put your Mum as far away as possible."

"Why would he suggest that?"

"He's frightened, or should I say Josh is frightened, that Myra might ask Josh's Mum to share a cabin with her and Josh doesn't want his Mum interfering in his time with Rob."

"Fair enough, but we can't stop her from asking whomever she likes. I'll see what I can do. Give me an hour or two and I'll go and book, then get back to you."

The phones were put down and Selwyn shouted through to Rob telling him that he'd spoken to Michael and that Michael was going to go ahead and book for them. He then went through to Rob's office, sat down opposite him, smiled and said, "Right, now fill me in on the details."

"You don't give up do you?" laughed Rob. "Josh is actually a very nice guy and seems to have quite a few good qualities about him."

"I bet he has," came a snide comment from Selwyn. "It's very rare for you to go on a date and to report the next day that you are over the moon, so to speak. So he must be really good."

Rob had decided that no matter what Selwyn or Michael tried to wheedle out of him regarding Josh, he wasn't going to tell them about Josh's porno movies. That was going to be their secret, if one could call it a secret having been in a couple of movies. In some sordid, yet romantic way, he enjoyed the fact that Josh was revealed to the world in all his glory through the medium of a film. He could be having a relationship soon with a film star! Now, how many people could lay claim to that, he wondered?

Selwyn really tried hard to coax and cajole information from Rob regarding Josh's sexual delights, interests, attributes, or whatever he could, but without success.

"Why won't you tell me any juicy bits?" he asked Rob.

"Because they're private, and I know you. You probably want to get your claws in if you could. I know you like a lot. Both you and Michael have made that clear, but he's not on the open market at the moment. I hope," Rob added.

"Tell me about his physical attributes," pleaded Selwyn.

"You're one helluva desperate tart! I'll tell you what; if we go to the coast, I'll ask him if he wants to come along and then you can see him in a bathing costume and form your own opinion. How's that?"

"What about taking him to the pool we go to."

"There you go. You see how desperate you are. You can't even wait until we go to the beach, which might only be in a month or two's time."

Selwyn knew that he wasn't going to win this one with Rob, so he gracefully gave in, just as the phone rang. He picked up the receiver to hear Michael on the other end of the line.

"Hi there. I've done the booking and everything is now in order."

"What did you get us?" asked Selwyn.

"I've got cabin 7630 for us and cabin 7632 for Rob and then I've put Mum down the front of the ship in cabin 7534," replied Michael.

"Oh we're not next door to Rob and Josh," said a disappointed sounding Selwyn.

Michael laughed.

"Do you really think I would do that to you or them? Their cabin is next door to ours and what's more they are connecting staterooms."

"You mean…"

"…Yes!"

"I love you. You're a star. I'll have to owe you big time now."

"Why such excitement Selwyn, anyone would think you wanted to get into their cabin with them?"

"Well, you never know," came the nonchalant reply.

"We're all on the seventh deck. We're basically across from the library, so we don't have any neighbor across the way from us and we're three decks above the dining room and theatre, so we'll be handily situated to get at the food and shows."

"Now I can't wait to get going on our cruise. Have you phoned your Mum and told her?"

"Yes and she seems equally excited as you, and probably for the same reason."

"And what's that?"

"Men! I asked her if she was happy with her cabin and she replied, 'sweetie, with all those men on board, who says I'm going to get any sleep'."

"She does know it's primarily a gay cruise and the men on board, perhaps with the exception of some of the crew, are all going to be gay?"

"Oh yes, she's well aware of that, but she thinks she's going to get herself a hunk, even if she's got to use me as bait to get him."

Selwyn collapsed with laughter as he envisaged Michael having to act as bait to catch a hunk for his mother.

"I thought I was desperate, but that takes the cake. I must tell Rob about that one. I'll see you later. Cheers." And with that, Selwyn hung up.

"Rob, everything's been booked and you're next door to us, but better still, it's a connecting cabin, so we might leave the inter-leading door unlocked. But the best is that Myra is at the other end of the ship and she's made it clear to Michael that he is going to have to act as bait for her to catch a hunk."

"A gay hunk?"

"Well, what other hunk are you going to find on that ship? And you said I was desperate!"

"Does that mean I can phone Josh and tell him?"

"Sure, go for it," replied Selwyn, leaving Rob's office and closing the door behind him, allowing his boss privacy.

Rob dialed the number and waited.

"Josh Green speaking."

"Hi there sexy," whispered Rob into the mouthpiece.

"Hi Rob, how're you doing?"

"Fine but tired. You exhausted me last night."

"I can't help it if you were up all night," he flippantly replied.

"It was you who kept me up all night."

"Oh no. It was your persistence that kept you up."

"Tell me," said Rob, "are we talking about the same thing?"

"Are you talking about keeping you awake, or keeping you up? If it was keeping you up, then perhaps I'm guilty of that, but keeping you awake; that was your choice."

"You are so clever. You have such a way with words. I can see that I'm going to have to watch what and how I say things in future. But listen, I've got great news for you. Michael has booked our cabin for the cruise. We're next door to them and it's a connecting cabin."

"Wow, that could be dangerous, don't you think?"

"Not if I keep the door locked, and take the key. But also, Michael's booked his Mum at the other end of the ship, so you've nothing to fear."

"That really is great news, Rob. I'm truly looking forward to sharing some time with you."

"Same here. I want to get to know you better and I think this might be a good time for both of us. Have you told either your Mum or Myra about us?"

"My Mum knew that we'd gone out to dinner because Myra had told her, but I haven't phoned her about our evening together, but I'm sure it must be killing Myra to know what happened."

"I'm sure it is and maybe that's why Selwyn was pumping me for information."

"What sort of information?"

"Oh you know. The usual stuff."

"No I don't know. Like what?"

"You know. Things like what were you like and did I like you."

"And what did you say?"

Rob could feel himself blush.

"Of course I told him I liked you."

"And what else?"

"Gee this sounds like I'm getting the third degree."

"I'd just like to hear what you thought of the evening," said Josh.

"I told you I had a really great time and I hope you did too."

"That goes without saying. But what other stuff did Selwyn want to know?"

"You must understand that although Selwyn is happily in a relationship with Michael, Selwyn is a compulsive sex freak. He likes a lot, to put it plainly. To paraphrase what I think Oscar Wilde once said in one of his plays, 'Selwyn can resist anything but temptation'. Do you catch my drift?"

"Very much so. But we all like a little temptation sometimes."

"Only Selwyn likes it a lot. With him you have to give all the juicy details. That's why I think he gets on so well with Myra. They're like two of a kind."

"Well, juicy details are good sometimes, as well," answered Josh.

"But not all."

"You must just give snippets and leave them drooling for more. Never show all your cards, as it were. Give them just a touch of spice and they'll be eating out of your hands for hours, no months."

"You sound as if you've done this before."

"I learnt all this when I was modeling and doing the movies."

"Rob!" came a shout from the outer office, "There's a call waiting for you."

"Josh, there's apparently a call on hold; I'd better be going. Listen, give me a call later and maybe we can go for a drink after work if you'd like."

"Sounds good. I'll do that, and don't forget, just give Selwyn a taste. See you later. Cheers for now."

The phone went dead and soon the waiting call was put through to Rob. When he had completed that, he called for Selwyn.

"How's Josh?" asked Selwyn as he entered Rob's office.

"He's fine and he said thank you for doing the booking."

"Did he say anything about last night?"

Selwyn was at it again, so Rob decided to take Josh's advice.

"The only thing I'll tell you about last night is that Josh is a big boy."

Selwyn's face lit up like a Roman candle. He was aglow and his mind must have been traveling at a speed of lightning.

"Come on, tell me more."

Josh was right. Rob smiled to himself and left the conversation at that.

"Selwyn, I've got to go out and I won't be back so will you please lock up and I'll see you tomorrow?"

"Are you going to see Josh?"

"No, you quizzy little imp. I'm going out on business."

Rob hustled up his things, picked up his car keys and waltzed out of the office, almost floating on air, oblivious of Selwyn's still pestering questions.

Chapter 7

The cold of winter was dissipating and the buds were beginning to break out on some of the trees, but spring hadn't really arrived. It was nearing the departure date of the cruise and Myra had been toying with the idea of asking a friend to accompany her, but was unsure as to whom to ask. She had decided to phone Michael and ask his opinion.

"Mum, I know it's too late to cancel, but I told you right from the beginning that the cruise was a gay cruise. Obviously there wouldn't be people of your age on board, although I suppose I shouldn't say that, because there might. However, it's up to you. There'll obviously be plenty of fun but unless you're happy to spend your time with a group of gay men, I don't see much joy for you."

"Michael dear, I'm not some old fossil that should be kept in hibernation in a musty old museum to be viewed by equally musty old people. I want to have fun. Life is fun and I intend to enjoy myself. In fact, you know what, I think if I took a friend along, she might just cramp my style."

"Mum, where did you hear that phrase?"

"Oh I often hear Selwyn using it. I do know what it means."

"I'm sure you do. So have you made up your mind to go it alone?"

"I think so, son. I'm bound to have more fun on my own than having some old female friend tagging along and not being able to keep up with the pace."

Michael smiled when he heard his mother say these words. Nobody could ever say that Myra wasn't prepared to have fun. He also knew that his mother could be the belle of the ball if she chose, and he was not the type to dissuade her from going on the cruise and probably flirting with all the gay men.

"Mum, I think you should go by yourself. We'll be there for you and I know you'll enjoy yourself, so don't even contemplate asking anyone. Have your cabin to yourself and if you meet a man there, well you can take him back to the comfort of your own cabin and not have to sneak to his."

"Oh, Michael. That all sounds so exciting. Do you know, I've actually packed my bag already."

"That's good, Mum. I know we're going to have a really fun time."

"Now tell me son, what's happened about Rob and Josh. I haven't heard a word and Mrs. Green is in the dark. She knows nothing."

"Rob and Josh are coming on the cruise with us."

"Oh that's wonderful. I'm so happy for Rob. I always knew that Josh was right for him. They suit each other, you know. It's almost like Beauty and the Beast."

"I'm sure they wouldn't like to hear you put it like that."

"You know what I mean. Josh is very good looking and Rob is so huge he's almost like a beast, that's what I meant. Do you think I should invite Mrs. Green to come with me, then?"

"I wouldn't Mum. If you did you might not have as much fun as you're anticipating."

"True, but do you think Josh would mind not having his mother along?"

"I'm sure he can cope quite happily with Rob."

"Has Rob said anything to you about Josh?"

"No, but I know that Selwyn would be trying to find out as much as he can."

"I must phone Selwyn then and see if he's found out anything. Who knows, we could have a wedding on the ship. Wouldn't that put Mona Liebewitz's nose out of joint."

"Why?"

"Remember I told you her Monty was getting married to his surgeon boyfriend, well, we'll be having a honeymoon and perhaps a wedding at the same time, and how many Jewish weddings have you been to where they've taken over an entire ship?"

"Mum, Josh and Rob are not getting married so don't get ideas."

"How do you know? Give me an opportunity and I could do wonders for their lives. I'd better pack an extra outfit in my suitcase in case we do have a wedding on board."

"By the way, Mum, don't overdo the suitcases. We're only going for a week, and I know when you go on holiday; you take an entire entourage."

"Darling, you know me. I must have a different outfit for each night. A woman should never wear the same thing twice, and certainly not when you're in a confined space like a ship. Just think, people would be saying, 'I saw her in that yesterday' and I can't have that. Now tell me, how are we going to the ship?"

"We'll have to fly to Miami, but I haven't made any arrangements with the others. As soon as I have, I'll let you know, Mum."

"Thanks darling. Mikey, are you sure I shouldn't invite Mrs. Green?"

"Mum, it's up to you, but personally, I wouldn't."

"Well if you think so, then I won't. Now enough of this idle chatter, I must phone Selwyn and find out if he has any news for me. Take care my darling and I'll see you soon."

"Bye, Mum."

***

When Selwyn returned home from work that day, Michael asked him if Myra had phoned.

"Oh yes, desperate for news on Josh and Rob, but I had none."

"Nothing! That's not like you. Normally you have more news than the *New York Times*."

"Rob's not saying a word. He's keeping very quiet and secretive about his evening with Josh."

"And he gave you no hints or clues?"

"The only thing he said to me was Josh was a big boy. Now how would you interpret that?"

Michael laughed.

"I know what he's getting at."

"You mean…?"

"Yes, your favorite object to discuss."

"Oh wow!" said an excited Selwyn. "Myra would love to hear that."

"No, Myra wouldn't, and you're not saying anything of the kind to Myra."

"You know, sometimes you can be such a spoilsport. It's scandal like that which keeps your mother in touch with her son-in-law."

"Did you speak to Rob about how we're getting to Miami?" asked Michael.

"Yes, he phoned Josh and apparently they're going to Miami the day before the ship's departure, so he said they would meet us on the ship."

"That's fine, then you, me and Mum can fly down on the morning of the departure. I'll book our flights tomorrow."

"Why not do it now on the internet?"

"Of course, I wasn't thinking," replied Michael, who promptly went into their bedroom where the computer was situated.

Michael looked up various flight times, chose a convenient one and booked all three of them on the flight, allowing them time to get from the airport to the harbor.

"Everything's set," said Michael emerging from the bedroom. "We fly early on the Saturday morning which will give us plenty of time to book in on board."

"What time is departure for the ship, so that I can remind Rob?"

"17:00," replied Michael. "Tell him to get there early so that we can have some fun seeing who's boarding before the ship sets sail, and maybe have a drink or two."

"Are you looking forward to the trip?"

"Absolutely. I haven't been for a holiday for quite some time," said Michael, thinking back to when he had his last holiday. "You know I can't even remember when I had my last proper holiday."

"We've actually never been away together for a holiday; and I'm not talking about the weekends we have at the coast. I mean a real holiday. I think it's going to be great fun, so long as we don't get sea sick."

"I don't think we will, Selwyn. These huge ships have good stabilizers so I think we should be fine. Hey, and if we don't feel so well, then we can just have a drink or two and that might take our minds off the possible rocking and rolling of the ship."

"I like that idea. It sounds like good medication."

"Do you think we're likely to see much of Rob and Josh, or do you think they'll be behind closed doors?" asked Michael.

"I don't know, but you might find that we're also behind closed doors most of the time," suggested Selwyn, sidling up to Michael and throwing his arms around Michael's waist.

"And what might you be after, may I ask?"

Selwyn winked, smiled and kissed his partner gently on the lips.

Chapter 8

The great day arrived. The sun was shining brightly and there wasn't a breath of wind. Both in Myra and Michael's homes, things were busily happening. Last minute packing was taking place and checks were being done to see that everything that might be needed was in fact packed.

"Towel, Speedo, shorts, T-shirts, tanning lotion, sunglasses, good book. There that's the lot," said Selwyn.

"I don't think you'll need a towel because I think they provide, and what do you want with a good book, because you'll be spending most of your time eyeing all the guys," said Michael, light-heartedly.

"Sweetie, the book's only there for decoration. It's an ice-breaker."

"How so?"

"Well, let's say this hunky man walks up to me and sees that I am reading…"

"…But you won't be reading!"

"Pretend. He's going to say, 'what are you reading? It looks interesting.' And that will be the ice-breaker."

"And when you've shattered the ice, what then?"

"We can sit and chat."

"Is that all? Because that's not like you."

"My dear sir, methinks you doubt my loyalty to you," replied Selwyn putting on his very British accent. "If he is indeed worth conversing with, I shall endeavor to entrap him and through gentle and subtle persuasion, lure him to the confines of our celestial boudoir where both you and I will entertain his desires."

Michael stopped his final checking and burst out laughing at Selwyn's antics.

"That's what I love about you; you're always full of fun."

"I do not jest, oh lord and master; it is for your desires that I secrete myself in various places in order to find my lord some form of entertainment, with which to amuse himself."

"I thank you for your concern and kindness, good servant, but methinks it is time that we departed to catch that bird in the sky that will wing us off to fabulous places," said Michael, imitating Selwyn's accent.

The cab arrived and they made their way round to Myra's apartment to pick her up.

"I just hope we have enough room in the cab for Mum and all her luggage," muttered Michael, as they neared her building.

Standing in the foyer was Myra, looking as lovely as ever in a pair of tailored slacks and matching top. Alongside her stood three identical suitcases.

"Oh, no! She's brought the wardrobe," said Michael almost in desperation.

"Hello my darlings," screamed Myra when she saw the boys. "This is so exciting. I can't wait to get on that boat."

"Ship! Mum."

"Same thing, they both float."

The poor cab driver squeezed and squashed suitcases into the trunk of the cab and then Myra took her place alongside the driver in the front. She glared at Michael on seeing the rotund, bald and elderly driver.

"Couldn't you have at least asked for something a little more pleasing on the eye, especially if I have to sit next to it," she whispered to Michael.

"That's why we're sitting in the back, Mum," he replied, causing both boys to grin at Myra's unhappy predicament.

The cab made its way through the hubbub of the city as it traveled towards the airport. Once they arrived, they booked in and made their way to the departure gate and waited to board the flight to Miami. All three, although they never mentioned it, were in a state of excitement at the prospect of starting their holiday.

The flight to Miami was uneventful, and Selwyn decided that there was nothing worth looking at on the flight, so he dozed a little while Myra and Michael chatted. On reaching Miami, they decided not to waste time looking around Miami, but rather to catch a cab and head for the harbor.

When they arrived at their destination and had unloaded the cab, Selwyn stood agog, admiring the sleek, gigantic, white liner that stood waiting for them.

"Wow! It's huge!" Exclaimed Selwyn.

"Don't say I don't think of you," said Michael. "I know you like big, so we're going on one of the biggest liners, especially for you."

Selwyn liked the manner in which Michael was joking with him.

"Ooh, and I like the name. Pretty appropriate don't you think, Michael?"

Myra looked up at the name on the side of the ship and laughed. In blazing black against the white of the ship stood the name, *Caribbean Queen*.

Already people were queuing up to check in and board the majestic ship, so the three of them joined the line of men.

"At the moment, you seem to be the odd one out, Mum," said Michael looking at the long line of laughing, chatting men who were gathered at the harbor.

Selwyn's eyes were like saucers as he glanced over the throngs, checking out the talent, or potential talent.

"Spot anything you like?" asked Michael.

"Hm?"

"I can see your mind has already gone and you're no longer in our dull world."

"Sorry, love, what did you say?"

"I just asked whether you'd seen anything you like?"

"There really are some hunky guys here, but nothing that I'd dump you for."

"Well, I'm glad to hear that; at least there's hope for me at the moment."

Myra had, at this time, left the queue and was wandering up and down it, admiring men. Michael and Selwyn watched with interest as she would stop every now and again to chat up some guy who she thought might be worth getting to know. By the time she returned to the boys in the queue, she was well acquainted with quite a few of the men.

"I like Reuben," she said to Selwyn. "He's the dark-haired young man over there," she said pointing to a man about six places in front of them. "He tells me he's an artist, and he's traveling alone, isn't that good?"

Again Michael and Selwyn made eye contact with each other. They weren't even on the ship yet and Myra was embarrassing them.

"Then there's Dirk, that very tall man. You can't miss him if you look down the line. He's originally from Holland and you know what they say about Dutch men?"

"No, Mum, what do they say?"

"Well look at him. He's tall and everything about tall Dutchmen is big!"

At this, Selwyn became more interested in the tall man down the line.

"Selwyn, control yourself," reprimanded Michael. "Don't believe everything my mother says."

"Michael, what was my cabin number again?"

"Why Mum?"

"Because I think I gave them the wrong number."

"Gave who the wrong number?"

"Those lovely young men I've been talking to."

"Mum, you haven't!" said an exasperated Michael. "I knew this was not a good idea, bringing Myra on this trip."

"Well, what's my number, Michael?"

"7534, Mum."

"Thanks darling," and off Myra rushed to check with her newly made friends that she had given them the correct cabin number.

When Myra returned, she had more information for the boys.

"Dirk tells me that he's a businessman. His family owns a diamond polishing works in Amsterdam, but he lives and runs a branch in New York. Just think of all those diamonds," said an excited Myra.

"Mum, he's not interested in you. He's probably here with someone. Those wealthy people always seem to have any number of hangers-on accompanying them."

"Well, he didn't say as much, but we'll see when he checks in."

The line of men moved slowly forward as people were checked in and started boarding. Eventually, Michael, Selwyn and Myra made their way onto the gleaming white ship to be greeted by a group of staff members, dressed smartly in neat, white uniforms.

They gave their names and they were then directed to their cabins. Michael and Selwyn were happy to explore to find their cabin, but Myra insisted that a young steward who was standing along with the welcoming party take her to hers.

They were all on deck 7, so they made their way to the correct level. Michael and Selwyn soon found their cabin and went in.

They were very pleasantly surprised by their cabin's appearance. The décor was a mix of blues and greens, with two twin beds pushed together, a sitting area made up of a sofa, two easy chairs and a small round table on which sat a bowl of fruit with a card attached. They read the card, which said, 'Happy Anniversary. Have a great time, love Mum' From the sitting area, there was a sliding door which led to a small balcony on which were two sun loungers and a fantastic sea view. Their luggage was already waiting for them in their cabin, but they wandered around inspecting everything, including the bathroom, which consisted of a shower, washbasin and toilet. All told, they were very happy with their cabin, and then they noticed a door in the wall adjacent to what would be Rob and Josh's cabin. Selwyn tried the handle but it was locked.

"Damn it, there's no key here," he said trying desperately to open the door.

"Maybe it's on the other side," remarked Michael. "We'll have to wait for Rob to arrive to find out."

Once they had surveyed their cabin to their satisfaction, they hastily unpacked their luggage and then set off to find if Myra had settled in. Myra's cabin was identical to the boys', the only exception being that hers was not a connecting cabin. Myra's cabin had a blue and white color scheme and also had the balcony on which she could sit if she so desired. Obviously with Myra's three large suitcases, she had not unpacked yet.

"You boys go exploring and leave me to unpack," said Myra, pulling dresses from her suitcases.

"I hope you're going to have enough hanging space, Mum."

This didn't seem to worry her, but she was happily unpacking when the boys set off to explore the ship.

They found an elevator and made their way up to the top of the ship where they found a lounge with majestic views around the ship. They then made their way, by foot, down a deck to find a small-scale golf course, a rock-climbing wall and a sports court.

"This looks good," said Michael.

"You won't catch me climbing up that thing," said Selwyn pointing to the climbing wall. From there they walked down, deck by deck until they reached the promenade where they found a variety of shops, bars and cafés. Still further down, they came to a theatre on a grand scale and even an ice skating rink.

"This is not a ship," remarked Selwyn, "This is a floating city."

In their travels of exploration, Michael saw a staff member and asked, "How many people are on this ship, sir?"

"On this voyage, sir, we're expecting two thousand four hundred guests."

Selwyn gasped. "Think of that, Michael, at least two thousand three hundred and ninety nine men."

"No, he said two thousand four hundred."

"That includes your mother!"

"Sorry, I forgot. Well, that should make your holiday viewing worthwhile."

The two boys made their way back up through the ship until they reached the deck on which they found the swimming pools and hundreds of men, lazing in the bright afternoon sun. They found themselves a couple of deck chairs and sat watching the passing parade, and what a parade it was. There were men of all shapes and sizes, all ages and all colors. Some seemed to be alone, while others were in groups.

After sitting in the sun for some time, watching the parade, Michael said he was going back down to their cabin, but Selwyn could stay man-watching if he so wanted to. When Michael got back to the cabin, he went out onto the balcony to watch the crowds flocking on the wharf side. There was no sign of Rob or Josh that he could see. He came back into the cabin and was just about to lie down when he heard a key turning and the connecting door opened.

"Rob, hi there! You made it."

Rob entered Michael's cabin closely followed by Josh. When Michael saw Josh, his face lit up.

"Josh! How are you? How nice to see you. How's your Mum?" asked Michael flinging his arms around both their necks and giving them each a kiss.

"She's fine thanks, but you're still looking good," replied Josh, managing to break free from Michael's grasp. "Do you know, I often used to see you on your way to school and my mother often spoke about you."

"Thanks, but you are also looking good. Have you been going to gym to get that body of yours into shape?"

"Sure I go as often as I can, but that's not very often."

"And I must say, I like the accent, it's quite sexy."

They all sat down in Michael's cabin and reminisced about Michael's school days under Josh's Mum's tutelage. Rob didn't mind Michael and Josh going on the way they did.

"Where's Selwyn?" asked Rob.

"Where do you think? Man watching up by the swimming pools."

"Why don't we go up and join him and then he can meet Josh as well."

The three set off up to deck 11 to find Selwyn. By the time they reached the deck, it was crowded with half naked men, some swimming, others drinking, but all in a pre-departure party mood.

"Michael!" shouted Selwyn, above the noise of laughter and the band, which had recently started up. "Over here!"

Michael heard and saw Selwyn and led Josh and Rob to where he was standing, leaning against the rail, watching the remaining passengers embark.

"Selwyn, this is Josh," said Rob introducing the two.

"I've heard so much about you," replied Selwyn.

"Liar," retorted Rob, "you know very little about Josh. Josh you must watch out for Selwyn, he loves a bit of gossip."

They hugged each other and Selwyn assured Josh that he was nothing like Rob might make him out to be.

"I'm pure and innocent," said Selwyn, looking angelic.

Both Michael and Rob roared with laughter at this exaggeration.

"You'll get used to him, Josh," said Michael.

At precisely 17:00, a loud, deep, resonant blast from the ship's funnel signaled the start of the cruise. The music somehow became louder, people cheered and streamers floated gently down to the wharf, creating a rainbow-color effect down the white side of the ship. Men danced and sang in time to the music, and slowly the giant ship began to move from its mooring. It was such a gentle movement from the ship, that unless one watched objects on land, one was not really aware that they were underway.

Among the many hundreds of men gathered on the pool deck, one tiny woman stood out. Dancing men in various stages of undress surrounded Myra and she was dancing along with them.

"Michael, check out Myra," said Rob, who, being the tallest in their group, saw her.

"Where?"

"Over there among that group of guys, dancing."

"Rob, I'm not even going to say anything to her about embarrassing herself," said Michael. "She's here to enjoy herself, so let her do just that."

"I heard that your Mum was quite a character," said Josh, "but I didn't know she was a red hot mama."

"Josh, just watch out for her. You must never say you're single or on the loose, because before you know it, she'll have a date for you, and I'm not being facetious with regard to you or Rob."

Just then Myra spotted Michael and the gang. She broke from her circle of men and headed towards her boys. Panting from exhaustion, and grinning from ear to ear, she wormed her way through the throngs.

"Hello boys, I see you're all here. Hello Rob," she said, kissing him and then turning to Josh, with a glint in her eye. "I'm glad that you're here with Rob; he needs someone like you," she added, kissing Josh on both cheeks. "Have I been enjoying myself? What a lovely bunch of boys that lot is," she said, pointing to the group she had just left. "They're so full of fun and what bodies some of them have got. If only I was twenty years younger!"

"Mum, even though you're not twenty years younger, it's still not stopping you. Just behave yourself a little."

The party, if one could call it that, albeit an impromptu one, was now in full swing as the ship sailed majestically from the harbor in Miami. Even Michael and the gang were joining in, Selwyn swiveling his hips like an Egyptian belly dancer. Rob and Josh stood on the sideline watching while Myra searched for a man to 'attack'. It wasn't long before Myra spotted Reuben.

"Ah, there's Reuben, the young artist I was speaking to before we boarded. I'll ask him to dance, seeing that you two aren't asking!"

She waltzed off having given Rob and Josh a look of disgust at their not asking her if she wanted to dance. Reuben was grabbed and whisked onto the makeshift dance floor. Reuben was a decent looking guy; not one of the Muscle Mary's, but attractive to look at and seemingly pleasant to talk to, because soon he and Myra were chatting and dancing happily together.

Josh snuggled closer to Rob as a bit of a wind had sprung up as the ship hit the open sea.

"Are you cold?" asked Rob, putting his arms around Josh to warm him.

"I was, but not any more, thanks. And thanks Rob, for asking me to come on the cruise, I think we're going to have a good time together, especially with the present company of Michael and his gang."

"Josh, do you want to stay up here or go back down to the cabin?" asked Rob.

"I don't mind staying here, if you'd like."

Rob accepted Josh's response, but had really hoped that they might go and have some quality time together in the cabin, but they still had a week ahead of them.

Once land began disappearing, people started drifting from the pool deck and heading to either their cabins to get ready for the evening, or going exploring around the ship. Myra made her way to her cabin while the four boys went exploring.

"I believe this ship even has an ice rink," said Rob.

"We found it," said Selwyn, "it's down in the belly of the boat."

"Ship!" reminded Michael.

"Well, it's down in the bottom. Quite nice actually, but you must see the promenade. That looks a fun area with shops and bars."

"Let's go there then and have a drink," suggested Josh, so off they set.

Although the promenade was crowded, they found a bar with a few empty seats. They sat and placed their order: beer all for all.

"Here's to us," said Michael raising his glass, once the drinks had arrived. "May we all have a horny, happy holiday together."

"I'll drink to that, especially the horny bit," remarked Selwyn.

They clinked glasses and then sat back to relax and enjoy the holiday.

"By the way, Mike, where do we eat tonight?" asked Rob.

"I think we're in the *Mozart Dining Room*."

"That sounds very smart," commented Selwyn, "but do we have to dress up?"

"That I'm not sure of, but I'll find out."

"Perhaps our cabin steward will know, but to be honest, I just didn't feel like dressing up on the first night," stated Selwyn.

"Otherwise, I'm sure that we can eat elsewhere," suggested Michael. "What about you Josh?"

"Michael, I'm easy."

"Josh, don't say that in present company, because Selwyn will take it literally."

"Anything that might have a sexual connotation, Selwyn will grab with delight," laughed Rob.

"It's not only the connotations that he grabs, Josh, so watch him!" chirped Michael.

"Josh, don't believe a word that these two lonely men say; they're only jealous of my good looks, charming personality and undying sexual athleticism," replied an indignant Selwyn.

"I believe you Selwyn," said Josh, feeling sorry for the 'attack' on Selwyn.

"What do you believe about him?" asked Rob.

"Well, the good looks … and…"

"Yes?"

"Well, he seems a really nice guy."

"That's how he gets round people, by being a really nice guy," observed Rob, "But we all love him, don't we Mike?"

Michael smiled enigmatically at Selwyn and replied, "Of course we do."

Most of the passengers seemed to have come indoors from the pool area and were wandering around the ship, getting their bearings. Although Rob, Josh and Michael remained deep in conversation, Selwyn's eyes drifted and watched every passing man. Just then they heard a "Yoohoo!" and Myra made a grand entrance, waving and moving hastily in their direction. When she reached them, Rob pulled up a chair for her and ordered her a whiskey.

"What are we doing tonight?" asked Myra.

"We haven't actually given it any thought yet, Mum. Did you have anything in mind?"

"I believe there's a disco on one of the top decks…"

"Mum, you're too old to be going to discos. In any case that's for the kids."

"Oh well, maybe there might be a show on. I believe they have a magnificent theatre here."

"It really is magnificent," said Michael. "Selwyn and I found it earlier and had a look; it's beautiful.".

"I'm sure they have an entertainment programme somewhere," volunteered Josh.

"You're right, Josh, I saw one in our cabin when we arrived," replied Rob.

"Well then we can have a look and take it from there," said Michael.

He noticed that Selwyn had been busily observing every walking male that passed them.

"Have you spotted anything you like, love?"

"A few are not too bad, but this is like a meat market. I've never been anywhere where you have so much meat to choose from," replied Selwyn, glowing as he said it.

"Selwyn!" exclaimed Myra. "You're not supposed to looking at other men, especially when you have my strong, virile son as your better half."

"Oh don't worry Mum, he's always looking. Rather look than touch, I say."

Both Josh and Rob finished their beers simultaneously and Rob suggested that they go back to their cabin and get ready for the evening.

"Good idea," said Michael, "at least then Selwyn will only have one man to look at."

They all rose and headed in the direction of their cabins. On the way they saw a steward and asked about the meals and the dress code for the dining rooms. Selwyn was very happy to hear that it was only the Captain's cocktail party and a couple of other restaurants where one had to dress up, so it was decided to meet in the *Mozart Dining Room* at 7:30p.m.

Back in their cabin, Michael asked Selwyn what he thought of Josh.

"I think he's very nice," replied Selwyn, "and I think he and Rob actually make a good couple. Do you like him?"

"Yes, I think he's a very nice person."

Meanwhile in Rob's cabin, the same types of questions were being asked and discussed.

"What do you think of Selwyn?" enquired Rob.

"I think he's very sweet," replied Josh, "but I haven't really had a chance to speak to him properly."

"And Mike?"

"Well I've always liked him. I always looked for him when he went to school. He seems to have become better-looking as he's got older, not that he's old or anything. You like them don't you, Rob?"

"I'd say that they're the best friends I've got."

"How did you meet them?"

"I was looking for an apartment, in fact my current apartment, and Mike is a real estate salesman and he took me to see the apartment. I fell in love with the place and bought it. At the same time, he'd gone into a relationship with Selwyn who was unemployed. No I lie; he was doing three nights a week at a club as a drag artiste."

"You're joking!"

"No, and a bloody good one at that. Any rate I offered Selwyn a job working with me and we've been buddies ever since."

"And the drag shows?"

"He's stopped doing those, although I think some times he might do the odd private show, but I haven't heard of any recently."

"I wouldn't have thought he was a drag artiste because he doesn't look that fem or camp."

Rob laughed. "He used to be, but I think since he and Mike have been together, he seems to have calmed down a bit."

Josh moved over to their twin beds, which had also been pushed together like in Michael's cabin, and lay down. "Do you want to join me?"

"I thought you were never going to ask," said Rob. "Since we arrived on board, I've wanted to get you on your own."

"Well, now you have, so what are you going to do about it?"

Rob lay down next to Josh, his gigantic frame making Josh's look small, then Rob leant across and placed his lips on Josh's. Their tongues met and each tried to invade the other's mouth. Soon Rob's muscular body slid on top of Josh and they could feel their aroused cocks rubbing together. Clothes began to be removed, clumsily. Arms, legs, mouths and hands fought for possession. Their naked bodies thrashed together, their moans and groans sounding like a unified chorus of pleasure as Josh gave himself over to Rob.

Next door, Michael smiled on hearing the sounds from his friend's cabin alongside, so did Selwyn, but neither said anything.

"I think I'm going to take a shower," said Michael, pulling off his clothes and entering the bathroom area of their cabin.

Selwyn watched the lithe naked body of his partner of two years. He always found Michael sexy. In fact, he found every bit of Michael's being desirable. Michael soaped his body and Selwyn watched through the open bathroom door as soapsuds slid down the wet, taut body of Michael. Selwyn felt himself getting an erection from watching Michael in the shower. He got up from the bed and also removed his clothes. He wandered over to the bathroom doorway and stood watching as Michael massaged his chest and pectoral muscles with his soapy hands. Watching Michael like this was arousing Selwyn even more, so when he couldn't contain himself any longer, he entered the shower and both young men massaged each other while their bodies slid effortlessly together.

Michael's lips found Selwyn's and Michael's hands slid onto the firm rounded ass of Selwyn. Michael pulled Selwyn closer to him, crushing their burgeoning cocks together. Selwyn writhed in Michael's clutches and then slid down to take Michael's hard cock deep into his throat. Michael began a gentle thrusting motion into Selwyn's throat and he could feel the suction that Selwyn created with his mouth on his thick stem. They continued like this for some time until Michael warned that he was nearing his climax. Selwyn released his mouth momentarily.

"Shoot, baby, shoot," he gasped, and immediately went back to pleasuring

Michael.

Michael couldn't contain himself any longer and with a loud groan, he fired the first of a number of volleys into Selwyn's throat. Selwyn swallowed as fast as he could, not wanting to lose any of Michael's juices, and he continued doing this until he could feel Michael's erection beginning to subside. Michael then went about doing the same for Selwyn and when they had finished their shower having pleased each other, they re-entered the bedroom area, where they heard the sounds of joy emanating from next door, and both Michael and Selwyn hugged and kissed each other, happy in the knowledge that they had each other to share their love.

Chapter 9

Dinner in the *Mozart Dining Room* was a sumptuous affair. The availability of dishes was unbelievable. They all realized that should they continue to indulge in the amount of food that was on offer, they'd all roll off the ship when it docked again in Miami.

After dinner, drinks were enjoyed in one of the bars along the promenade and then it was off to the theatre for a show. The *Crimson Theatre* took up three decks of the ship and the performances were on a par with anything one saw on Broadway. The show was a typical musical-type review, which suited most of the gays on board, who applauded thunderously after each act.

Of the group, Selwyn sat watching the show more intently than the others, perhaps to take tips in case he ever decided to go back to being a drag artiste. Josh sat between Michael and Rob and on one or two rare occasions, either by accident of perhaps intentionally, Josh's leg touched Michael's, not that Michael minded, as he never objected or moved away from Josh's leg.

After the show was completed, everyone headed off to the bars, casino, out onto the deck and a few even ventured to the disco, where Myra was longing to go.

"What do you want to do, Rob?" asked Josh, feeling refreshed after his early evening lovemaking with Rob.

"I'd be quite happy to go back to the cabin and carry on from where we left off this evening."

Michael overheard this and smiled. Rob noticed Michael's smile and asked, "What are you smiling about, little Mike?"

"Not so much of the little. Did you enjoy this evening?"

"Yes, the food was great, the show even better …"

"No, I mean earlier?"

Rob grinned like a Cheshire cat.

"How do you know?" he enquired softly.

"We heard you and because of that, it got us going as well."

"In that case, I'm glad we both hit the jackpot!"

"Do you know what I'm glad about? You. You seem so much more relaxed and happy, now that you've met Josh."

"Mike, I must be honest with you, I did get a little worried by something that Josh said when we first met."

"And what's that Rob?"

"Do you know that he had the hots for you when you were at school?"

Michael looked surprised.

"You're joking of course, aren't you?"

"No, I'm not."

"But that was a long time ago."

Michael had found Josh attractive, more now as an adult than he did as a young boy, and there was no denying that Josh had a lot going for him. He had charm, charisma, a good body, good looks and he was just a very nice person, but Michael was not about to drop Selwyn in favor of Josh.

"I don't know what to say Rob."

"You don't have to say anything. I'm just telling you what Josh told me."

"What are you two so deep in conversation about?" interrupted Myra.

"We were just discussing which man we could get to propose to you Myra," replied Rob.

"Liar! You're more likely to ask the guy to propose to you," retorted Myra. "Josh, don't take any notice of these men here, come with me and we'll go and see where the action is."

Myra took Josh by the hand and led him off in the direction of the elevators.

"Now where do you think those two are off to?" asked Rob.

"With Myra in tow, anywhere."

"Well, what are we going to do, after all we don't have to get up early tomorrow because we're not docking anywhere?"

"I think I'm going to go up on deck," said Selwyn, "if anyone's wanting to come with me."

"You go, Selwyn," said Michael. "I think I'm going to go to the casino. What about you Rob?"

"I'll come with you Mike. Maybe I might get lucky and win some bucks."

They all dispersed in their different directions. As Michael and Rob wandered off to the casino, Rob said, "What if Myra and Josh come looking for us, they won't know where we are."

"Well, we don't know where they are, but I have a pretty good idea," replied Michael.

"Where Mike?"

"In the disco. She just loves dancing. Do you think we should go and see if they're there then head down to the casino? At least we can tell them where we'll be."

"Good idea, Mike. Lead on."

They caught an elevator up to the top deck where the disco was situated. As they approached, they could hear the music pumping loudly and when they went in, it was almost deafening. In the dim lighting, they managed to locate Josh and Myra on the dance floor, giving their all among a number of shirtless men, all sweating.

"Mum," shouted Michael above the noise of the music. "Rob and I will be in the casino if you're looking for us."

Myra merely smiled and nodded. Michael, however, wasn't sure whether Myra was nodding to him or in time to the music. Rob and Michael caught the elevator back down and went to the casino where they started to gamble. While they were gambling, Michael caught the eye of a steward and asked him to bring a beer, which he duly did. Michael played a couple of machines and finished his beer.

"Would you like another one, sir?"

Michael looked up to see the same steward standing next to him.

"Sure, why not. What's your name? I hate calling you guys that work on the ship 'steward' all the time?"

"It's Brent, sir."

"Well, thanks Brent I will have another beer."

The drink was fetched and given to Michael, who thanked Brent. After about half an hour of gambling, Rob approached Michael.

"Mike, I'm giving up. I seem to be losing too much. Maybe tonight's not my lucky night."

"No, your luck all happened this afternoon, didn't it?"

"Cheeky! But then so did yours, didn't it?"

The two friends laughed together as their thoughts flashed to their enjoyment earlier with their partners.

"So where are you going, in case Josh comes back here?"

"I don't know. I think I'll just wander about and see what's happening."

"OK. I'll see you later."

Rob left the casino and made his way up to deck 11 where the swimming pools were situated. The cool night air was a light relief from the near stuffiness of the casino. He wandered along the deck towards the pools and the whirlpools. In one of the whirlpools sat three guys, chatting together and laughing. As he stood against the railing of the ship, looking out over the dark ocean, a voice came close to him.

"Hi there. Lovely evening, isn't it?"

Rob turned to see who the speaker was.

"Derek, is that you? What on earth are you doing here?"

"Probably the same as you, enjoying the cruise and the night air."

"Are you here alone?"

"No, I brought a friend along. I don't know if you remember Chris who works for me?"

"Yes. He was the guy who helped Selwyn when he was attacked."

"That's right. Well, things blossomed and we're now living together."

"That's wonderful for you, but where is Chris now?"

"You know what these youngsters are like. He wanted to go off dancing, and I'm afraid I think I've passed that stage in life."

"Rubbish, Derek. You've got a lot of go in you still."

"So tell me, are you here alone, Rob?"

Rob smiled because for once he was able to say he had a partner, albeit still in the early stages and they weren't actually in a full-time relationship.

"No, Derek. I've also got a friend with me, but he too is dancing."

"We sound like a couple of old folks. Both our partners dancing and not with either of us."

"I'm also here with Selwyn and Mike and Mike's Mum."

"Oh, where's Michael?"

"Gambling. I started out there this evening, but I'm afraid I don't seem to have much luck tonight. Listen, instead of us standing out here in the sea breezes, how about joining me for a drink?"

"Sounds great. There's a bar back there towards the aft of the ship, shall we go there."

"Lead on, you obviously know your way around this floating hotel."

The two headed off in the direction of the bar, went in, ordered their drinks and settled down to chat.

Meanwhile, Selwyn had been sitting having a drink in the *Sky Bar* on the same deck as the disco. He had met a couple of guys and sat talking to them for a while, then decided to go down one deck to where Rob and Derek had been just a little earlier. When Selwyn reached the deck, the three guys in the whirlpool were still enjoying the warmth of the water and each other's company.

"Do you mind if I join you?" asked Selwyn.

"Not at all. The more the merrier," said a blonde guy of about Selwyn's age.

Selwyn stripped off in the limited light and hopped in between the blonde and a tall, lean man of about thirty-five. The conversations continued, but only after they had introduced themselves.

"Hi, I'm Gary," said the blonde, extending a hand to Selwyn.

"And I'm Bert," replied the tall, lean man.

The third man's name was Novak and he sounded foreign.

"Hi, I'm Selwyn," then turning to Novak, he said, "you sound foreign."

"Correct, I am from the Czech Republic and I'm on holiday in the States."

"And are you enjoying your stay here?" asked Selwyn.

"Very much thank you," replied Novak.

Novak had an appealing face; handsome without being overly beautiful. His smile was open and broad and he seemed to be very friendly, but alone. It seemed to appear to Selwyn that perhaps the blonde and the tall, lean man might be together.

The conversation was typical of that when people meet for the first time;

where do you come from, are you alone, what do you do, those types of questions.

As the jets of the whirlpool pounded water against their bodies, Selwyn felt a knee touch his. He glanced to his left and noticed that Gary was smiling at him. He returned the smile. A little later, the knees touched again, and again there was the smile. Throughout all this, conversations continued as per normal. Eventually Gary stood up and said he was going to dry off and go downstairs. As he rose from the bubbling water, Selwyn noticed the evidence of an erection on Gary. Obviously the touching of knees had done something to arouse Gary, and Selwyn wondered if his getting out of the whirlpool was meant to be a signal that Selwyn should do likewise and follow Gary. However, Selwyn chose to remain in the water. No sooner had Gary departed, than Bert excused himself and also left. Novak and Selwyn remained in the bubbling water.

Selwyn slid, surreptitiously, closer to Novak, until the jets of water forced his leg against Novak's. This time it was Selwyn who was making the advances. Novak's leg remained 'glued' to Selwyn's then Selwyn felt a hand rest on his thigh. This feeling aroused him and soon it wasn't only his legs or arms that were bouncing and bobbing in the bubbling water. Novak's hand slid a little higher until it reached its target. Selwyn closed his eyes as he felt a warmth flood through his body. He stretched out a hand and felt something long and hard bobbing close to him. He squeezed and heard Novak groan in ecstasy. The two men lay luxuriating in the warm water, their hands massaging the other until the bubbles grew to a fury. Two gasps emanated from the whirlpool and two men lay relaxed for a while and then both stepped from the warm water.

"I'm afraid, I don't have a towel," said Selwyn, the evidence of his excitement still apparent.

"Here, share mine," said Novak, and both men stood side by side with the towel wrapped around them until Selwyn and Novak had dried themselves.

Once they had dressed, Novak said, "I hope I see you around."

To which Selwyn responded, "Thanks Novak that was great. See you."

Then both men disappeared in the dark.

Selwyn found the bar in which Rob and Derek were still drinking and approached them.

"Hello Mr. Campbell," said Selwyn on seeing his former part-time boss.

"Hello Selwyn. How are you?"

"Very well thanks. Sorry to disturb you both, but do you know where Michael is, Rob?"

"If he's still at it, in the casino."

"Thanks, I'll make my way down there."

Selwyn thereupon made his way down to the casino. He knew that Mr. Campbell and Rob knew each other, so thought nothing of their being together, but he did wonder why Mr. Campbell was on the cruise and if he was alone. When he found Michael, who by this time had acquired a fair sum of winnings, he said, "You'll never guess who I've just seen on this ship!"

"Who?" answered Michael.

"Old Mr. Campbell. You know the clothing store guy. I saw him chatting to Rob in one of the bars up near the disco."

"I wonder if he's here alone or with someone."

"We'll have to ask Rob when he comes back."

"Selwyn would you like something to drink?"

"Please. That would be nice. A beer thanks."

Michael looked around, spotted who he was looking for and shouted, "Brent, could I have two beers please?"

The steward hastily got the beers from the bar and returned to where Michael was gambling.

Selwyn's eyes caught sight of Brent as he neared.

"Oh my God!" exclaimed, Selwyn.

"What?" asked a perturbed Michael.

"It's him," hissed Selwyn, who immediately turned his back on the approaching Brent.

"Your beers, sir," said Brent, handing Michael the two beers.

"Thank you Brent."

"Don't I know you, sir?" Asked Brent to Selwyn.

Selwyn turned to face the steward and their eyes met. Brent smiled, but Selwyn remained stony.

"I thought it was you. Well isn't that interesting, both of us on the same ship!" replied Brent.

Selwyn ignored the snide comment and Brent turned and still smiling, headed off back to the bar.

"Where do you know him from, Selwyn? Is he from your past?" asked Michael.

"Michael," said Selwyn in a chilling tone. "That is the guy who beat me up and threatened me when I did that stint at the clothing store. It was his friend that I bust."

"Oh hell. I'm sorry. I think we'd better tell Rob about this and you'd better watch out for him."

Selwyn gulped his beer down almost in one continuous swig. He was afraid, having seen his accuser. Immediately Michael suggested that they leave the casino and look for Rob.

"He's upstairs having a drink with Mr. Campbell."

"Come, we're going to find him."

The two boys hurried up to the bar where Rob and Mr. Campbell were still sitting.

"Hi guys," greeted Rob on seeing his two friends.

"I'm glad that we've got both of you," replied Michael.

"Why, Mike, what's the matter?" asked Rob.

"The guy who attacked Selwyn at your store, sir, is on this ship. He's a bar steward."

"What!" exclaimed Mr. Campbell.

"Where did you see him?" enquired Rob.

"I've been ordering drinks from him while I was gambling, not knowing who he was and it wasn't until Selwyn joined me that he told me who the person was."

"Michael, I think I just want to go back to the cabin," bemoaned Selwyn.

"Take Selwyn back to your cabin and lock the door, because I assume when you ordered drinks, you gave your cabin number," said Rob, being the epitome of a good P.I.

Michael and Selwyn left immediately for their cabin and did as Rob had suggested. Selwyn got undressed and climbed into bed while Michael sat alongside, comforting him.

"Babes, we're not going to let this guy ruin our holiday and we're going to carry on doing what we want and try to take no notice of him, even if he serves us."

Selwyn closed his eyes and tried to go to sleep while Michael lay next to him, stroking his hair.

Later that evening, there was a light tap on the connecting door and Rob popped his head in.

"How's he?" he whispered.

"Sleeping," replied Michael.

"Listen tomorrow morning, we'll go and see the chief steward or the purser and explain the situation. After all, I don't think the ship wants to get a bad reputation should anything untoward happen here. Now get some sleep, both of you."

"Thanks Rob. Has Josh come back yet?"

"Yes, he's also sleeping. He and Myra exhausted each other by the sounds of it. But go to sleep and I'll see you in the morning."

Chapter 10

The following morning, the ship's newspaper was slid under each cabin's door and in it were explained the activities for the day. Michael slid from the bed while Selwyn remained sleeping, and picked up their copy of the newspaper. He climbed back into bed and started reading.

The morning was made up of a variety of lectures to be conducted by certain people, dancing lessons being held, but the thing that caught Michael's eye was what was planned for the afternoon: Sports Games.

There were to be teams of not more than ten members who would participate in a variety of 'unusual' sporting games to be held in and around the pool area. That would be fun, he thought.

As he was reading, Selwyn stirred and opened his eyes.

"Hello, beautiful," said Michael, kissing Selwyn on the forehead.

"Hi there," groaned Selwyn.

"How are you feeling this morning?"

"A bit of a heavy head, but otherwise, fine. How are you?"

"Rearing to go," said Michael. "Time to get up and smell the sea air and have a hearty breakfast."

His energy and enthusiasm only made Selwyn feel more tired.

"Where's all this energy come from?" asked Selwyn, getting up and going off to the bathroom.

"I've been reading the ship's newspaper and there're going to be some fun sports games this afternoon, so I thought we should put together a team."

"Are you mad?"

"No. There's you and me, Rob and Josh; Mum might be able to do a few things, perhaps, but even if she can't there're four of us."

"How many in a team?"

"The paper says no more than ten in a team."

"I suppose it's something different. Where are they doing it?" enquired Selwyn.

"On the pool deck."

"Let's ask Rob and Josh and see what they think."

The two boys dressed and then tapped on the connecting door.

"Come in," boomed Rob's voice.

Michael gently opened the dividing door and peered around it. Both Rob and Josh were still in bed, but they told Selwyn and Michael to come in.

"Aren't you two getting up today?" asked Selwyn, leaping on the bed.

"We're on holiday, so what is the rush?"

"What have you got there, Mike?" asked Rob.

"The ship's newspaper. Oh there's yours still on the floor," replied Michael, picking up their newspaper and handing it to Josh. "There are sports games this afternoon and we were wondering if you two were keen to make up a team with us?"

"What do we have to do?" asked Rob.

"It doesn't say. It only says Sports Games to be held in and around the pool area. Should we do it for fun?"

"Go on, let's do it, Rob," pleaded Josh.

"OK. For you, anything."

"So what must we do Michael?" asked Josh.

"I don't know, but I'm sure they'll tell us during the morning or we can ask at the purser's desk."

"That reminds me," said Rob, "I must speak to him about last night's episode."

"Are we going for breakfast? I'm hungry," moaned Selwyn.

"Well if you two would get out of our cabin then we might be able to get dressed," commanded the booming voice of Rob.

"Sorry, but it's nothing we haven't seen before, except for Josh," snickered Selwyn, leaving their cabin.

Michael followed immediately and phoned Myra's cabin to see if she was awake and if she was going to join them for breakfast.

By 8:30 a.m., all five of them were seated around a table on the pool deck enjoying not only the glorious sunshine, but also the bounteous amount of food on offer.

"Michael, I might be able to dance the legs off most people," said Myra, "but I don't think I can do sport. Why don't you ask Reuben and Dirk?"

"Who?"

"You know those two nice young men I spoke to while we were waiting to board the ship. You know the quiet one and the large Dutchman."

"Oh yes, I know which ones you mean. Do you think they'd want to join us?"

"I'm more interested in them wanting to join each other," retorted Myra.

"The matchmaker's at it again," said Michael. "You see what I mean, Josh, give my mother half a chance and she'd have had the entire world either married or partnered."

"I think they'd make a lovely couple and besides, both are on their own on the ship. It would be nice if they could be friends."

"Mum, you want them to be more than just friends, as you put it. Whenever you see anyone on their own, you think that they have to be matched up with someone. Maybe they like being on their own, have you thought of that?"

"Of course I have, but I know that they don't want to be on their own."

"I suppose that you've asked them that, and that's what they told you."

"Both said they were hoping to meet someone nice on this cruise."

"I don't believe it. And when did you ask them?"

"Last night."

By this time, the others were almost collapsing with laughter at Michael's frustration at his mother's behavior. Say what you like, but Myra seemed to always be concerned for the underdog.

"Oh look!" exclaimed Myra, jumping up from the table and hurrying across the deck.

"Now where is my crazy mother off to?"

Soon she was scurrying back with a man in tow.

"Boys, this is Reuben. I saw he was about to sit down on his own so I asked him to join us. Reuben these are my boys; well they're not all mine, but it feels like it sometimes. This one here is mine. He's Michael and that's his partner, Selwyn. And over here we have the giant, Rob and his partner, Josh. Boys, this is Reuben."

Josh smiled and leaned closer to Rob. "I like the sound of me now being your partner."

"So do I," he replied.

Myra then took over all the organizing of the Sports Games.

"Reuben, we want you to be part of our team for the sports games this afternoon. We don't know what we have to do, but at least you look strong and athletic. Has any other team asked you yet?"

"No, Myra."

"Good, then you're ours. Right boys, that makes five."

"Are you on your own here or have you got a partner?" enquired Selwyn.

"No. All alone in the world," he answered, "but I don't mind it."

"Just don't let Myra get her claws into you because she'll have a partner for you in no time at all."

Reuben laughed. "I know. She was trying her best last night and becoming very frustrated because I wasn't interested in the guys she was pointing out to me."

"Well, I didn't want to see you unhappy."

"I appreciate that, but if I want a guy, I'll find one, thanks," said Reuben without sounding cheeky.

"Well I'm very glad that someone has at last told my mother to keep her nose out of other people's affairs."

"But he's not in an affair," respond Myra.

"You know what I mean, Mum."

Breakfast proceeded without any other incidents and once everyone had eaten their fill, they all departed in various directions, Michael, Rob and Selwyn heading to the purser's office and Myra taking Josh for a walk along the deck.

"I'm sorry to hear of your complaint, Mr. Clayton, but according to my staffing list, we don't have a person employed by the name of Brent on board this ship."

"Then he has to have given you a false name," commented Michael.

"Sir, if he has, there's nothing I can do about it, because we wouldn't know what name he was working under. The only thing that I can suggest is that should you see him again, to call me and then point out the young man to me."

They knew that the purser couldn't do any more, so they thanked him and left.

"Selwyn, don't you worry about a thing. Remember, I'm a P.I. and I'll do my own investigations to find out who he's going as."

"Thanks Rob."

They made their way back to their respective cabins, slipped into their bathing costumes and headed back up to the pool deck for some sun and swimming. Myra and Josh saw them when they arrived at the pool area, so Josh retuned to his cabin to get changed.

Back on the pool deck, Selwyn, Michael and Rob, found themselves some pool loungers, plus an extra one for Josh when he arrived, lay their towels on them, stripped off and lay down to enjoy the warmth of the sun. They were not the only people enjoying the sun. The pool area was becoming crowded with semi-naked men. The aroma of tanning lotion pervaded everywhere. If Selwyn thought their farewell on the deck as the ship departed was like a meat market, he was mistaken. There were bronzed bodies everywhere, some even lying on the actual deck for a lack of chairs and loungers on which to lie.

Selwyn was almost drooling and both Rob and Michael noticed this.

"Down boy!" said Rob to Selwyn.

"Do you realize how painful this is for me?" said Selwyn, licking his lips. "All these beautiful hunks parading in front of me."

"Temptation! Don't let it get to you, babes. I know what you must be going through, but just imagine that they are metallic robots without feeling."

"I can't," whimpered Selwyn. "And they're all so big. Just what I like!"

"You know Rob, I think we'll have to send him back to his cabin for safety sake, or what do you think?"

'Well, it would leave more of them for us."

"True."

Suddenly Selwyn burst out laughing and pointed towards one of the whirlpools.

"Look at Myra."

Myra was seated on the edge of the whirlpool, bottle of tanning lotion in her hand and was busy oiling some hunk's shoulders and back.

"I don't believe what I'm seeing," remarked Michael. "Do you realize that if she were a man, she'd be worse than Selwyn."

"Damn cheek. What do you mean?" asked Selwyn, indignantly.

"Well I think she's attached herself to more men since she arrived on this ship than you have, and to do that takes some doing!"

Josh arrived and put his towel on the vacant lounger that Rob had saved for him. He peeled off his T-shirt and then slid his shorts down to his ankles and stepped out of them. His body was definitely athletic and toned and he had on a canary yellow Speedo, but it was what was encased within the Lycra that caught Michael and Selwyn's eyes. They both stared, Michael actually smiling at what he saw. To say that Josh was 'big' would be considered an understatement. Josh lay down on his towel and proceeded to pour tanning oil on his chest. A thought flashed through Michael's mind: how nice it would be to offer to massage the oil in for Josh, but he daren't. He watched as Josh's hands slowly and almost seductively slid over each pectoral muscle and then down the taut stomach to run across the waistband of his Speedo. Once again Michael's attention was drawn to the package encased in the tight Lycra.

Josh happened to glance up and saw Michael watching his every move. Josh gave a subtle smile to Michael, who instinctively looked away hurriedly as though not to be caught looking. Josh poured some oil onto each thigh, and once again massaged it into his skin. Michael's glances became fleeting, in case someone might be watching his intense interest in Josh's action. Josh's hands once more glided effortlessly over his smooth skin, his fingers running ever so gently against the crotch area of his Speedo. Michael was beginning to become worried as he was also growing in size from looking at Josh. Josh noticed this and became even more seductive in his massaging, until it became unbearable for Michael, who flipped over onto his stomach to hide his embarrassment. Josh smiled at Michael and lay down on his back to enjoy the sun's rays.

"I'm going for a swim," said Rob, "anyone coming?"

"I'll join you," replied Selwyn.

When they had gone, Michael turned his head to face Josh and found the young man, beaming at him. Michael returned the smile. They remained looking at each other and then Josh's hand moved down to his thigh. Michael's eyes immediately followed in the same direction, and he noticed that Josh was looking bigger than before in the package area. Josh seemed to feel no embarrassment about having an erection in public, but then Michael didn't know that Josh had been a porno star and was used to this state of excitement in public. Michael shifted slightly and rolled onto his side to face Josh and in the process his state of excitement was evident to Josh.

"I think you've got a big problem there," whispered Josh.

"I'm not sure if you might not have an even bigger problem," retorted Michael.

They smiled to each other, but Michael was worrying that Rob might see what was happening and take offence. He had to do something to get out of this situation, but what?

"There's a gym on the ship, isn't there?"

"I think so," replied Josh. "I think they have a sauna there too."

That was it!

"That's a good idea. I think I'm going for a sauna," said Michael, standing up and wrapping his towel around his waist.

He moved off away from the pool area and headed towards the beauty salon and gym area to find the sauna. It didn't take him long to find it, removed his towel and was soon sitting in his Speedo on the wooden bench in the sauna, heat warming up the environment. Michael closed his eyes and thought about what had happened at the pool. Suddenly the door opened and Josh stood in the doorway. He entered, smiled at Michael, dropped his towel and sat down beside him. The two young men sat silent, until Josh reached across and touched Michael. Michael's eyes closed once more as he felt the tender touches of Josh on his body.

"It's not safe here, Josh," whispered Michael, still with his eyes closed.

Josh continued to run his finger tips across Michael's chest caressing each nipple and then down to the stomach, slowly trailing them down over the six-pack stomach until his fingers ran over the bulge that was protruding from Michael's Speedo.

"You know I've always admired you," continued Josh, whispering in Michael's ear.

Michael never moved but delighted in the gentle touch and eroticism that Josh was creating. He felt the waistband of his Speedo being pulled down to release his engorged cock and then he felt the warmth of Josh's mouth encompass his length.

Michael felt a pleasurable feeling charge through his body, causing him to brace himself. He gasped as the feeling of Josh's mouth sliding effortlessly along the length of his thick cock reached a climax and his breathing increased. Slowly he felt the warm movement of Josh's mouth come to an end, and then heard the sauna door close. He opened his eyes for the first time; the sauna was empty. Josh had left. He looked down at his crotch, pulled his Speedo back over his still engorged cock, stood up, wrapped his towel around his waist and walked out of the sauna.

"Where were you?" asked Selwyn when Michael got back to the pool where Josh and Rob were lying.

"I just went for a stroll around the deck," answered Michael, but without catching Josh's eye.

"Mike, have you heard anything more about the sports games this afternoon?" asked Rob.

"No and I don't know if Myra is still looking for more team members for us."

"But we can cope," remarked Selwyn.

"Of course we can," said Josh adjusting his position on his towel so that he could view Michael better.

"Speak of the devil," quipped Michael, "and she's sure to appear. Mum, we were just talking about you. Have you got your team ready for the games this afternoon?"

"Yes, Darling, everything is in order. I've managed to get Dirk involved as well."

On hearing this, all four boys roared with laughter.

"What's the joke?" enquired an innocent Myra.

"Mum, I love you. You really are the sweetest person I know. You're always more concerned for others, rather than yourself. So tell us, is Reuben and Dirk now in some sort of relationship?"

"We'll see what happens," was all Myra said.

While they were all lying near the swimming pools, Chris and Mr. Campbell ventured past.

"Chris!" shouted Selwyn, leaping up to meet his friend.

"Selwyn, hi there. How are you? Derek told me that he'd seen Rob and that you guys were on the ship. It's so good to see you again."

"I've been fine, but did you hear that Brent is on board."

"So I believe, but more importantly, which of these hunks is your partner?"

Selwyn pointed out Michael.

"Oh, yes, very nice I could go for that; in fact I could go for anything, you know me!"

"Someone after my own heart," murmured Selwyn. "But tell me, have you been behaving yourself while you've been here?"

"Let's go for a walk to the railing," suggested Chris. When they reached the rail, Chris confided in Selwyn. "Last night was such fun. I went to the disco because Derek doesn't like dancing and I met this guy there. Very dishy! So we went for a walk up on the top deck, you know where the sports court is?"

"Yes!"

"Well we went behind the rock climbing wall. Ooh it was great fun."

"And you weren't caught or seen."

"No, there's a toilet behind the wall."

"That's very handy," replied Selwyn. "I must remember that, should I need it."

"And what about you, or can't you misbehave here?"

"Michael knows I can't behave myself. I met a guy in the whirlpool last night, a Czech guy."

"Does Michael know?"

"Of course not. He has this philosophy: 'out of sight out of mind,' so as long as I don't let him see, he doesn't mind."

"Is that how you interpret it?"

Both laughed heartily.

Just then Michael came over to where they were standing.

"What are you two up to? Hi, I'm Michael."

"Hi Michael, I'm Chris. I used to work with Selwyn."

"Oh I remember, you're the guy who looked after him."

"I don't know so much, I think he looked after me, especially that day in the change room with the customer."

"Well, thanks any way. It was good of you. Listen Selwyn, I'm going down to the cabin for a while."

"OK, I'll see you later."

Michael trotted off leaving Chris with Selwyn.

"You see that young guy lying with us, the one with the yellow Speedo, I think Michael had a thing with him just now, or perhaps he's off to have one with him now, should the guy get up and go."

"Ooh, scandal. What makes you say that?"

"They were eyeing each other earlier on and both had roaring erections," chuckled Selwyn.

"So who is that lovely thing in the yellow?"

"That's Rob's boyfriend. You know the guy who picked me up after work everyday."

"Good taste he's got, but then so have you."

"Thanks. Tell me, are you going in for the sports games this afternoon?"

"Are you crazy? I and sport don't go together. I only go together with the men who play sport. Why? Are you?" asked Chris.

"Sure."

"Quite manly are you?"

Selwyn flexed a muscle.

"Sweetie I wouldn't do that here, not with all these muscular men around, you might make a fool of yourself."

No sooner had Michael left, than he was back on deck.

"Sorry to disturb you two," said Michael interrupting Selwyn's conversation with Chris, "but Selwyn, did you go back to the cabin at all this morning?"

"No, why?"

"It looks as though someone's been rifling through our things. Rob, could I borrow you for a minute?" asked Michael, moving to where Rob, Josh and Myra were lying.

"Sure, what's the problem?"

"I think someone's been going through our stuff in the cabin."

"What! Come let's go and have a look."

Both Josh and Rob accompanied Selwyn and Michael back to the cabin. It was clear that their things had been tampered with and not by their cabin steward. Clothes were scattered all over the floor, an empty suitcase lay on the balcony and the drawers and cupboards had been left open.

"Check to see if anything is missing," instructed Rob, "but try not to get fingerprints on everything, just in case. I'm going to get the ship' security for you.

Josh, check our cabin and see if anything has been touched."

The first thing that Selwyn and Michael checked for were their passports and money. That hadn't been stolen; in fact the more they checked the more they realized that nothing seemed to be missing. It was only when Selwyn went into the bathroom that he discovered something. He emerged from the bathroom with a small plastic bag and in it was some white powder.

"Michael, I don't have to be a rocket scientist to know what this is, and it's not flour or baking powder."

"Where did you find that?"

"Hidden behind the toilet."

"Then someone's stashed it there on purpose. Hide it until Rob returns and then we'll speak to him about this."

Very soon Rob, accompanied by a security officer, arrived. The security man asked various questions, looked around the cabin and then left.

"Rob," whispered Michael as though someone might be listening at the cabin door. "We found this hidden in the bathroom, but I didn't want to say anything with security here."

Rob took the plastic bag and studied its contents.

"We all know what this is, don't we, and I know that neither of you use it?"

"Who would plant it here and why? asked Michael.

"Think!" suggested Rob. "Who on this ship has a grudge and would do anything to get his own back?"

"Brent!" echoed both Selwyn and Michael together.

"Exactly, but I'd like to know how he got in, unless, being a steward he had access to the cabin keys. Somehow I think we have to set a trap for him. Give me some time and I'll think of something."

Chapter 11

"Ladies and gentlemen, could I have your attention please," said the voice over the ships' loudspeakers. "Those planning in taking part in the Sports Games, please assemble at the sports court on deck 13 to register your teams. You have ten minutes to do so, as the games will be commencing at 14:00 precisely. Thank you."

"Did you hear that, Michael? I think we better get moving," said Myra, gathering her team members together.

The four boys, along with Myra, hurried up to deck 13 where crowds of teams were already gathering. There was an air of excitement as banter and challenges were being thrown from one team against another. They soon found Dirk and Reuben waiting for them, so their team consisted of six strong young men and their female captain.

"Myra, we apparently have to have a team name. Any idea what to call us?" Selwyn asked.

"Any suggestions, boys?"

Names were being bandied about, but no one was happy with any as they sounded too effete or ridiculous.

"What about the 'PI's'?" asked Rob

"That's quite good, Rob," Michael remarked, and all agreed to it, including their captain.

They registered their team name and the names of their team members, and then they were given their instructions as to how the games were to be run. They were going to have the first events on the jogging track on deck 12 and then move down a deck to the pool area to complete the games.

The rules were simple; each event must have a competitor from each team, but the number of events a team member took place in was not restrictive. So a team could consist of one, but that one person would have a great deal of exercising to do. Points would be awarded at a rate of 10 for a win, 8 for second, 5 for third and 3 for the remainder of the finishers. The added fun incentive was that for certain races props would have to be used by contestants as part of their race, so it could mean that before they actually got to running or swimming they had to get used to the objects which could delay or hamper them.

Non- participants were gathering around the pool area and those who couldn't find space there, went up to the jogging track deck.

The entertainment's officer took charge and announced the first event which was to be a two-lap run around the jogging track, one round forwards followed by their second lap, backwards.

"Who's good at running backwards?" asked Myra.

"I'll do it," replied Josh.

He took his place at the start line along with fifteen other runners. The starter got them under his orders and soon they were running and jostling for positions along the running track. As they came round after their first lap, Josh was in fourth or fifth position. The cheering and shouting was, to say the least, vocal. Myra was jumping up and down, screaming for her man. Once they crossed the start line, they had to turn around and run the route again, but backwards. This caused some consternation as runners collided with one another or ran into objects because they couldn't see where they were going. It was in this leg of the race that Josh began to come into his own. He would glance over his shoulder to get his bearings and run. Some tripped over their own feet and fell, causing more obstacles for the runners, but Josh kept going. As Josh and another runner neared the finish line, the shouting and screaming increased to a crescendo. Josh crossed the line, spun around and in his momentum, ran into the arms of Michael who caught him and held him. The gasping Josh smiled into Michael's face and they remained glued to each other.

"Well done Josh!" exclaimed Michael and soon the others were gathered around their runner.

"In first place, Team P.I. In second place, Team Handbag and in third, Team Muscles," announced the master of ceremonies. "The next event will need two entrants per team. It's the piggy-back race."

Teams hurriedly decided on their entrants and it was decided that Rob would carry the lightest who happened to be Reuben.

"The only difference about this race is that the people being carried will not be on the backs of their team mate, instead they will be over their shoulder."

All those competing began to try lifting and carrying their partners. Some were managing, while others were not. It was no problem for Rob to pick up Reuben, but when he flung him over his shoulder, Reuben began complaining.

"My balls! You're squashing my balls!"

When Rob adjusted Reuben's position, Reuben then complained that he couldn't breathe because his stomach was being squashed. However, other bodies being carried were echoing the same complaints.

The competitors came under starter's order and were then off. It was only once around the track, but before they had even gone a quarter of the way, all could hear the cries and groans from those being carried. Obviously the spectators were enjoying this immensely.

Rob found the going tough. He was not a fast runner, but he was strong so he didn't have to stop to adjust his partner's position, unlike other teams. Rob plodded along, not worrying about his position, so long as he didn't drop Reuben.

Poor Reuben was beginning to find himself in a slightly compromising position because with the constant rubbing of his crotch on Rob's shoulder, he was getting the start of an erection, and Rob could feel it, but it wasn't going to stop him from trying to win the race. Reuben was grunting and groaning and trying to reposition himself on Rob's shoulder to avoid the rubbing, but without success. As they came into the home straight, the cheering rose in volume again.

As they crossed the finish line, the announcer gave the results.

"First goes to Team Kitchen, followed by Team Muscles and in third, Team P.I."

Rob lowered Reuben to his feet and the poor young man immediately grabbed his crotch and groaned.

"Ooh that was sore," wailed Reuben.

"Right ladies and gentlemen," interrupted the announcer. "We come to race number three. For this event, two runners will be attached to each other by means of a rope, except they will be one behind the other and will have to run together."

Naturally there were gales of laughter at the idea of the two runners being one behind the other. Of course, snide comments were flowing and partners were being sought. Team P.I. looked at each other. They obviously needed fast runners, but they were also thinking of who wanted someone's crotch up against their ass!

"I think we need two people of approximately the same height," suggested Myra, "then it'll be easier to move together."

"Good point Mum."

"I thought of giving Dirk a chance, but he'd have to be paired with Rob, because they're both tall, but Rob may still be tired from his last race. Selwyn, you and Josh seem to be of similar height, and Josh has had a rest, so you two do it."

"Who's going at the back?" asked Josh to Selwyn.

"Josh! What a silly question! Now get behind me."

Josh positioned himself up against Selwyn's ass while the judges, who happened to be crewmembers, wrapped a rope around them.

"Ooh, that feels good," whispered Selwyn.

"Shut up and concentrate," whispered Josh back to him.

"If your ropes come undone during the race, the team will be disqualified," announced the M.C.

"Listen," said Michael going up to Selwyn and Josh. "Start on you left foot and begin slowly until you're used to each other's strides and then you can speed up. Good luck."

"On your marks! Go!" shouted the starter.

Bodies fell instantly while others got their footing muddled, while a few others, Selwyn and Josh included, managed to get moving and stay on their feet. Josh and Selwyn did as Michael had suggested and moved off slowly, but they soon increased their speed.

"This is fun," gasped Selwyn as they headed down the straight. "Rob was right. You are a big boy."

"Shut up and concentrate," said Josh into Selwyn's ear.

They ran a little further in total synchronicity, while Selwyn continued to pass compliments to Josh.

"I bet you've never done this before," said Selwyn thrusting his ass a little closer to Josh's crotch.

"Concentrate, Selwyn."

"I'm trying Josh, but I feel you're getting harder and it's making me lose concentration."

Josh knew that what Selwyn said was correct. Their close contact was a stimulus for him, and yes, he was getting harder, and yes, it did feel good.

"Hold onto me!" shouted Selwyn. "Put your arms around me so we don't lose contact."

Josh did as he was requested which, in doing, brought them even closer to each other, but still they ran. As they headed to the finish line, the laughter from the spectators was deafening and cameras were being clicked. As soon as they crossed the line, the rope was untied for them and Selwyn turned to Josh, gave him a kiss on the cheek and said, "Thanks that felt amazing!"

Josh blushed and went over to where Rob was standing, who gave him a kiss as well. Selwyn sidled up to Michael and whispered in his ear, "He is a big boy."

Michael glanced at Selwyn, as though not quite understanding the relevance of the statement.

"He had an erection from rubbing up against my ass and I could feel how big he is."

Michael smiled and hugged Selwyn to him.

"You're incorrigible!"

"The winner of the race was Team P.I. and second was Team Muscles," announced the M.C. "Unfortunately all the other teams either lost their ropes or lost their way! The scores after the first three events are as follows: in first place is Team P.I. on twenty-five points, followed closely by Team Muscles on twenty-one and then Team Kitchen on thirteen. As for the rest, I think they have problems with their teams. Right ladies and gentlemen, it's now down one deck to the swimming pool."

Everyone traipsed down one deck and tried to find places around the pool area. When they reached the pool area, they found that eight water-filled buckets were waiting.

"Ladies and gentlemen, for our next event, each team may have a minimum of two and up to three competitors each. The first will have to dunk his head into the bucket to retrieve an apple, get up and by means of his mouth, pass the apple to his team mate who will then replace it in the other bucket, then run and retrieve an apple from the original bucket and pass it to team member number three who will do likewise. The first team to get all three apples in their second bucket wins. For this event we're dividing the sixteen teams into two groups of eight each."

The teams were called and the first group positioned themselves. While their event was taking place, Myra was busy organizing her team.

"Dirk you must pass to Rob, because you have the same height, then Rob you pass to Michael, who will then pass the last apple back to Dirk."

Team Muscle, their closest rivals were in the first group and won their event, giving them ten points, so Team P.I. had to win to maintain their lead.

Team P.I.'s race started and Dirk battled to get a firm grip on the apple, which kept falling out of his mouth. Myra was screaming at him, coaxing him on. Eventually he managed to pass it on to Rob who dropped it into the second waiting bucket. At that stage they were lying fourth. Rob opened his mouth wide, taking in water, but not choking, gripped the apple and, dripping water headed towards Michael.

"Now don't get into a passionate kiss," shouted Selwyn, "just take the apple!"

Michael could feel the start of the desire to laugh at Selwyn's comment but fought hard to concentrate. He bit into the apple and ran for the bucket.

He then ran back for the last apple, but he couldn't get a firm grip. The crowd was shouting and cheering their friends on, but still Michael battled. At last, he managed to get a grip and with the apple firmly stuck in his mouth and looking like a stuck pig, he ran to deposit their last apple.

"The result of the second group is as follows: first Team Kitchen. Obviously they're used to bobbing in pots. Second Team Stiletto and third, Team P.I."

"That puts us one point behind Team Muscles," said Myra, having done her calculations.

"Ladies and gentlemen, we come to the final event of our games. Each team will allocate three members and across the pool are three poles. Each team will compete against another team and whichever team has the most members still on their poles, wins. As this is a knock out competition, we've split the teams up into groups. Based on the current scores, Team Muscles and Team P.I. are seeded one and two respectively, followed by Teams Kitchen and Handbag. The scoring will be as follows: the winners will get ten points with the losing finalist getting eight. The two losing semi-finalists will each get five and the losing quarter finalists, three points. The others, I'm afraid get nothing."

The first teams were called and they climbed on the poles where each member was handed a pillow in order to fight with.

Both Team Muscles and Team P.I. won their first and second round matches with ease.

In their semi-final match Team P.I. came up against Team Kitchen.

"Rob, I want you, Michael and Selwyn to take this match," said Captain

Myra.

Each of the three boys had on his Speedo and slid slowly across their pole to the center of the pool to face their challengers. Selwyn watched as his opponent slid nearer.

"Oh, Hi. I haven't seen you around much."

It was the blonde whose leg had been rubbing up against his in the whirlpool the previous night. The blonde, Gary, smiled at Selwyn.

"I'm going to get you," he smirked.

"Not if I can help it, Gary."

Each person faced an opponent and waited for the referee to start them.

"Fight!" shouted the referee.

Pillows swung in all directions. Heads were hit, upper torsos were walloped and generally, bodies hovered on the slippery poles.

Gary tried sliding closer to Selwyn, all the time, pounding Selwyn's head with his pillow. Selwyn was blindly trying to retaliate, but it appeared that Gary's blows were more telling.

Rob took an almighty swipe at his opponent, sending him crashing into the water. Team P.I. were one up, but Selwyn was taking strain.

Gary's face was no longer one of fun and enjoyment, but rather one of hate; he was like an animal possessed. Selwyn watched as the blonde, breathing heavily tore into him and continued to get closer to him, until they were virtually crotch-to-crotch.

"I'm going to get you!" hissed Gary, and as he said that, so the rain of blows intensified until Selwyn felt what to him seemed like a punch and he went flying from his pole into the water. As he surfaced, he saw Gary laughing almost hysterically and then his eye caught sight of something else. He wiped the water from his eyes and looked up. There on the deck above, leaning over the railing to watch the events was Brent.

Michael continued to fight hard, knowing that each team had lost a member, so it all rested on him. In a way, he too became aggressive having seen Selwyn beaten. He gave one almighty swing of his pillow, which connected the head of his opponent and dislodged him.

"Team P.I. wins!" shouted the M.C.

Michael, Rob and Gary slid from their poles while Selwyn emerged from the pool, dripping water.

"Bad luck, son," said Myra, "but you put up a good fight. I'm proud of you."

"Me too," echoed Josh.

Selwyn never smiled nor said anything to them. He waited until Michael and Rob came back to the group.

"I was pushed in," said Selwyn.

"Don't take it too seriously," said Michael, comforting his partner.

"No I mean it. I was punched off that pole to be precise."

"Hey, buddy, I see a red mark on your face, what's that?"

"Where I was punched."

"You mean by the blonde?" asked Rob.

Selwyn nodded.

"But I heard you speaking to him. You called him Gary. Where do you know him from?" enquired Michael.

"Babes it's a long story and I'll fill you in sometime, but more importantly, I spotted Brent on the deck above laughing his head off when I was knocked off the pole."

Rob and Michael instinctively looked up to see if they could see Brent, but to no avail.

"Don't worry, Selwyn. He's not going to try anything in public, not with all these people as potential witnesses," Rob said, reassuring his young friend.

In the other semi-final, Team Muscles had very little opposition. The three burly men removed their opposition with ease and Team P.I. was able to watch to see their tactics. The two top seeds were now about to come up against each other to decide the winners.

"Rob, we have to think this one out properly," said Myra, calling her team together. Obviously I want you Rob, and Michael, you're strong, but who's our third going to be?"

They huddled and discussed.

"Dirk might be tall, but I don't think he's that strong," observed Myra.

"I'll do it if you like," volunteered Josh.

"Fine, but we have to see which of their guys they put on the pole against you. If it's one of those Muscle-Mary's you won't have a chance."

"Myra, leave it to me," said Rob. "Come here guys," and he moved away from Myra. "Now listen carefully. So long as you use the pillows and no physical part of your body we won't be disqualified, just don't let then frustrate you. Mike and Josh don't aim for the head; aim for the balls."

"But it's hard to get there because of the way they cling to the pole with their thighs."

"Mike, don't worry about that. Aim for the stomach and go a little lower. Once you hit them in the balls, they'll buckle, then you attack their upper body because they'll be too busy worrying about the pain to concentrate on their balancing. Just remember, they might be all muscle, but they've got a weak spot – aim for it."

The two teams were called forward and they slid onto their poles facing each other.

They waited, glaring at each other.

Josh tried something different. He smiled at his opponent, who was actually very good looking and who smiled back, but neither of their looks was vindictive or threatening, it was more the look of desire. Josh slid a little closer to his opponent, and then let his hand drop down to his crotch where he adjusted the lie of his cock. His opponent's eyes fastened on the wholesome package that confronted him. Again he smiled at Josh who returned the smile and continued to adjust his lie, except this time he inserted his hand into his Speedo and did it. The opponent could clearly see the circumcised outline of a substantial length, closely guarded by the tight Lycra. His eyes watered and he licked his lips.

"Fight!" shouted the starter.

Josh took one swipe at his opponent, who was so engrossed in Josh's well-hung appendage, that he never knew what hit him.

"Team P.I. is one up!' shouted the referee.

Michael and Rob fought their opponents furiously. Michael was taking a pounding from a Mr. Universe clone, but he remembered what Rob had said. He kept ducking to avoid the blows, but aimed for the target. He took a long slow back swing and let fly. The corner of the pillow connected Mr. Universe right on the target. A low grunt emanated from him and he buckled slightly. Immediately, Michael delivered a barrage of blows to Mr. Universe's body, causing him to wobble. The cheering had risen to a crescendo as the crowd saw that Michael was close to dislodging the muscular giant. A second blow hit Mr. Universe in the balls; this time Michael clamped his thighs tightly around the pole, almost lifted himself off the pole and delivered the coup de grâce. The water splashed as the second muscular giant fell into it and the crowds cheered. Both Michael and Josh smiled at each other, while an exhausted Rob, shook hands with his opponent still on their pole.

All three Team P.I. members slid back off their poles and gathered with their captain, who they immediately threw into the pool as a celebratory occasion. Myra surfaced, grinning, hair plastered flat on her head.

"You were brilliant," said Rob, congratulating Josh. "You had him off so quickly. How?"

Josh smiled and casually replied, "Charm."

"What did you do?" enquired Rob.

Josh giggled, and then replied. "You know I always said to you that I had learnt never to reveal all your cards as it were, well I saved the best for last. I was sure that I couldn't beat him, so I grabbed my crotch."

Rob roared with laughter when he realized what this poor man must have been going through.

"I know that crotch of yours and it's no small ornament."

"Eventually, I put my hand into my Speedo, adjusted my cock's lie and left it to him. He was totally transfixed by what he saw and that's when I struck, while he wasn't focusing on the fight."

"No he was obviously focusing on a bigger thing!"

Michael and Selwyn came and stood between Josh and Rob and put an arm around each of them.

"I think we did bloody well, don't you?"

Both agreed, but more so, it had somehow brought all four boys much closer together.

Once Myra had been fished out of the pool, the prize giving ceremony started.

Each of the team members was given vouchers to some of the shops on the ship and a *Caribbean Queen* cap, and then the drinks flowed.

Chapter 12

Monday afternoon and the elegant liner sailed into San Juan, Puerto Rico. Myra and the boys had decided to go ashore to explore. The five found a taxi, piled into it and having told the driver to show them the place, sat back to relax. They visited the old town with its pastel colored houses, wrought iron balconies and narrow streets of cobbles of blue stone and then they set off to visit the lush and spectacular *El Yunque* rainforest. In the forest they came across numerous exotic species of birds and plants and within this tranquil environment, they were able to have quality time with their loved ones.

As the ship was only departing at 22:00, they decided not to eat on the ship, but rather enjoy the tastes the old city could offer. On their travels around the city in search of a restaurant, they came across some of the Team Muscles boys, Josh's opponent in particular. Both Rob and Josh smiled at him when they saw him, Rob because he knew of Josh's strategy that he used to win his fight.

"Hi," said the muscle guy. "I'm Chad."

"Hi, Chad, I'm Josh and this is my partner, Rob."

They greeted each other, then Chad added, "I think you had an advantage over me in that fight."

"I wouldn't know," replied Josh, grinning, as he knew what Chad was referring to.

"I know what you mean," said Rob.

"I was distracted," continued Chad.

"I know that feeling too," replied Rob.

"Are you guys enjoying the cruise?"

"Loving it," responded Rob. "Are you on the cruise by yourself?"

"As you know there's a whole gang of us, but yes, I'm by myself."

"At least you've got the others for company, even though you might not have a boyfriend with you," said Josh, sympathetically.

"Unfortunately my boyfriend and I were booked to come on the cruise and we had a bust up, so I decided to go it alone, after all, I wasn't going to waste the money."

"I'm sorry to hear that," commented Rob.

"My problem is that I'm sort of on the rebound so to me this trip is more a sex-crazed cruise. The more I can get involved with people, the better for me because it takes my mind off the situation."

"Why don't you join us for dinner, Chad, we're actually busy looking for a restaurant."

"Thanks, Rob, I'd like that."

Then Josh thought of something. "Chad, if you're really desperate to find a man, we've got the ideal person to do that for you."

Rob looked horrified at his lover.

"Well, I'm not that desperate, but who?"

"The captain of our team."

"Oh you had a lady. Where does she fit in?" asked Chad.

"Ask Mike, over there; it's his mother, but she's very sweet and very into gays. In fact we warned her about this cruise, but she insisted on coming."

"She actually looks like she enjoys life and fun."

"Oh yes! She does, but never let her know you're on the search for a partner. She's a typical Yiddisher mama who likes matchmaking," answered Rob.

They didn't have to wander around too long before they came across a restaurant. They went in and found a table for six. Once at the table, Rob and Josh introduced Chad to everyone. They obviously recognized him from the sports games, so he wasn't such a stranger to them and soon everyone was drinking, eating and enjoying each other's company.

"What deck are you on, Chad?" enquired Josh.

"Six. I'm in one of the cabins that overlook the promenade."

"That must be fun because you can watch all the people below you."

"Are you sharing with anyone?" continued Josh.

"Well it was going to be me and my boyfriend, but as I told you we split up, so I'm there on my own." Chad felt the gentle touch of a knee against his leg. He smiled at Josh, who returned the smile. "And you?"

"Rob and I are sharing. We're next door to Selwyn and Michael, and Myra was put down the other end of the ship so we could have peace, not so Myra?"

Myra laughed at Josh's comment. "You see, Chad, they think I'm going to cramp their style, but that's not me."

The leg remained against Chad's leg.

Dinner was brought and during the placing of the different meals in front of each person, Chad felt the gentle touch of a hand on his thigh. He turned and again smiled at Josh. He remembered what he'd seen in Josh's tight Speedo and that conjured up visions in his mind. He felt a constriction in his jeans as his blood pumped through his body to his cock. Slowly it was getting harder. The hand slid ever so slightly upwards, closer to the tautness of his crotch. He had goose flesh and his lips were becoming dry, so he leant forward, picked up his drink and took a swig. In leaning forward, the hand had easier and better access to his crotch. Chad nearly choked, but controlled himself. As he replaced his glass he felt a gentle squeeze on his now swollen cock and then Josh's hand returned to pick up his knife and fork.

After dinner, they caught their taxi, along with Chad, back to the ship. When they boarded, Chad found a pen and a piece of paper on which he wrote '6275' and slipped it into Josh's hand. Josh glanced at it, smiled and placed it in his pocket.

Back in their cabin, Selwyn and Michael found that once again their belongings had been searched, and once again nothing was missing. Having found the plastic bag earlier, they decided to search for another one just in case. They went back to where they'd found the earlier one, and sure enough, another one was hidden away. Selwyn took this plastic bag and knocked on the connecting door to Rob's cabin.

"Come in," shouted Josh.

Michael and Selwyn went in, both looking somewhat depressed by these constant upheavals in their cabin. All Selwyn did was hold up the plastic bag.

"What are you doing with that?" asked Rob.

"This is a new one, Rob. Our cabin's been ransacked again," sighed Michael. "Someone is definitely trying to set us up."

"Tonight, as late as it is, I'm going to see what I can do," said Rob, getting of the bed and marching out of the cabin.

The other three merely stood speechless.

"Josh, why don't you come and sit in our cabin until Rob comes back?" suggested Selwyn.

"I might as well," he replied and the three went back through the connecting door.

Half an hour later, Rob came into Michael's cabin with news that the staff was going to be lined up once the ship was underway and a search for Brent would be made.

"Selwyn, you and I will go and do the search. Josh you stay here with Michael," said Rob, angrily. "We need to find this bastard tonight so that we can have him arrested tomorrow in St. Thomas when we dock."

Selwyn and Rob left in a hurry, leaving Michael and Josh together.

There was a slight tense moment as they left and Josh and Michael stood staring at each other.

"Do you want to do something?" asked Josh.

"I'm easy," replied Michael.

"You're not supposed to say that; isn't that Selwyn's favorite line?"

The tension was broken as both boys laughed at Josh's comment.

"Do you want to stay here or go for a walk around the ship, Josh?"

"I'm happy to stay here with you, if you'd like."

Michael switched on the TV that was in the cabin and lay on the bed. He patted the bed next to him, inviting Josh to come and relax there. Josh sprang onto the bed and the two lay side by side.

The only sound came from the TV, but after a while Josh spoke, "I think they might be quite some time having to get the whole crew together."

"You're probably right, Josh."

Again there was an awkward silence between the two boys as the TV continued to make the only noise.

Josh stretched an arm in Michael's direction and let it touch, ever so lightly, Michael's thigh. He left his hand gently touching Michael, but said nothing. They both stayed watching the TV screen. Michael lowered his arms, which he had been resting his head on and let one touch Josh's hand. Josh's fingers felt for Michael's and when he'd found them, he clasped Michael's hand. The two lay holding hands, but not speaking.

Inwardly both boys were experiencing different emotions but neither was showing it. Josh wanted Michael to make love to him, but Michael, although he wanted to do something with Josh, was trying to avoid the temptation.

Josh felt a tiny squeeze of his hand and he turned to look at Michael, who was staring at him.

"Josh," whispered Michael, "I want to make love to you."

"I'd like that."

Nothing more was said.

Michael released his grip on Josh's hand and rolled over so that he and Josh were face to face. Michael slowly lowered his face to Josh's until their lips touched tenderly, and then he raised his head and looked into Josh's eyes. Once more their lips met and each time they became a little more urgent in their passion.

Soon two beautifully chiseled and tanned bodies lay naked on the bed, their touches to each other being gentle and erotic; their mouths searching each other's erogenous zones. Michael slid down Josh's body until he reached the now famous cock. He admired it like one might admire a glorious painting, and then slowly allowed his mouth to encompass its thickness and length. Josh merely groaned softly as Michael's mouth began a journey of pleasurable exploration.

There gentleness was soon building to a more urgent desire and Michael was edging closer to the desire that Josh had wanted. Michael positioned himself between Josh's open thighs and slowly sank into his waiting warmth. The deeper Michael sank, the more Josh groaned and smiled. A steady, yet slow rhythmic movement started up and both boys were soon thrashing like two sharks fighting over the same piece of meat. Their mouths clamped together and their tongues searched each other's mouth.

Michael continued thrusting into Josh's tight ass until they rolled over and Josh found himself sitting on top of Michael, but still deeply attached to each other. Josh leaned forward and as his mouth clamped onto Michael's, so he began to rise and fall on Michael's thick cock.

The perspiration on their bodies made them glide effortlessly against each other, until that moment of ecstasy arrived and both boys knew no bounds. As their climax was reached and their supplies of love juice were fired, their actions became more frenetic and wild.

As their breathing began to return to normality, they lay in each other's arms, caressing each other tenderly, their lips resuming their opening advances, gently touching.

"Thank you," was the tender, soft whispering that Josh said into Michael's ear as he nibbled gently at it. "That was beautiful."

Michael kissed Josh once more.

"It was only beautiful because we both wanted it. Thank you Josh."

For a long time they lay in each other's warmth, still caressing and gently kissing, until Josh said, "I think we'd better get dressed."

Michael slipped gently from the warm cavity that had kept his cock hard for so long and before getting off the bed, Michael gave Josh one last kiss.

They pulled on their clothes and Michael then asked if Josh would like a drink.

"I think I need one after all that exertion."

"Let's take a walk to the promenade and have a drink in one of the bars. Maybe we'll see Rob and Selwyn."

They departed from the cabin and made their way down to the promenade deck to have a pleasant drink together.

Down in the staff quarters, Rob, Selwyn and the head of security went through a file containing photos of every member of staff on the ship. It was a long and tedious task, but worth it if they were to catch Brent. They searched and searched and were about to give up when the head of security said that he had another set of photos in another file as these people were late comers to joining the ship's crew. He fetched the file and the whole process began all over again.

"Rob, this looks like that guy who punched me when I fell off the pole in the sports games today, or am I wrong?"

Rob took the file and looked carefully at the photo.

"I don't think it could be sir, because the crew may not fraternize with the passengers, so he couldn't have taken part."

Rob looked even more carefully.

"I think it's him all right."

"You must be mistaken, sir."

"What section of the ship does this man work in, sir?" asked Rob.

The head of security looked at the file.

"He's part of the kitchen staff."

Rob and Selwyn shared glances.

"He was part of the kitchen team at the sports games," muttered Selwyn.

Nothing more was said about the blonde. They looked in the file and saw that his name in the file was not Gary, as the blonde had said. It was Kevin.

Rob and Selwyn continued to look for Brent.

They turned pages and got tired of looking at photos, but it had to happen. They eventually saw the face they were searching for.

"That's him," said Selwyn, quietly.

Rob looked at the name under the photo. "Grant? Well if that's the name he's going under then I wonder if in fact Brent was his real name."

"What section does he work in, sir?" asked Selwyn.

Again, the head of security looked up the information.

"He's also in the kitchen."

"It makes sense," commented Rob. "The kitchen staff don't work twenty-four hour shifts, not even on a ship like this."

"You're right," agreed the head of security, "but again they are not allowed to mingle with the passengers."

"That's what you say, sir, but I'm telling you that this man is harassing your passengers. He also has a suspended sentence hanging over his head, are you aware of that?"

"Sir, I don't employ these people."

"I hear what you say, but tell me, are you going to do anything about these two men?"

"Sir, with all due respect, do you have evidence of them doing anything untoward on this ship?"

Rob knew that he didn't have a case and the security guy was right.

"Come Selwyn," said Rob, rising from the seat he'd been sitting on and marching out of the office.

"Where are we going?"

"Anywhere. To have a drink!"

Rob was angry.

They made their way to the promenade and bumped into Josh and Michael also having a quiet drink together.

"Hi guys," said Michael on seeing them. "How did it go?"

"Don't even talk to me about these clowns on this ship. They're not interested because as far as they are concerned our two friends have done nothing wrong because we can't prove it's them."

As frustrating as this was, Michael knew it to be true. To calm Rob's anger, Michael immediately got the barman to get beers for both Rob and Selwyn.

"Another drink for you, Josh?"

"Thanks Michael; same again."

Michael ordered the drinks and once they all had their drinks, Michael raised his glass. "A toast," he said. "To us; to the fabulous friendship we have with each other and to the happiness of this cruise."

"To us," echoed everyone.

"So what did you two do while we were looking for crooks?" asked Rob.

"Oh, we sat and chattered for a while, watched a bit of TV and then we came down here to have a couple of drinks," replied Josh.

Michael merely smiled at Josh and concurred with him.

"Tomorrow we land at St Thomas," said Selwyn, "Are we going on shore because we're there for the whole day until 18:00?"

"I believe they've got fantastic beaches," stated Michael, "and duty-free shopping. That should suit Selwyn and Myra."

"Does she know about that?" enquired Selwyn.

"I don't think so. Maybe you'd better tell her and the two of you can go shopping together."

Josh emptied his glass and said, "Guys, I'm off to bed. It's past my bedtime and besides it's nearing midnight and I don't want to turn into a pumpkin. I'll see you all at breakfast. Goodnight all."

"Hang on Josh, I'm coming too," said a tired Rob.

"It looks like we might as well all hit the sack," suggested Michael.

And so it was that another eventful day came to an end; Michael and Josh having been wonderfully satisfied, while Selwyn and Rob bitterly annoyed.

Chapter 13

Early the following morning, Michael was woken to hear someone knocking on Rob and Josh's cabin door. He opened his eyes and saw the sun shining through their balcony sliding door. He could hear voices next door and thought perhaps the boys had ordered breakfast in bed. Michael got out of bed, without disturbing Selwyn who was still asleep, and went to open the sliding door. The ship had docked in St. Thomas and the wharf side was already a hive of activity. Michael heard a soft rapping on their connecting door, and the door open.

"Can I come in?" whispered Rob, who only had a towel wrapped around his trim waist.

"Sure. Hi Rob, what's the problem?"

"There was an attack that took place on the ship last night or in the early hours of this morning."

"That sounds bad, but what's that got to do with us?"

"You know Chris, the young guy that worked with Selwyn?"

"Yes, he seems a nice guy."

"Well he was stabbed last night."

"No! Are you serious, Rob."

"Look, it wasn't fatal, but the fact remains that something odd is happening on this ship."

"Where's he now?"

"Down in the ship's hospital. Apparently he's adamant he's not getting off the ship to go to a local hospital here, but a doctor is coming on board to check up on him."

"But surely they have a doctor on board?"

"Oh yes, but he wants a second opinion, and I believe, the local police are also coming on board."

"Who told you this?"

"You know Derek Campbell, the CEO of the store who was on the cruise with Chris; well he came round just now."

"I thought I heard voices in your cabin, but wasn't sure if it was you and Josh talking. But what happened?"

Just then, Selwyn stirred and Michael went to him and told him what had happened. Selwyn sat up in bed listening to Rob's story.

"Apparently at some time during the night, after we departed Puerto Rico, Chris and Derek had gone to have something to eat, and after that, Derek said he was going to bed. Chris then decided to go to the disco."

Immediately Selwyn's mind kicked into action and he thought that Chris might have gone there to find someone to have sex with, like he had explained to Selwyn about the toilet behind the climbing wall.

"Well, he apparently saw someone that he liked and they went out on the deck…"

" … By the climbing wall," interjected Selwyn.

"Yes. According to Chris, they went outside and they were talking to each other and one thing led to another, and soon they were kissing. The guy he was with suggested that they go somewhere less public …"

" … So they went to the toilet behind the climbing wall," said Selwyn.

"Yes. How do you know?" enquired Rob.

"Better still, how do you know about the toilet there?" asked Michael.

"Chris told me."

"How could he? He was only attacked last night," answered Rob.

"No Rob. He's done this before. Michael do you remember when he and I were talking and you came over and met him?"

"Yes."

"Well, he was busy telling me about how he met a guy in the disco and they went to the toilet together and had a bit of fun."

"So he has done this before, but I wonder if it was the same guy that he'd gone with before?" thought Rob.

"Where's Chris now?" enquired Selwyn.

"Down in the hospital."

"Can't we go and see him?" asked Selwyn.

"We must," insisted Rob, "because I want to get to the bottom of this."

Selwyn hopped out of bed, naked, not that it bothered Rob, because he had seen Selwyn naked before, when they had to go on a case in Miami and they had slept together. Selwyn hurriedly pulled on some clothes and said, "Come on let's get down there."

Rob went back to his cabin to get dressed and then he, Selwyn and Michael made their way down to the hospital.

The doctor on duty allowed them in because Derek was sitting there with

Chris and he vouched for them as being close friends.

"Chris, how are you doing?" asked Selwyn going to his bed and taking Chris's hand.

"Sore, but OK."

"Where did he get you?"

"Here in the shoulder," replied Chris, indicating with a nod of his head.

"Rob," said Derek, rather seriously. "I know that the police are coming on board to question Chris, but will you do something to help us find his attacker. For all I know the person might already have left the ship once we docked this morning."

"Sure thing, Derek. Don't worry about a thing; we'll do the best we can for you and Chris."

"What happened, Chris?" asked Selwyn, hoping to hear not only some juicy details but also to get an idea of how he could help Rob in their search for the attacker."

"Chris, speak freely. Don't leave any detail out so that Rob can get the complete picture," requested Derek.

Chris swallowed, cleared his throat and began his tale.

"As you know I went to the disco after you went off to the cabin. Well, I was enjoying myself dancing, and during the evening, a guy came up to me and asked if I'd like a drink. I said I would like a beer, which he bought for me. We were standing chatting and then the music changed, so he asked me if I wanted to dance. We went onto the dance floor and started dancing. Everything up to that point seemed fine. We were enjoying ourselves and then he pulled me closer to him. We danced like that for a while and I could feel that he was becoming aroused. Naturally, it turned me on and so he obviously could feel my erection. As we were dancing he slipped a hand down to my crotch and started feeling me up. He then whispered in my ear suggesting that we go outside. As I was now quite horny, I agreed. You must understand, I also thought he was quite good looking, so we went outside. We went to the area by the climbing wall and that's when he suggested that we go into the toilet there. Once we got inside, I unzipped his jeans and started giving him a blowjob and it was during this time that I felt the sharp pain in my shoulder. I screamed and fell to the floor. I noticed that he quickly zipped up and fled, then I crawled out of there back to the disco area and that's when someone saw me and they got me down to the doctor."

"Chris, what did this guy look like?" asked Rob.

"Probably about my height, not one of the muscle guys, but then I didn't take his shirt off so I really wouldn't know. Um, I think his hair was fair or light … no, blonde…"

Selwyn and Rob caught each other's eye.

"Chris, I think I might know this person. If I can persuade security on the ship to let me show you some pictures, do you think you might recognize the guy?"

"Rob, I can only try."

"You guys stay with Chris, and I'll be back soon," said Rob, leaving them in the ship's hospital.

"I'm so sorry Derek," whimpered Chris, tears beginning to form in his eyes.

"Baby, it's OK. I'm just thankful that you're alive. You could have been killed."

Derek held Chris's hand and kissed him gently. Selwyn watched in amazement. He'd never seen such gentleness from Mr. Campbell. He had thought him as an aloof, pompous man, but here was a different man altogether.

"Chris I don't mind you going with other guys, but be careful. I understand how I might not be able to please you sexually as you might want to be pleased, and I understand that you might have needs and desires, but rather bring them back home or in this case to our cabin, rather than creeping around toilets."

By this time, the tears were streaming down Chris's face. Michael took Selwyn's hand as they stood watching and their eyes met. Michael could see the glistening tears beginning to well up in Selwyn's eyes. Selwyn couldn't contain himself, and left the hospital ward that Chris was in. He went outside and stood in the corridor, sobbing. Michael joined him and hugged him to his chest. Gently, Michael stroked Selwyn's head.

"Don't cry, love, but I hope you listened to what Derek said to Chris. I think our situation is much like theirs, so we must both be careful. I'd hate to lose you. I think we must make a pact that if either of us goes with a stranger, we need to make the other aware so that we can safeguard each other."

Selwyn simply nodded, because he was choked with tears and couldn't speak. Rob suddenly appeared carrying a file, and being followed by the head of security. They walked into the ward where Chris was and placed the file on the bed. Selwyn and Michael also re-entered the room.

"Chris, I want you to look at the photos in this file, but take your time," said Rob, handing over the file to Chris.

Everyone stood around the bed watching as Chris flipped through the photos. It wasn't long, when Chris stopped flipping pages and looked long and hard at a photo. He then looked up at Rob and pointed to the photo.

"That's him, Rob."

Rob took the file with the photo, looked at who Chris had pointed at and turned to the head of security.

"Now are you people going to do something?"

"Mr. Clayton, we don't have any proof that he did it. All we can do is question him."

"Well, when you do, I demand to be present."

"Certainly. As soon as the police arrive, I'll call you and we can start our questioning."

During all this drama, Rob had completely forgotten about Josh, whom he'd left in the cabin.

"Michael, please do me a favor. I've forgotten all about Josh, won't you and Selwyn go and see that he's OK?"

They left the ward and made their way up to Josh's cabin. When they arrived there. He was sitting on their balcony watching the goings-on in the harbor.

"Josh," said Michael, "Rob's probably going to be busy for some time so he asked us to come and see that you were OK. Do you want to come with us for some breakfast?"

"That sounds great, thanks Michael. How's your friend Selwyn?"

"He'll be fine. I think it was a helluva shock. I know it would have been for me, but I'm sure that he'll pull through."

They made their way up to the pool deck to have breakfast alfresco. While they were sitting eating, Chad came strolling along the deck, looking fresh and sprightly.

"Hi Chad," said Josh greeting his new friend. "Have you had breakfast yet?"

"No."

"Do you want to join us?" asked Michael

"Thanks guys, that's good of you. Where are the others?"

"Haven't you heard?" asked Selwyn. "A friend of ours got stabbed last night."

"What!" Exclaimed a shocked Chad. "Where? On the ship?"

"Yes," continued Selwyn. "He picked up a guy last night at the disco and the guy stabbed him."

"You mean one of the passengers did it?"

"We actually think it's a crew member, but the police are coming aboard this morning, so Rob's waiting for them."

"But why would he be waiting for them?" enquired Chad.

"He's a private investigator," said Josh.

"Are you going ashore today, Chad?" asked Michael, trying to change the topic.

"I suppose I will. Go and see what the island's got to offer. Are you guys going or are you staying on board?"

"I'd like to go," replied Michael, "but I don't know about the others."

Both Josh and Selwyn said that seeing they had come on the cruise to see new places, it seemed silly not to go ashore.

"But what about Rob?" asked Josh. "Won't he want to tag along?"

"Maybe the police might arrive early and get this whole thing out of the way fairly quickly, and then he might be able to see St. Thomas," suggested Michael.

They continued eating their breakfast and then Josh said that he was going down to ask Rob if he was going ashore and should they wait for him, while the others remained on the pool deck. Both Michael and Chad watched as Josh walked away, his cute ass gently tightening and then relaxing as he walked along the deck in his white shorts. When they realized that they were both looking at the same object, they grinned at each other, but said nothing.

Down in the ward, unbeknown to those on deck, the police had arrived, Chris had been questioned and Kevin, or Gary, whichever name he was going under, was busy being interrogated. Josh arrived at the ward as they were asking Gary where he'd been the previous night.

"In my cabin," he replied.

"Can anyone vouch for that?" asked the police inspector.

"Yes, my cabin buddy."

"Did you or did you not go to the disco last night?"

"No, I didn't."

Chris's face was a picture of shock. He couldn't believe what was being said.

Rob intervened.

"May I ask a question?"

"Certainly," replied the officer.

"Gary, did you take part in the sports games? Now remember I did and I know who we competed against."

Gary was silent for a while.

"Answer the man," commanded the police officer.

Gary hung his head. "Yes."

"But you're a member of the crew aren't you?" asked Rob.

Again, a subdued 'yes' came forth.

"Isn't it illegal for the crew to fraternize with the passengers? Isn't that written in the contract you signed?"

'Yes," came a very soft reply.

"I beg your pardon?"

"Yes," said Gary a little louder.

"I thought as much," continued Rob. "And doesn't it stipulate in your contract with the shipping company that anybody admitting to or getting caught fraternizing with a member of the public on board a ship will have his or her contract terminated with immediate effect?"

Gary remained silent.

Rob then turned to the head of security.

"Am I not right, sir?"

"Yes," came his subdued reply.

"Then I think that someone in a superior position needs to do the necessary, and if it is not done with immediate effect, heads will roll."

Rob sounded very authoritative and also his height was in his favor. He towered over those in the room and therefore made them feel intimidated. Josh watched with admiration as his lover took command of the situation.

"If nothing else, I think that this man should be taken ashore, charged with contravening his contractual duties and questioned in more depth about the stabbing incident," suggested Rob.

The police inspector agreed and the head of security, who was totally intimidated by Rob's attack on his staff, didn't have much choice but to agree. Just as the police were about to march Gary from the room and off the ship, Rob said, "Could I ask one more question?"

"What is it, Mr. Clayton?" replied the officer.

"Gary, look me in the eyes and tell me; do you know a man on this ship by the name of Brent. And remember that if you're lying in your answer and we find out, you'll be in even more trouble. Do you know him?"

Everyone waited in silence while Gary stood, head hanging low, declining to answer.

"Remember what I said, Gary, because we're going to question Brent now, so you'd better say something."

Gary raised his head when he heard Rob say they were going to question Brent. Rob of course had no right to question Brent because he hadn't been implicated, but it was a ploy that he was using.

"Yes," came the answer.

"So you know him? How do you know him?"

"We're cousins."

It came as a surprise to Rob and those in the room to hear this because they had no idea of their relationship.

"Take him away," said Rob, finally.

The police officer and the head of security handcuffed Gary and led him from the ship.

Derek, who'd been party to the entire questioning stood up went to Rob and shook his hand.

"Thanks Rob. That was very clever of you."

"Thank you Rob," said Chris from his bed, while Josh still stood in awe of his lover.

For the first time since this event started, Rob smiled.

"Come here and give me a hug," he said to Josh, who gladly obliged.

Chapter 14

Myra was like the Pied Piper of Hamlyn, leading the gang through the streets of the town in search of duty-free goods.

"Chad, come and walk with me," commanded Myra.

The boys all laughed on hearing this instruction.

"Now you've had it," quipped Michael, "she's going to do her match-making on you."

"Just ignore them Chad. Now tell me my darling, have you met any nice men on this cruise?"

Chad could feel himself blushing because the others were waiting to hear his answers.

"Yes, Myra," replied Chad, choosing not to elaborate.

"Who?" continued Myra with her interrogation.

"A few," came the non-committal answer from Chad who caught Josh's eye and smiled.

"Don't hedge the issue my boy, who?"

"Well, all these guys here," replied Chad, taking the safe route. "I like them all, and they've been good to me."

"No, no, no. I'm not talking about friends. Sure we all need friends, but what I'm talking about is a partner for you. Someone to share your life with," said Myra, taking Chad's hand and dragging him along with her.

Again Chad blushed.

"You blush very easily," laughed Rob, putting an arm around Chad's shoulder and pulling him away from Myra's clutches.

"I can't help it. I'm actually very sensitive."

"Whatever you do, don't let Myra bully you or intimidate you, Chad. You pick whomever you like. I know Myra was instrumental in fixing Josh and me up, but when we met we clicked and we're very happy together. I'm sure that you'll find Mr. Right sooner or later. You might even find that when you get back home, your ex might want to get back together with you."

Chad looked sadly at Rob, tried to offer a smile, but couldn't. Rob noticed this and pulled him a little closer to his gigantic body. Chad knew that he wouldn't be getting back with his ex.

"I'm sorry if I upset you; I didn't mean to, but you're a great guy and you deserve somebody good. If your ex wasn't up to it, then get on with life and find the next one. Usually when men talk about their girlfriends, they say, 'there're plenty more fish in the sea', well I'm telling you there are plenty more studs on the farm."

Josh hustled up to join Rob and he and Chad walked on either side of the big man.

"Hey, this looks great," said Rob looking on either side of him. "Two of the hunkiest guys on my arms. What more could a guy ask for?"

Chad glanced to Josh who returned the smile.

"Selwyn!" shouted Myra, "Come, it's time for my son-in-law to go shopping with his Jewish mother-in-law. We're off to find duty-free goods. We'll see you back at the ship for afternoon tea. Michael are you coming with us?"

"Sure Mum. We'll see you guys later."

Rob, Josh and Chad wandered around aimlessly until Rob suggested they get a cab to one of the beautiful beaches they'd heard about. Having grab a cab, they set off, Chad in the front and Rob and Josh in the back.

"Now Chad, keep your hands to yourself, no touching up the driver," joked Josh.

They soon reached a pristine beach of the whitest sand imaginable and crystal clear water. They paid the cab driver and walked onto the soft, white sand. It almost trickled between their toes as they walked. They hadn't brought towels with them as they hadn't anticipated going for a swim, but each had on a Speedo under his shorts. They undressed and lay of the gleaming soft sand, again, Rob in between Chad and Josh.

Although Chad was part of the Muscles Team, he wasn't overly muscular, like the Mr. Universe that pounded Michael, but he was clearly the type who'd enter minor bodybuilding competitions. In comparison to Rob, Chad had a more defined muscularity, whereas Rob had broader shoulders and chest, but that might have been as a result of his general physique, which was large. Josh, on the other hand had a natural gymnastic type of build, but all said, together they made a wonderful sight.

"You've got quite a neat body there, Chad. Don't you agree, Josh?"

"Absolutely," replied Josh, turning to admire the Adonis lying next to his lover.

"Have you been going to gym for a long time then?" Rob asked.

"About two and a half years."

"What do you actually do, Chad?" enquired Josh.

"I've got my own business back in New York."

"Doing what?" asked Rob.

"I've got an interior design business I run."

"That sounds great. You should hook up with Michael because he's in the property business. Maybe he can buy the apartments and you can decorate them," stated Rob.

"And you guys? Well I know that Rob is a P.I. but you Josh?"

"I'm a bum!'

"No seriously, what do you do?"

"I'm an architect by profession."

"Hey that's terrific. Now we can include Josh in the company along with the interior designer and property developer," laughed Chad, turning to Josh. He looked at the large bulge in the front of Josh's Speedo. He recognized the object that made him lose the fight on the pole in the pool to Josh.

Josh sat up, resting on his elbows and caught Chad's eyes fixated on the bulge in his Speedo. Rob lay with his eyes closed absorbing the sun's warmth. Josh let a hand surreptitiously slide over the heavily packed bulge as he watched Chad. Chad's eyes lit up and a broad smile emerged across his face. As though like a secret message being passed on, Chad ran his hand over his own crotch for Josh to see. This was like a sign of willingness between the two men. Chad could feel himself heading for a possible embarrassment so he quickly jumped up and, adjusting the lie of his ever-growing cock, ran to the water's edge and dived in.

Rob sat up when he heard Chad's scramble to the water and watched the bubble-butt move sexily towards the water.

"He's quite nice, isn't he?" commented Rob, when Chad had dived under the water.

"Hm!" replied Josh.

Rob turned to Josh and grinned at him.

"I think that package of yours is looking a little swollen, wouldn't you say? Been looking at something nice?"

Josh giggled out loud. "I don't know what you mean?"

"I think you do," came the sly remark. "I know you're a big boy, but at the moment I think you're a bigger boy, so to speak." Rob continued to watch Josh, and then added, "and I think it's getting even bigger as we speak. Maybe we should go for a swim and the cold water might get it back to normal." Rob winked and laughed as he said these final words.

The two lovers trotted over the silky soft sand into the crystal water. The coolness of the water did in fact relieve some of the pressure that Josh was experiencing. Rob swam to where Chad was treading water, dived under and grabbed Chad's legs, pulling him under. Both men resurfaced, Chad spluttering and Rob laughing.

The three of them began playing in the water, diving and grabbing each other's legs and pulling the person under the water. They were completely relaxed in each other's company. Rob grabbed Josh and threw him high into the air and watched as he came crashing down into the water, then it was Chad's turn to fly through the air and crash into the water. The giant man was having fun. At one stage, Chad picked Josh up and threw him in to the air to watch Josh splash back into the water. They were like children, and then they slowed down in their activities, bobbing gently in the swells. They moved a little closer to shore where they were able to stand on the sandy bottom, yet remain floating in the cool water.

Rob dived under the water, went in between Chad's legs and lifted him onto his shoulders and then surfaced.

"It's a pity we don't have another person here because then we could have some fights on each other's shoulders here in the water," said Rob, carrying Chad a little way and then throwing him off his shoulders. He then dived again and repeated his game with Josh.

Chad liked the idea, so he dived between Josh's legs and then surfaced. He wiped the water from his eyes and felt the bulge on the back of his neck.

"Should I try to pick you both up?" asked Rob.

"No," shouted Josh, "you'll hurt yourself."

No trouble to Rob, he dived between Chad's legs and tried to lift both of them. The weight was too much and Chad and Josh landed up in the water, laughing as they did so. After what seemed like an eternity, they emerged from the sea, exhausted and went to lie on the soft sand and let the sun dry them.

"What's the time?" asked Chad, looking up at the sun in an effort to try to work out the possible time.

Rob looked for his watch, checked the time and suggested that they start heading back to the ship.

They pulled their shorts back on and headed off looking for a cab to get them back to the ship, but without success. An old truck came rambling along the dusty road, so Rob decided to try to hitch a ride with the driver. The truck pulled over and the three men ran up to the driver's window.

"Could you give us a lift to the harbor; we need to get back to our ship?"

The driver, who couldn't have been more that nineteen or twenty, obliged. Rob and Josh climbed in alongside the driver while Chad hopped in the back. It was Chad who was worst off. The dust circled around him and the bumps left his lovely bubble-butt somewhat in discomfort.

Rob and Josh, in the meantime, were squashed up against the young driver who, every time he tried to change gears found his hand rubbing Rob's leg by mistake. For Rob and Josh, they found this amusing, but for the driver he was finding it difficult. The basic reason for the discomfort was that the gear stick was on the floor and when they had climbed in, Rob found it necessary to sit with his legs on either side of the gear stick. Rob sat waiting for the driver's hand to slip when he was changing gears, and to land in his crotch.

"It's your lucky day," murmured Josh, nudging Rob in the ribs.

"It won't be if that gear stick hits me in the balls."

Every time the young man needed to change gears, Rob tensed waiting for the painful jar, but it never came. Somehow they all arrived back at the harbor in one piece. They thanked the driver profusely and Rob even gave him some money for his effort. They waved their young driver goodbye and boarded the ship.

"Rob, Josh, thanks for a really fabulous day," said Chad. "I really appreciate your friendship and kindness because you didn't have to take me along with you, after all you could have had a really special time alone."

"Hey, Chad, we both like you a lot. If we didn't, we wouldn't have asked you along, so don't worry about it. Buy me a drink instead," said Rob, giving Chad a pat on the back.

"Only with the greatest of pleasure," replied Chad. "Do you want to go for a drink now, or later?"

"Let's make it later," said Rob, "because I want to see Chris in the hospital and find out if anything else has happened since we left. Shall we meet for dinner at eight?"

"Sounds great to me. Eight it is, but where?"

"Downstairs on the promenade where we had drinks last night, hey Josh?"

"Why don't we meet at the Champagne Bar," suggested Josh.

"Ooh, are we being smart tonight?" joked Rob. "Right eight it is."

Chad made his way back to his cabin overlooking the promenade, while Josh and Rob went down to the hospital to see Chris, but he wasn't there.

"He's gone back to his cabin," said the doctor.

"I don't know what their cabin number is, do you Josh?"

"No."

"Doctor, do you have their cabin number please?" requested Rob.

The doctor gladly gave it to them and they headed back a couple of decks until they reached Derek and Chris's cabin. They knocked and waited. Derek opened the door.

"Hello, Rob, please come in."

"I don't know if you've met Josh. Josh, this is Derek Campbell; Derek this is my partner, Josh."

They greeted each other and shook hands.

"Where's Chris? I was told he'd left the hospital."

"He's out on the balcony, Rob, but feeling much better."

Josh and Rob went out onto the balcony to see how Chris was feeling.

"Although I'm in some pain, I really feel better. I think it might also be because I'm in my own bed and not in one of those hospital beds."

"So no action for you, hey Chris," said Rob with an element of humor in his voice.

"No you're wrong there it's only my shoulder and not my dick."

Even Derek laughed at Chris's sense of humor under his painful condition.

"In fact," continued Chris, "I'm rearing to go. I've told Derek we should go to dinner, but he's insisting on dinner in the cabin."

"That sounds romantic to me," stated Josh; then he leant to Chris's ear and whispered, "Maybe he wants to give you something nice after dinner, have you thought of that?"

Chris grinned and looked at Derek, almost for confirmation.

"Maybe. I'll let you know tomorrow if I get lucky."

"Tell me Derek, have you heard anything more from the police?" asked Rob.

"Nothing Rob, but then I must be honest, I haven't been up to the purser to find out."

"Well, we're going for dinner later, so I'll make enquiries then. Is there anything either of you want?"

"No thanks Rob, but thank you for your concern; and it was nice meeting you Josh," said Derek.

Rob and Josh left them and headed back to their cabin. When they entered they could hear Selwyn and Michael laughing together next door. Rob knocked on the connecting door.

"Come in," shouted Selwyn.

"What are you two laughing about? We could hear you through the walls here," said Rob walking into their cabin and sitting on the edge of their bed.

"We were just talking about Myra and her bargaining tactics."

"Did you have a good time shopping?" enquired Josh.

"Oh yes. Selwyn and Myra spent a fortune on rubbish," said Michael in jest.

"Why, what did you buy?"

"Apart from a few shirts, just some mementos to take back home with us, like the inevitable coffee cups with touristy pictures on, a straw hat, which will probably never be worn, a nice pair of sandals and then some tacky shit to give to friends back home," replied Selwyn.

"Just remember, we're not friends of yours, so don't palm all your junk off onto us," said Rob, looking concerned.

"What did you guys do?" asked Michael.

"We got a cab and went to one of the beaches. Wow, but you should have seen that water; it was crystal clear and the sand on the beach was like walking on silk. It was so soft and white, it was amazing. We spent the day there, then we had fun coming back because we couldn't get a cab, so we waved down a truck, and this poor young guy who was driving was totally frustrated because he had a problem trying to change gears."

"Why Josh?"

"Well, Chad was in the back of the truck and Rob was sitting next to the driver ..."

" ... Because he was young?" interrupted Selwyn.

"Probably. But the problem was that there was very little room up front in the cab, so Rob had to sit with his legs on either side of the gear stick. The poor driver, whenever he tried to change gears, either touched Rob's leg or very nearly whacked him in the balls."

All four laughed at the scenario that Josh had painted.

"And Chad, how was he?" asked Michael.

"He actually seems a helluva nice guy," answered Rob. "We had a great time with him, swimming, and in fact, we're meeting for dinner tonight. Do you two want to join us?"

"We haven't got anything planned, so yes that would be nice. Don't worry about Myra, she's got a date," said Michael.

"A date!" exclaimed a surprised Rob.

"Yes, one of the guys on the boat has invited her to dinner."

"A gay guy?"

"Oh yes, Rob, a very gay guy," said a very jocular Selwyn.

Rob was puzzled.

"She's having dinner with Chris and Derek."

"Are you serious, but they didn't say anything to us when we spoke to them."

"Maybe they were either too embarrassed or too excited."

Josh turned to Rob and said, "Oh well, there goes Chris's dessert!"

"Dessert?" queried Michael.

"It's a joke Mike. Chris was hoping that he might get lucky with Derek tonight, but not with Myra around he won't."

The ship's sonorous hooter sounded and the liner began to slip slowly from its moorings and proceed on its journey to Phillipsburg on the island of St. Maarten. The four went onto the balcony and waved to the unknown people along the wharf, until their arms became tired.

"Come Josh, we must go and shower and get ready for dinner. Also we must leave these two lovebirds; who knows what they might want to do before dinner," said Rob with a sparkle in his eye.

They went back through their connecting door and left Michael and Selwyn alone. Back in their cabin, Rob lay down on the bed as Josh stripped off his clothes.

"Are you going to have a shower first, Josh?"

"I was hoping you might come and wash my back for me!"

Rob chuckled to himself and blew Josh a kiss.

"Tell me seriously; what do you think of Chad?"

"Rob, that's the second time you've asked me that, why?"

"I just wanted to know what you thought of him, especially after having spent time with him today."

"I like him, as I said. I think he could be a good friend and could be interesting once you really get to know him."

"And physically? Does he do anything for you?"

Josh hesitated and thought.

"I think he's got a beautiful body and he's obviously kept it in good shape."

"Is that it?"

"What else did you want, Rob?"

"Do you find him sexy, for example?"

"Yes, he does have a sex appeal about him. I like his smile."

"Yes, I agree with that. He really looks handsome when he smiles. Could you have a thing with him?"

"Do you mean could I go to bed with him?"

"Yes?"

Josh looked deep into Rob's eyes. What was he leading to?

"Yes, Rob, I could. And you?"

Now the shoe was on the other foot, metaphorically speaking.

"Very easily I could take him to bed. I think he exudes sexuality."

Josh wasn't sure whether Rob was not subconsciously comparing him with Chad, nor did he know what Rob's ulterior motive was.

"Rob, why are you asking me all these questions. Are you tired of me?"

"For fuck sake no! I love you. You drive me crazy with your sexuality but I also find Chad very appealing."

"If I understand you properly, are you then hinting at having an affair with him, is that what you're saying."

"No, not at all. If anything, I'm asking if you'd like to have a scene with him, together with me."

"You mean a ménage à trois? The three of us?"

"Yes. Does that offend you, Josh?"

Josh shook his head and smiled at Rob. He went over to the bed and lay down on top of Rob so that they were face to face.

"Is that what you would like?"

"But only if you agree to it. I would never go behind your back and have an affair with him, without you."

"Why him?"

"When we walked together, arms around each other I realized that I had the two most handsome men on this ship next to me; the two men I could gladly go to bed with and be happy."

Josh kissed Rob gently on the lips and felt Rob's thick, muscular arms wrap around his waist.

"I'll do whatever pleases you, Rob, you know that."

Rob kissed Josh and rolled him onto his back so that he was lying on top of him, then he slid slowly down Josh's body, kissing every part with tenderness and showing his love for his partner.

Chapter 15

Rob, Michael, Selwyn, Josh and Chad, all sat toasting one another in the Champagne Bar. The ship was a buzz of excitement as men strolled along the promenade, drank in the bars and enjoyed meals in the various restaurants. A couple of decks higher, Chris, Derek and Myra were enjoying a meal in Chris and Derek's cabin, and even higher up the ship other men were engaged in sitting in the whirlpools, disco dancing or simply enjoying the tranquility of the top deck lounge and bar. The atmosphere was that of the start of the tour; jollification, excitement and happiness.

While they were sitting drinking, the purser approached Rob.

"Excuse me for interrupting you, Mr. Clayton, but I just wanted to give you some news of the arrest of the crew member who you called Gary. Apparently his name is Gary and the name he used to register with us was a false name, however, he refuses to acknowledge the stabbing. He is pleading not guilty, but the police say they don't buy his story. I want to apologize for our head of security not listening to you in the beginning, but as there was no real evidence, there would have been nothing we could have done."

"Do you think that he might confess and implicate his friend on the ship?"

"That I can't say, but the young man that you named Brent is not saying much, so much so, that he denies that he and Gary are cousins as Gary had said."

"Well, I appreciate your concern and thank you for keeping me posted. If you hear any more, please let me know."

"I will Mr. Clayton. Enjoy the rest of your evening."

With that the purser departed.

"What's the story, Rob?" asked Michael.

"Still nothing. Gary's not admitting to stabbing Chris, but I have to come up with some sort of plan to catch Brent. I think he's behind all this."

"What makes you say that, Rob?"

"Michael, I just have this gut feeling that Brent is too clever to do things himself and he gets others to do his dirty work. However, I'm still not sure why he's targeting the people who worked in the store. It was Bobby's girlfriend who bought those clothes back at the store. Neither Bobby nor Brent took the clothes, so they couldn't be directly held responsible, even though Bobby had planned it with the girl. Why would Gary stab Chris; they didn't know each other. Would you stab someone giving you a blowjob?"

"Depends who's giving it to me," said Michael, grimacing at the thought of stabbing someone.

"However, if they are cousins as Gary stated, then I wouldn't put it past Brent to get someone to do his dirty work for him. But the burning question is: what is the connection between Bobby and Brent?"

"Rob, do you think it might be some sort of revenge?" suggested Chad, who'd been quietly listening to all the discussion. "Perhaps this Brent guy and this Bobby guy were part of a gang and Bobby got nailed and now Brent is seeking revenge on his gang member's behalf."

"Chad it sounds feasible, but I don't really know. But hey, we're here to have fun and not sit philosophizing. Are we going for dinner?"

"Yes," came a chorus.

"And then perhaps a show," said Selwyn.

They made their way to the Rossini Dining Room where they found a table for five. The environment was plush and elegant, and to match, the waiter brought an equally interesting and sophisticated menu. There was none of the usual fast food type offerings. Instead they were offered a menu which could possibly put them in gastronomical heaven.

First on the menu was crab and spring onion risotto, followed by Parma ham with fresh black figs and a Turkish dried fig infused balsamic. Not to be outdone, three-bird galantine of chicken, duck and quail with basmati rice and pomegranate sauce followed. The dessert, unlike that which Chris was hoping for, consisted of almond tiramisu, blood orange crème brûlée and a light cranberry and chardonnay sorbet as a palate cleanser.

The boys' taste buds were doing back flips as they read the menu. It was as if they could smell and taste the food before it was even brought to the table. They placed their orders, plus two bottles of white wine and sat back to enjoy.

Meanwhile, a couple of decks above them, Chris, Derek and their glamorous guest, Myra Bloomberg, were sitting in Derek's cabin, having had their dinner delivered to them. Of course it was not quite the same as the boys in the Rossini Room were getting, but it was also no fast food cum take away. Derek had ordered a bottle of wine to accompany their dinner and although Chris was still in some pain from his stabbing, they were determined to enjoy their time together.

"Now tell me Derek, where did you two meet?" enquired the mistress of matchmaking.

"Chris came in for an interview, along with a couple of other young men and I liked his flippant, yet sophisticated approach to life. Obviously, I also needed someone who could sell my products, but at the same time, could win over the customers. I always say, it's easy to sell something; it's difficult to get that customer back."

"You're so right," twittered Myra.

"I suppose, if I'm honest with myself, there was also a mystique about him that intrigued me. Although I come across as someone aloof and arrogant, so I've been told, I think that deep down there is a heart beating in me and that heart went out to Chris from the first day I met him."

"Ooh," cooed Myra, "this sounds so romantic."

Chris merely blushed.

"For some time I spent my days watching Chris to see how he was getting on, but you must remember, I wasn't openly out in my work environment, nor was I one hundred percent sure of Chris's interests, if you know what I mean."

"Oh yes," crooned Myra.

"Well an incident took place in the store one day. No, that's wrong of me to call it an incident. Let me put it to you this way. I saw Chris go into a change room with a customer and wondered why. Well, after the customer had left, I called Chris to my office to enquire why he had gone into the change room together with the customer. Well, after a little consoling, Chris told me."

"Yes? Why did he go into the change room? Asked Myra.

"I would say, to see if the customer wanted anything else," replied Derek diplomatically.

"Like another garment?" continued Myra.

"Yes, yes, that's it," said Derek, much to Chris's relief. "Well, as we were discussing the customer, we found that we were talking about similar interests, men, and that's how we got to know each other."

"I love it. I really love it. Your story is really so romantic. Love in a store," crooned Myra, her face alight with happiness. "But tell me Derek," asked Myra, stuffing a fork filled with meat into her mouth, "Have you and Chris thought about having a wedding?"

Chris and Derek looked at each other.

"I have," said Chris, "but I don't think Derek is into those types of things, are you?"

"Not really."

"I think a wedding would be wonderful; it would be like the icing on the cake so to speak," replied Myra, already scheming in her brain, how she could do the catering. "I can see it now," said Myra, dropping her knife and fork onto her plate with a clatter. "I can see it now; both of you in matching outfits, a large, but not excessive ceremony, nothing over the top, and a happy, festive reception for a couple of hundred people."

Derek looked a little shocked, but Chris was grinning at Myra's ideas.

"Derek, are you Jewish?"

"No Myra, but Chris is, why?"

"Oh Chris, darling that makes it even better. I tried organizing a wedding for my Mikey and Selwyn, but they wanted nothing to do with it. In fact that's why we're on this cruise; it's like their belated honeymoon."

"But Myra, why's it better that Chris is Jewish?"

"Because there's nothing to beat a Jewish wedding. Oi vey! What a happy day this will be. I can see you both in white; white designer suits, with a pink rose or orchid in each buttonhole. Must have pink! We must have flowers, yes flowers everywhere, and a chuppa..."

Myra was on a roll, but Derek's face was becoming more and more sullen. He was thinking of costs.

"...Myra, the cost!" exclaimed Derek.

"Darling Derek, don't be a schmuck. It's one day in your life and besides, you must think of Chris."

Chris battered his pretty eyelids at Derek who only rolled his eyes to heaven or some higher power.

"You must always consider the bride," chirped Chris, smiling angelically at his lover, who was getting a little peeved with Myra's fantastical journey that she was taking them along.

"Think about it; perhaps it might be nice to have a rabbi and a priest. Have you thought of that?"

"Myra, dear, I haven't thought of any of this, because Chris and I are happy together. I don't really think we need to go through the motions of a wedding ceremony."

Myra wasn't about to have her dreams shattered, and the knowledge that Mona Liebewitz was organizing a gay wedding for her Monty was the determination that Myra needed. She couldn't be outdone. Michael and Selwyn had let her down, but here was another opportunity to save face in the Jewish community.

"Darling Derek, just say the word and Myra Bloomberg will have everything organized for you," said Myra, beaming from ear to ear.

Derek cleared his throat as he thought of how to tell Myra, as politely as possible, that he wasn't into weddings be they gay or otherwise.

"Myra," he said, coughing a little to clear his throat. "Myra, I thank you for your concern and I'm sure so does Chris, but I think we need to discuss this; Chris and I, I mean. I'm really grateful for your offer, but it's not just a ceremony and a lot of people having a party... I just think Chris and I must talk."

A silence fell on the cabin. Chris looked a little despondent, but then so did Myra. Suddenly a grin appeared on Myra's face; she wasn't one for giving up.

"Talk about it and let me know tomorrow morning. OK?"

That put a despondent look on Derek's face.

For the rest of the dinner, silence was on the menu.

Down below in the Rossini Room, the food was being praised by all around the large table, and the wine was flowing, resulting in a festive atmosphere. Rob and

Chad were ensconced in deep conversation about sport, while Michael, Selwyn and Josh were discussing the merits and demerits of having pets.

"I'd love to have a dog," said Michael, "but it's obvious we couldn't keep one in the apartment."

"Maybe a cat," suggested Selwyn. "They're not too bad in apartments."

"True, but can you imagine what our curtains would look like with all the clawing that would go on, not to mention what the furniture would be like."

"I'm really a doggy person," said Josh, "you know the small cuddly types. I reckon it would be cool to get home from work and have a happy wagging tail and smile to greet you every day and then at night, when you're on your own, to have your dog curl up with you on the bed. I think I could get to like that."

"But you don't need a dog, Josh, you've got Rob to curl up with."

"But he doesn't have a waggy tail!"

"Sure, but his 'tail' isn't that bad," replied Michael.

Rob, in the meantime, was busy discussing American football with Chad.

"I couldn't be a professional football player," said Rob, shaking his head. "Can you imagine how frustrating it must be in the change room with all those muscular men running around half naked? I think I'd have a permanent hard-on."

"It's the pants that get to me. Have you seen how tight they are? Some are so tight you can actually see their jockstraps through the material. To me that's such a turn on. I'd probably spend all my time in the change room offering to wash their jockstraps for them."

Both Rob and Chad laughed at the ridiculous ideas that they were coming up with.

"But all said and done, I wouldn't mind putting on a pair of those silky Lycra type pants that they wear," said Chad.

"Didn't you play football at college or high school?" enquired Rob.

"No, did you?"

"Sure. In fact," said Rob after a little thought, "I've still got a pair of my pants back at home. Maybe if you come round to our place, I'll let you try them on."

Chad blushed at the thought, but deep down there was a deep-seated desire to do just that.

"What do they feel like, Rob?"

"Smooth to the touch. Your body feels totally encased and everything seems to be held in place by the tightness of the material. In fact I would go so far as to say it's a very sexual feel to it. But I'm serious. If you come round we'll put you in a jockstrap and slide those pale blue pants on you."

Rob became aware that just speaking the way he had been to Chad and describing the feeling of the material against his skin, was actually turning him on. He grinned at Chad and whispered, "I think we'd better cut this conversation; it's not good for what's happening down below in my groin."

Chad smiled knowingly.

"I know the feeling," was the confidential reply, as Chad adjusted the lie of his cock in his jeans.

"Tell me Chad, what's your view on relationships?"

"What do you mean Rob?"

"Well do you believe in monogamous ones or would you be willing to have a three-some with someone provided your partner was also involved, or what?" Rob was delving for answers, particularly after his discussion with Josh.

"I don't really know. Sure it would be nice to meet some that you could have a lasting relationship with. As for the monogamous thing, I don't think gays are capable of that. Come to think of it, I think you'll even find straight guys having affairs with women other than their wives or girlfriends. I think the only difference between the gays and straight monogamy thing is that with straights, they're bound to each other by the laws of marriage, whereas gays aren't. I don't know any couple who hasn't flitted on the side with someone else during their relationship, do you?"

"You're right about that. No I don't know of anyone," replied Rob.

"Can I ask you a personal thing? Have you slept with anyone outside of your relationship with Josh?"

Rob smiled, guiltily. "Yes, of course I have, but I don't think he knows. And you?"

"Of course. As I say, all gays do it."

"But how do you feel about it. I mean guilty or not?"

"Rob, I think that's up to each individual, but personally, I don't feel guilty because I see it merely as a way of getting my rocks off if my partner isn't in the mood to have sex with me."

"And what about having a threesome?"

"To be perfectly honest with you, Rob ... I dig threesomes."

Immediately Rob's face lit up broadly. The thought of him, Josh and Chad being together excited him. He loved Josh and found him very sexy, but with Chad, it was purely lust. He lusted after the young man's body and looks. Obviously he hadn't got to know Chad that well in the short time since they had met, but that didn't stop him from liking what he saw and heard. He never, at any stage, saw Chad as a replacement for Josh; rather, to Rob it was an addition, a bonus, possibly for both him and Josh.

Chad then asked; "Why are you asking me these things, Rob?"

"It's just that Josh and I were talking about it and I wondered what your views on it were."

Chad remembered the day they had lunch together, and Josh's leg constantly rubbed up against his and the feeling was pleasurable to say the least. A thought ran through his mind: was Rob coming onto him and was he suggesting, in a subtle way, the idea of him having a scene with Rob and Josh?

"What are you two so intently engrossed in?" asked Josh, turning his attention to Rob and Chad.

"We're just talking sport, honey."

Rob gave Josh a broad smile and winked at him.

In the meantime, Selwyn was whispering into Michael's ear so that none of the others would hear.

"They're having a talent competition on the ship tomorrow night and I think I'm going to enter," said Selwyn, confidentially.

"What were you thinking of doing, babes?"

"Part of my drag act. I haven't done it for years and I think I might have a pretty good chance of winning. Of course, I've no idea what other people here can do, but don't say a word to the guys, I want it to be a surprise."

"But you didn't bring any of your stuff."

"Not a problem. Beg, borrow and steal is my motto. I'll see if the beauty salon has a spare wig and if I have to I'll ask the entertainment's crew if they have any spare outfits that I could use."

"So you've got it all planned, hey?"

The two boys chuckled together as they plotted Selwyn's re-emergence as a potential budding talent.

After indulging in a most pleasant dinner, the five boys made their way down to the ice rink to see if there was a show on. They were in luck because the ice show was starting in ten minutes of their arrival. They made their way in, found seats quite close to the rink's edge and settled down for some entertainment.

The lights dimmed, the music played, building to a crescendo, and the first of the skaters emerged from the dark into the spotlights. The five boys sat entranced by what they saw. This was no second rate show put together to please tired and bored ship passengers; this was professional. The talent was evident, the costumes spectacular and the male and female skaters, beautiful. This was a gay man's dream, seeing these athletic males skimming effortlessly over the glistening ice. The applause after each act was thunderous and at the end of the show, the skaters all received a standing ovation from the crowd.

"Wow, that was some show," said Selwyn, totally mesmerized by the spectacle.

"You can say that again," concurred Michael.

"Are we all going for a couple of drinks?" enquired Rob, leading the way to the elevators.

"I think so," said Josh, buzzing with excitement at the sheer sparkle and talent in the ice show.

They found their way to Cleopatra's Lounge where they ordered a round of drinks and sat discussing the ice show.

Selwyn couldn't contain himself any more, so he asked the others if any of them were going to enter the talent show the following night.

"Are you mad?" asked Rob, looking around the group. "Do you honestly think that any of these people here have any talent, other than having sex?"

A riot of laughter reverberated around the lounge.

"Well, that's where you're wrong," said Selwyn, defending his talents. "I'm entering."

It was then that Rob remembered Selwyn's skills as a drag artiste, but the others who didn't know about Selwyn's past, laughed.

"Guys, don't laugh. You ain't seen anything yet," said Rob, now defending Selwyn.

"What are you going to do, Selwyn?" enquired Josh.

"You'll see tomorrow night, then we'll see who's laughing! Rob, if you have an idea of what I'm going to do, say nothing, I want it to be a surprise."

The boys continued enjoying each other's company until well past midnight, when five tired men, sauntered off in the direction of their cabins, ready to crash onto their waiting beds.

Chapter 16

The ship docked at precisely 8:00 a.m. to unpleasant, rainy weather. Rob got out of bed and opened the curtains to their cabin. The sky was gray and rain was constantly falling. He looked out through the cabin sliding doors to their balcony, saw the wet harbor of Phillipsburg below and decided that there wouldn't be much touring today. He crawled back into bed and snuggled up closer to Josh who was still asleep. Rob pressed his hefty body against Josh's and they lay breathing in unison. Rob looked at Josh's peacefully sleeping face and gently kissed his forehead. He was very happy with Josh. They complemented each other; the one gentle while the other, not being brutish, was strong; as Myra so succinctly put it, Beauty and the Beast. He knew that Josh loved him and although their relationship was still in its youthful stages, they were meant for each other, in Rob's opinion.

Josh stirred and in doing so, the duvet covering him, slipped from his chest, revealing the young mounds of pectoral muscle. Rob viewed these and gently ran a hand over them, skimming each nipple ever so lightly.

"Hmm!" came a groan from Josh.

Rob immediately stopped what he was doing.

"Don't stop. That feels so nice," murmured Josh.

Rob chose to refrain from his actions and Josh opened his eyes.

"Why did you stop? That felt so good."

"Because I thought you could do with a bit of teasing, so I chose to let you suffer for a while."

"You're quite a mean bastard, aren't you?"

"Not really. I love you don't I?"

"If you say so, but what proof do I have of that?"

"Are you playing hard to get?"

"No. Not yet, but wait until I do get hard," smiled Josh.

Rob's hand slid down between Josh's legs.

"If you ask me you are hard already."

The two began a mock fight, grabbing each other and rolling all over the bed, first one then the other on top. After some time of this activity, with both now on top of the bed instead of under the duvet, and both fully aroused, they lay panting in each other's arms, laughing.

"Josh, I must tell you, I spoke to Chad last night."

"What about?"

"You know what we'd discussed about having a threesome."

"Oh yes, and what transpired?"

"It was very interesting. Chad said he liked threesomes." Rob grinned at Josh. "Do you know what that means?"

"Yes. He's into more than one guy!"

"No! He's willing to do it, but I never got to ask him if he wanted to do it with us."

"Did he honestly say that he's into threesomes?"

"To quote him he said 'I dig threesomes', so what does that say to you?"

Josh gave Rob a sweet smile. "Are you going to ask him if he wants to spend some time with us and to come to our cabin? We've only got three nights left before we get off the ship, you know."

"If you're happy to do it, I'll ask him."

"Sure I am. I like him and I know that you fancy him, so what more do you want?"

Rob leant over Josh and kissed him long and hard.

"I think this could be the start of something interesting," whispered Rob into Josh's ear.

"Are you two awake!" came a call from the adjacent cabin.

Rob and Josh looked at each other, shrugged their shoulders and pulled the duvet back up over their arousals.

"Come in Selwyn," replied Rob.

Michael and Selwyn bounded into their cabin. When Michael saw their naked upper torsos, he asked, "Sorry, were you two busy?"

"Nothing that we can't start up later," answered Rob, winking at Michael.

"Listen guys," said Selwyn, sitting on the bed next to Josh, "are you doing anything today because I see it's raining?"

"We actually haven't given it much thought," said Josh, stretching and yawning.

"Because I was going to get my act together for tonight, which should take me the morning, and then hopefully it will have stopped raining, but Michael isn't doing anything, so I thought if you were going anywhere, you don't want to take Michael with you, do you?"

Rob screwed up his face and looked at Selwyn.

"I don't think we want to take Mike anywhere; he only cramps our style and never wants to do anything outrageous with us."

Selwyn at first was taken aback by Rob's comment until he realized that Rob was merely joking with him, and then he played along.

"I quite agree with you. He's actually quite a party poop, a drop out, a bore, a fader, can't take the pace or the talent that's on offer. In fact, I'd just leave him here on the ship if I were you."

"Thanks for that wonderful vote of confidence," replied Michael, also playing along with them. "I think I will stay on board in search of a hunk who would appreciate my lustful, masculine body; someone who's dying to have a man making love to him; someone who appreciates tenderness, care and is prepared to take it over and over."

"If that's the offer, we might all stay on board," laughed Rob.

"There, you see Selwyn. I've already had an offer."

"Seriously, what are you guys doing today?"

"Seriously Selwyn, we haven't decided, but you go ahead and get your things ready for tonight and don't worry about us. If you like we can all meet at lunch time," said Rob.

"Come, Selwyn, let's leave these two lovers to go back to sleep," said Michael, sensing that the two wanted some quality time together. "Rob, don't worry about me, I'll organize myself if Selwyn is going to be busy this morning."

The two neighbors departed and left Rob and Josh to cuddle up together. Just as they were beginning to doze off to sleep again, there came a knock on their cabin door.

"Now what does that queen want?" muttered Rob. "Come in!" He shouted.

The cabin door opened and in came the purser.

"I'm terribly sorry to disturb you Mr. Clayton, but I have the St. Maarten police on board. They were in contact with the police in St. Thomas and they received a message from them informing us that Gary has finally admitted to the stabbing, so formal charges will now be laid against him for attempted murder."

"I'm very glad to hear that. Does Mr. Campbell know of this?"

"Yes, we have informed him."

"Thanks, and please thank the police officers from us. I would do it, but as you can see, I'm a little undressed for the occasion."

The purser grinned, nodded and departed from the cabin.

"One down; one to go," said Rob, referring to his determination to flush out Brent.

The rain continued to pound the sea and land, and most of the passengers chose to remain on board, so the entertainment's group was busy trying to put together programs for potentially bored tourists. Selwyn was busily trying to get an outfit together and had approached the crew for help. He found himself, with permission, down in the crew's quarters trying on outfits which were spares for the ice and theatre shows. He also managed to get a wig, some shoes and the girls of the ice show offered him some of their make up. Selwyn was ready.

When everybody met at lunchtime, Selwyn was like an excited child given a surprise gift; he couldn't contain himself. Along with his excitement was Myra's, who was very much like Selwyn.

"What are you two on?" asked Michael. "If I didn't know you both better, I'd have thought you were either on drugs or been smoking something. What's with the excitement?"

They were all seated in the restaurant when Myra stood up and spoke.

"I have the most exciting good news for you. There's going to be a wedding."

The boys, with the exception of Selwyn, all looked surprised by Myra's comment.

"Whose, Mum?"

"Chris and Derek!"

"What? Mum, what have you been up to now?"

Now the excitement flowed from Myra.

"You know I had dinner with them, well I got to telling them how nice it would be if they had a formal ceremony, like you and Selwyn refused to have."

"Mum that was our choice."

"Well, after very little effort, I persuaded them to have a wedding," said Myra excitedly. "And Chris is Jewish so we can have a wonderful Jewish wedding."

The boys battled to keep straight faces as Myra rambled on.

"Can you picture it Michael? I told them they'd wear white designer outfits with a pink flower in each button hole and we can have a rabbi as well as a priest, only because Derek isn't Jewish, and a chuppa that they can stand under and I'll organize the catering… Ooh, just think of the fun we can have."

"You mean the fun you can have, Mum."

"Chris is very excited about it," continued Myra, not allowing anyone to stop her while she was on a roll. "I've told them I'll organize the catering such as the food and wedding cake, but they'll have to organize the drinks and maybe Michael, you can organize a band for the reception …"

"…And have you hired the venue for the reception yet, Mum?"

"Don't be facetious. You're just jealous because someone is getting something that you didn't get."

"What? A wedding! Selwyn and I don't need all the frills and trappings, we've got each other and that's all that matters. Mum you were determined to con someone into having a wedding because you didn't want to lose face to Mrs. Liebewitz, isn't that the truth?"

"Michael, if it makes two people happy, then it makes me happy."

"And where is this wedding going to take place, on the ship?"

"I never thought of that. That would outdo Mona Liebewitz's wedding. That would mean we'd have about two thousand guests! You see how exciting this is!"

"By the way Mum, have they actually agreed to this?"

Myra hesitated before answering.

"I told them to give me an answer by today."

By this time, Rob, Chad and Josh were almost collapsing from laughter at the way mother and son were going at each other. As the battle of the Bloomberg's raged on, Chris and Derek emerged from their cabin and came up to the restaurant where the gang was seated.

When Myra saw them, she rushed over to them and hugged Derek and gave Chris a kiss.

"Darlings! So good to see you both up. What's the verdict Derek? Wedding or …"

"Myra, we've both given it a great deal of thought," replied Derek solemnly.

"Yes, yes, yes!"

"Myra, we really appreciate your kindness and thoughts…"

"Yes, yes, yes. Derek, cut the crap."

"Myra we think that we'd rather use the money that would have gone into a wedding and reception to either take another trip or to refurnish our apartment."

Myra was silent. Stunned seems more the word. This would have been her second rejection. First by Selwyn and Michael, her own flesh and blood, and now by Chris and Derek.

"What is it with you Jewish boys when you marry a non-Jewish boy? You know how much a wedding means to us mothers, we thrive on them. It's bad enough knowing that you won't have children so we can't become bobbas, but to take away our organizing skills, oi vey, but that is painful!"

Poor Myra had once again been foiled. She was getting desperate to be able to match, if not better her arch rival, Mrs. Liebewitz, but knowing Myra's determination to bring happiness into other's lives, this little hurdle was not going to get her down.

Most of the morning was chaos on the ship as the entertainment crew hastily arranged events because of the rain, but Rob and Josh remained in their cabin, enjoying their own entertainment. Michael had wandered around the ship, but there's only so much one can see and do on a ship, so he wandered off to one of the lounges and sat there.

It wasn't long before Myra found him sitting alone in the lounge

"Mikey, darling. What are you doing all alone here in the lounge? Where are Selwyn and the others?"

"Selwyn's flitting around somewhere and as far as I know the others are in their cabins, Mum."

"Tell me, are you enjoying yourself?" asked Myra, sitting down next to him. "After all this is your honeymoon, remember."

"Thanks Mum, but we're having a wonderful time. I think this was actually a wonderful idea to come on a cruise. I mean not only do you rest, but you visit interesting places and meet fabulous people."

"Oh, and there are some fabulous people on this ship! The other day, I met some very handsome men and we all got on very well together. In fact they invited me to go and have drinks with them."

"And did you?"

"No. I didn't want to cramp their style; you know like Selwyn always says."

"You wouldn't have cramped their style Mum, because their 'style' as you put it, would have only come into play later when you weren't around."

"Oh, I see. I must remember that for future."

"Future? Are you planning more cruises?"

"No. Some of them gave me their telephone numbers and said when we got back to land, I must keep in touch."

Michael smiled at the thought of his mother doing the gay socializing rounds.

"You never know, I might be able to become a gay wedding organizer when we get back home."

Now Michael burst out laughing, unable to contain himself.

"What are you laughing at? I'm serious."

"That's what worries me, Mum, but if it keeps you happy, then you do it."

"I could make a lot of money, Mikey. Just think. You know how some gays are flighty, so I've been told, and present company excluded…"

"So?"

"Well, that means that they must go through weddings quite often and the more often they get married, the more money I'll make."

"Mum, I don't think it's quite like that. Gay guys are more likely to arrange a wedding when they're truly involved with their partner, not when they've just met someone and spent a month or two together. How long did you and Dad go out before you got married?"

"But that's different."

"How's it different? It was two people who fell in love, dated and then decided to get married. How different is that to what gays do? We are human you know!"

"I don't mean that."

"Well, what do you mean then?"

Myra was aware that she was getting herself deeper into a discussion on which she knew very little.

"I just thought that I might bring some happiness into some gay men's lives by taking the pressure off them if they wanted to have a wedding."

"Mum, there's absolutely nothing wrong in doing that, but don't think that this is going to be a killer job where Myra Bloomberg is going to become a millionaire out of it. If you want to do something like that, then I think it's good, but see it more as a part-time job."

"I really was hoping that Chris and Derek might have a wedding," said Myra, still living in hope.

"Mum, most gays are like Selwyn and me. We meet, fall in love, learn as much as we can about the other person to make our relationship a happy and workable one, we move in together and live happily ever after. Now how does that differ from your heterosexual relationships? You see we really are no different."

"I suppose you're right Mikey. It's just that I never thought of it like that."

"Unfortunately Mum, most people don't. They see two men together and condemn them. They don't see us as being human beings the same as them, who have the same emotions and the same desires. We want happiness just as they do. We want love the same as they do and we want to be left alone, the same as they do."

Myra had never had a conversation like this with Michael before. She had accepted his being gay but probably looked at Michael's relationship with Selwyn as something different from hers and her husband's.

"Mum, think of Shylock's speech in *The Merchant of Venice*, when he defends his Jewish heritage, and says 'If you prick us do we not bleed? If you tickle us do we not laugh? If you poison us do we not die?' Well, the same applies to gays. We are no different from straights except for who we choose to sleep with, so why should that small detail determine how we should be shunned or loved by others?"

"Michael you know I love you and have no objections whatsoever about you being gay, it's just that I've never given your being gay much thought. I see you as my son and you'd be no different whether you had a wife or Selwyn."

"I understand, Mum. It's just that so many people misunderstand gays and because these people choose not to find out about them, they continue to have preconceived stereotypical views of us."

As they were speaking, Selwyn came along to join them.

"So this is where you two are?" he said, giving Myra a kiss and sitting down next to them.

"Where have you been?" enquired Myra.

"Here and there," was Selwyn's no-committal answer.

"Doing what?"

"Nothing in particular," replied Selwyn, still maintaining his secrecy about his planned talent show entry.

Michael and Selwyn gave each other a knowing wink. Myra had no idea that Selwyn had been a drag artiste and was about to reveal his hidden talent that evening in the ship's theatre.

"Have you been anywhere or done anything, Michael?"

"No, I've been sitting here and then Mum came along and we've just been chatting. Have you seen any of the others on your travels?"

"No, but it looks like the rain's stopping and the sun's coming out. Maybe we'll be able to go for a swim or take a trip off the ship. By the way, what time do we sail tonight?"

"17:00, so it's not really worth going on a tour," said Selwyn. "Anyone want a drink?"

"Not for me thanks, babes, but Mum might have something."

"My darling, I'll just have a tiny whiskey, if that's OK with you?"

Selwyn trotted off to get a drink for Myra and himself and while he was busy at the bar, Chad arrived, having braved the rain to go around St. Maarten Island.

"Hi Chad, if you want a drink, catch Selwyn, he's just gone to the bar."

"No, I won't have one thanks Michael. Hi Myra. Did you guys stay on board today?"

"Yes, we decided it was too miserable to go out in the rain. Did you go anywhere?"

"I took a quick trip to Mullet Bay to see the beaches, but obviously it was miserable so no-one was swimming, then I came back to Phillipsburg and had lunch at a little Argentinean restaurant called *Los Gauchos*, then came back to the ship."

Selwyn returned with Myra's whiskey and his beer, sat down and joined in the conversation. As they were casually chatting, the purser came up to the group and spoke to Myra.

"Excuse me Mrs. Bloomberg I wonder if I might talk to you in private?"

Myra looked somewhat puzzled but agreed, so the two wandered a little way away from the boys. They could see both deep in conversation, and then Myra roared with laughter and started nodding her head. The purser shook her hand and departed, leaving Myra to return to the boys.

"What was all that about?" queried Michael.

"Nothing darling," giggled Myra, looking smug.

"What do you mean 'nothing'? You spoke, you laughed and then you say you spoke about nothing!"

"Michael, we spoke privately. In other words it has nothing to do with you young people."

"Are you having an affair with the purser, Mum?"

"Don't be silly, he's too old for me."

"Mum, he can't even be fifty."

"You see, that's far too old!"

"So what were you two talking about? Was it anything to do with the police investigations into Chris's stabbing?"

"Michael, what part of what I said to you didn't you understand? It was a private conversation between the purser and me. Period."

Michael knew that he wasn't going to get anything else from his mother, so he gave up trying to inveigle the information from her.

Once again on their trip, the loud sonorous sounds of the ship's hooter blasted informing all that they were about to get underway. From the lounge windows they could see the slow movement away from the wharf as the liner began to make her way out into the open sea. They would be sailing for a long time before they reached land again, in fact the whole of the following day would be spent at sea.

"That means it's 17:00," said Selwyn, "time to go and have a shower and get ready. Michael, are you coming with me to help?"

Michael gladly obliged and the two set off to start the transformation of Selwyn.

Chapter 17

Ask any woman how long it takes her to get dressed and put on her make up and she's bound to tell you : 'a long time'. Well, Selwyn, or Princess Selena, as he was going as, took just as long, if not longer. Dinner had been ordered in the cabin so as not to reveal the lovely lady before she was due to be seen. Michael and Selwyn sat talking about the cruise, about the people they had met on the ship and the trip in general. In fact, they talked about anything and everything, just to kill time. At one stage, there had come a knock on their connecting door and they had wondered whether to open it. Eventually, Michael sent Selwyn out onto the balcony and closed the sliding door curtains so that no-one would see him out there, and then let Rob and Josh in.

"Are you two going down for dinner?" asked Rob.

"No, Rob, we're having a little intimate meal here."

"Oh!" said a surprised Rob. "Where's Selwyn?"

"He just stepped out for a while."

"What time are you two going down to the theatre for the talent contest?" asked Josh.

"It starts at nine, so we'll probably go down at about half past eight to get a good seat."

"Shall we meet you there?" enquired Rob, still unsure as to why Michael was sounding a little cagey with his answers and demeanor.

"Come on Josh, let's go and feed our hungry stomachs," and the two departed.

"You can come in now, Selwyn. They've gone."

"It's cold and windy out there. I could have died from exposure."

"Please, you've exposed more than that before and you haven't died."

Their dinner was delivered, and once again Selwyn had to escape to the outside world while the steward delivered the meal. After they had completed eating, and as it was nearing 20:30, they decided it was time to make their move to the theatre.

"Michael, you go first and then I'll follow. In any case, the contestants have to go backstage, so I can't go in the main entrance with you."

"Good luck, babes. Knock 'em dead!" said Michael, giving Selwyn a kiss for luck.

Selwyn waited a minute or two before exiting their cabin and mincing down the corridor towards the elevators. Now as Princess Selena, Selwyn exuded elegance and charm. Her wig was perfectly coiffured, her make up immaculately done and the spring in her step indicated her excitement to get going.

Michael waited outside the theatre until he saw Rob and Josh.

"Where's Selwyn? Asked Rob.

"Backstage," replied Michael.

"I hope he's going to be fine," remarked Rob.

"You know him. He'll be absolutely fabulous!"

Chad and Myra soon joined them and all five made their way into the elaborate theatre and found seats as close to the stage as possible; three rows from the front, in fact.

There was sense of excitement in the theatre. People were laughing and talking, some shouted across the venue to other friends seated elsewhere. Even up in the gallery, they recognized members of the crew who weren't on duty, seated waiting to see the passengers make fools of themselves. The theatre filled, the houselights dimmed and there was a buzz of excitement. Suddenly a spotlight appeared on stage and the Master of Ceremonies, who was the purser, appeared.

"Ladies and gentlemen. Welcome to a show never to be experienced again. Thank goodness, some of you might say, but welcome anyway. Before we get under way with the various acts, I would like to introduce our judges for the evening. First, let me introduce you to our captain, Captain Leonard Montgomery."

The captain appeared on stage in the spotlight and bowed to the audience, who cheered and then someone shouted, 'who's steering the ship!' There were peels of laughter at this inane comment.

"Second of our judges is our own medical doctor, Doctor James Smith."

He too got a thunderous applause. The same voice that shouted earlier, shouted again, 'are you here because we'll be sick of the acts!' A little less laughter followed this comment.

"And last, but by no means least, we have a true artist in our midst tonight as judge number three. It gives me great pleasure to introduce you to Mrs. Myra Bloomberg, match-maker to the stars."

"Match maker to the stars!" gasped Michael. "Where the hell did that title come from?"

The men in the audience cheered and whistled when they recognized her. Myra made her way up on stage, bowed graciously, blew kisses to everyone and took her seat at the front of the auditorium along with the captain and the doctor.

"Ladies and gentlemen let me tell you what will happen tonight. Each competitor will perform for the judges, who will score them. At the end of the show the three performers with the highest scores will be brought back on stage and you will have a chance to vote for your favorite. From your votes and those of the judges, we will announce our winner. The prizes tonight have been gratefully sponsored by businesses and restaurants on our ship. Added to which, a cash prize of $500 will be given to the winner. Ladies and gentlemen, without further ado, let's get on with the show."

The first act was a comedian who tried, for three minutes, which felt like a lifetime to the audience, to tell jokes, which were less funny than the heckler at the start of the evening during the introductions. Gays can be nasty if they want to be. The catcalls and boos echoed round the theatre, so he departed very hurriedly.

Second on was a gay couple, probably aged between sixty and death, who waltzed around the stage with stumbling elegance. At one point the audience thought the couple were about to fall off the stage because they got so close to the edge, but the sad thing was that the man, acting the woman's role, had his toes trodden on at least six or seven times because he yelled each time it happened.

The night was still young, but the audience was already rolling in the aisles with the antics they saw on stage.

Item three was a singer. Not a bad voice. The only problem was that he chose to sing *The Phantom of the Opera* and when he tried to reach the high notes, he neither hit them nor reached them half way; he shattered them! People screwed their faces as if in pain as he tried desperately to reach the magical notes. Perhaps had he chosen another piece of music, he might have fared better.

Following on came a juggler. Nice idea, but not so nice performance. Either because of a lack of practice or because of nerves, the balls that he was juggling with got lost in the auditorium, so although he started with eight, by the end of his act, there were only two left.

Two guys called Mitch and Mike did a tap dancing routine which was greatly appreciated by the audience. Their performance was very slick and they looked appealing in their black pants and black waistcoats. They were in step with each other and their timing was perfect, not to mention the six-pack abdomen that both had and which appealed to the audience.

Item six was a short, bald, dumpy man who waddled on stage with a suitcase and announced to the audience that he was going to do a ventriloquist act. He opened his suitcase and produced a fluffy yellow duck. He inserted his hand and arm into its ass and this was how he manipulated its beak.

"Do people really take these sorts of things on holiday with them?" asked Michael in all innocence.

"Looks like it," chuckled Rob "If I knew we could stand on stage with our hand up someone's ass, I would have entered too."

The duck's beak opened and shut, but then so did the ventriloquist's. There was no subtlety in his performance.

"Did you hear the joke about the duck and the chicken?" Quacked the duck, the ventriloquist's mouth moving furiously in time to the duck's.

The joke fell flat. No one laughed, not even the duck. This didn't faze the man; he just carried on until everyone was once again rolling in the aisles. The sad thing about this act was that he was serious. If he'd done it with humor as his intention, it would have been good. At the end, the duck was packed away in the suitcase and the man waddled off stage.

Although the audience was expressing their opinions with cheers and boos, the judges were expressing theirs by busily wiping tears from their eyes from the laughter.

A drum roll sounded. The spotlight hit the curtain at the back of the stage and the music started. Through the curtain came entrant number seven. The minute the voice started singing and the audience identified the song, the auditorium erupted. Princess Selena, looking ravishing, strutted to the front of the stage singing her theme song, *Sisters are doing it* by Annie Lennox. This was a clever move on Princess Selena's part, because this piece of music had become a gay anthem, so, soon the entire audience was on its feet clapping and singing along with the Princess. She worked the audience well and even ventured into the auditorium to mingle with the audience, sitting on people's laps and stroking their faces and hair. At the end of the song, there was a thunderous applause with much cheering. Michael beamed with pride at knowing that Selwyn hadn't lost any of his touch.

Item eight was more subdued. A tall, gangly, middle-aged man walked solemnly onto the stage, took center stage and stared at the audience. He was dressed in black with a black cape and top hat. Silence fell over the audience in anticipation of what he was about to do. An assistant ran on stage carrying a small round table on which stood a square box, and then the assistant disappeared off stage. The tall man opened the box and took out a blue handkerchief. He showed the audience that his left hand was not holding anything and then he threw the handkerchief over his empty hand. He held it there for a moment and then removed the handkerchief and in his hand was a dove, which remained there fleetingly and then flitted off his hand and into the audience.

"This must be part of Noah's ark," shouted someone form the audience as the dove swooped in ever-widening circles over the heads of the audience.

The man on the stage remained straight-faced. He then replaced the handkerchief over his empty hand again, waited a moment and removed it once more. This time he had a bunch of plastic flowers in his hand. Still no smile crossed his face. The audience politely applauded. He then dug into his coat pocket and withdrew a pack of playing cards. Without speaking, he signaled someone in the front row to join him on stage. The member of the audience was to pick a card from his pack, without showing him, hold it in his hand and think of the number.

"Seven of hearts," said the magician.

The young man looked at his card and shook his head. The magician remained stony faced.

"Are you sure it's not the seven of hearts?"

Again the young man shook his head.

"Let me see," said the magician.

The young man held up his card for all to see, not only the magician. It was the queen of clubs.

"Pick another card," said the magician.

The young man duly did as he was requested. Again he was not to show the magician.

"Ace of spades," said the magician.

The young man looked at his card and shook his head. Now the audience began to laugh heartily. The magician looked very perplexed.

"Not the ace of spades?"

"No," replied the young man. "Seven of hearts."

The magician smiled for the first time.

"I told you that you were holding the seven of hearts, didn't I?"

"Not now. That was the first time."

"But I got it right, didn't I?"

"Second time round," replied the young man.

The magician thanked his helper and sent him back to his seat. The magician then took off his top hat and laid it on the round table. His helper ran on stage with a jug of water, which he handed to the magician. The magician showed the audience the water and then proceeded to pour it into the top hat. When the jug was emptied, the magician picked up the hat and placed it on his head. A shower of silver confetti fell from the hat over his head and shoulders. The audience applauded wildly for this trick. The magician bowed to his audience and departed from the stage.

The M.C. came on stage and announced that the acts were completed and now it was up to the judges to decide on their three best performances. This was a signal to the audience that they could chat casually while the judges discussed the merits and demerits of each act.

"I thought Selwyn was performing tonight?" asked Josh.

Rob and Michael smiled to each other.

"He did," replied Michael.

"But I didn't see him."

"Were you sleeping honey, or looking at the other talent sitting around you?" mocked Rob.

"Seriously though, where was he?"

"Wait and see if the judges liked him, then you can see him again," answered Rob.

"Ladies and gentlemen, could I have your attention please. The judges have made their choices," said the M.C. over the microphone.

An envelope was handed to him by the captain and the M.C. opened it.

"When I announce the top three acts, in no specific order, will they please come back on stage. First could we have Mitch and Mike our tap dancing duo."

Cheers and applause reverberated around the theatre.

"Second, we'd like our magician on stage."

The gloomy looking man strode onto the stage.

"And the third act we'd like to see again is Princess Selena."

Whistles, cheers and applause greeted Selwyn as he glided onto the stage.

"Is that Selwyn?" asked Josh.

Michael and Rob nodded simultaneously.

"I don't believe it. He actually makes a bloody good woman."

"Ladies and gentlemen, it's now your turn to participate. We have an applause meter which will record the volume of your support for each act, and based on that, we will combine the result with the judges. Can we have applause for act number one," said the M.C.

There was an enthusiastic response to their act. Cheers, whistles and cheering were offered for Mitch and Mike.

"Now act number two."

Polite but limited applause and very few whistles were offered.

"And finally act number three."

There was a thunderous applause accompanied with whistling, shouting and foot stomping.

"Thank you ladies and gentlemen. If we count the judges scores with your responses, our winner of the *Caribbean Queen* talent contest is Number three, Princess Selena."

Once more the cheers echoed around the theatre as Selwyn was presented with his prizes. Everyone stood and cheered, asking for an encore of his song, which he obligingly gave to the audience. The other two finalists also received prizes and after the prize giving, everyone started to filter from the theatre. Selwyn remained dressed as Princess Selena and rushed over to Michael, flinging his arms around his neck.

"Well done, babes. I knew you could do it."

The whole gang crowded around Selwyn congratulating him, but parted slightly with the advance of Myra.

"Selwyn, is that you?" she asked in disbelief.

"Yes, Myra."

"Good God! I never recognized you, but I must say, you make a beautiful woman; with an exquisite singing voice as well. I never knew you were so talented."

"You see Mum, he's got hidden talent."

They headed off to the promenade to go to one of the bars to celebrate, Selwyn sashaying along the ship's corridors with charm and panache. Men were turning to look, admiring not only how beautiful he looked as a woman, but also the group of men that accompanied him were equally eye catching.

They found a bar which was relatively empty, as it seemed most of the people had gone up to the disco, gathered enough seats for themselves and ordered celebratory drinks. Princess Selena was the belle of the ball and champagne flowed freely, especially considering that Selwyn had won, among his other prizes, $500,00.

"How long have you been doing drag acts?" asked Josh, who was still dumbfounded by Selwyn's transformation.

"Quite a few years. I've forgotten to be honest. I used to do it for fun, but then I managed to get a part-time job in a club three nights a week. That's when I met Michael and soon after that, I landed a job with Rob, so my three nights a week diminished until it came to a stop altogether. However, I don't really think I've lost my touch."

"You certainly haven't," said Rob. "I still find it amazing what you do. I remember the first time that I saw Selwyn doing his act. I didn't even know it was him until afterwards when I was standing at the bar chatting to Michael, and Selwyn came up to me and I actually asked him when he was going to do his act, not realizing that I'd been watching it."

Michael stood listening to all the praise that was being heaped on Selwyn. He was proud of his partner's achievement and proud of the attention that he was being given by those around them. The clock ticked merrily on towards midnight. The music still thumped in the disco, the midnight buffet was being prepared for those who had a desire to put on more weight, while the casino was still eating up patrons' money, and a sense of joie de vivre was in the air.

Thursday, the following day, was to be spent at sea as they traveled towards the Bahamas. According to the ship's newspaper, a *Mr. Caribbean Queen* competition was to be held at the swimming pool in the early afternoon of the Thursday and all were wondering who was going to enter.

"Why don't you enter, Rob," asked Michael.

"You're joking. With all these hunks on this ship I wouldn't stand a chance. What about you, Chad?"

"I thought about it, but I'm not really into those sorts of things."

"But you've got a brilliant body," complimented Josh. "You should enter, shouldn't he guys?"

They all concurred that Chad had as good a chance as any of the guys on the ship. One of them also suggested that Josh should enter, but he was a little reticent about entering.

"Darlings, if I can expose myself to this ship, then so can you," said Selwyn. "It's not all about winning, it's about having fun, and that's what we're doing on this ship. By the way, Myra, are you one of the judges for tomorrow's competition?"

"No, more is the pity. I think they did it on purpose, making me a judge for the talent contest rather than for the bodybuilding one."

"You see, Mum, you've been so busy chatting up all the young men, that it wouldn't be fair for you to be a judge because you'd be biased."

"Rubbish, Michael. I wasn't biased towards Selwyn in making him the winner; I didn't even know it was him."

"That's the point, without half their clothes on you'd know all the contestants in tomorrow's contest, Mum."

The whole gang laughed but it was apparent that Myra was not a happy lady. She had wanted to be a judge so that she could have been close up to the contestants.

"Myra, don't you worry your pretty head, we'll find you a seat as close to the action as possible, tomorrow," said Rob.

As they were sitting enjoying their drinks, a steward brought a note to Selwyn.

"Must be an admirer," joked Michael.

Selwyn opened the note and read it. He tried to remain casual as he read it.

"What's it say?" enquired Myra.

"Oh, nothing exciting Myra, just a note saying how they enjoyed the performance, that's all."

Selwyn folded the note and placed it in Michael's shirt pocket as he hadn't anywhere to put it on himself as he was still dressed as Princess Selena. He resumed his conversations with the others as though they had not been interrupted. After chatting for about fifteen minutes, Selwyn excused himself under the pretext that he wanted to go to the cabin and get out of his Princess Selena outfit and into something more comfortable. The others told him to hurry and rejoin them as they had all decided to go up to the disco for some music and dancing.

Selwyn hurried off and Rob and Michael got into conversation. At one stage, Rob looked at his watch and said to Michael, "I wonder what's keeping Selwyn?"

"I suppose it's a mission to get all his war paint off," chuckled Michael.

"Michael, do you think that note was from an admirer?"

"Rob, I wouldn't know."

"Well have a look. He did slip it into your shirt pocket."

"Hell, I forgot."

Michael took out the note, opened it and read. His face was ashen. He handed the note to Rob, who read it: *Meet me in cabin 7866 in fifteen minutes. An admirer.*

"Michael, don't take this too seriously. You know what Selwyn's like; he likes a lot and maybe this guys offering him a little bit of pleasure." Suggested Rob

"He can get that from me, Rob. He knows that, so he doesn't have to go looking for it elsewhere. I just hope it's not some crank."

"Well, that's easily remedied. Come, we're going to cabin 7866."

Rob and Michael excused themselves and told the others to wait for them as they were going to find Selwyn. They made their way to deck 7 and searched for the relevant cabin. When they found it, they listened at the door. They heard some groans coming from within and this caused Michael to grow angry with suspicion.

"Rob, if I have to, I'm forcing my way in."

As Michael, hastily followed by Rob, burst through the cabin door into the darkness of the cabin, a figure darted past them. All Rob managed to see, thanks to the light in the corridor was that the intruder or person was African-American with a clean-shaved head. Michael fumbled for the light switch and on turning it on, saw Selwyn, sans wig, lying prostrate on the floor of the cabin, blood oozing from a gash in the back of his head. Immediately, Rob gave chase of the person who'd fled the cabin, while Michael went to Selwyn's assistance. The cabin had been unoccupied, so he pulled some bed linen from the bed and tried to stem the bleeding. Selwyn was out cold. Michael shook him in an effort to revive him. A groan was heard and Selwyn began to come round. Instinctively Selwyn put his hand to his head to ease the pain.

"Don't touch it," said Michael, "but what happened?"

"I don't know, other than feeling a crack on the back of my head."

It looked worse than what it probably was, because head wounds tend to bleed more profusely than other wounds, but Michael was still perturbed. He placed the linen under Selwyn's head.

"Don't touch it and don't move. I'm phoning the doctor to come and take a look."

He dialed from the cabin's phone and got Doctor Smith, telling him what had happened and the kind doctor was up in the cabin in a flash. He looked at Selwyn's gash and said that he didn't think stitches would be needed, but he cleaned up Selwyn's head, bandaged it and gave him a sedative and told Michael to take him to his cabin and put him to bed.

"You might have a headache tomorrow, but I think you'll be fine," said the doctor.

Michael explained what had happened and that Rob had run off after the alleged culprit, but the doctor told then to get to their cabin and not to worry as he would phone security and warn them.

Michael helped Selwyn to his feet and the two, who must have been an ugly sight with blood smeared all over them, slowly made their way to their cabin where Michael put Selwyn to bed.

"Selwyn, why did you go to that cabin?" asked Michael, trying to find out what had actually happened.

"I was flattered," he replied, "so I thought I'd go and see who this admirer was, but when I knocked on the cabin door, a voice shouted for me to 'come in'. When I opened the door, I could see it was dark inside, but I thought maybe they were just fooling around. As I went through the doorway, I felt something hit me and I fell to the floor. Obviously being dark I couldn't see anything. I could feel someone trying to kick me on the floor, but I tried to scramble away. Then you and Rob burst in."

"You realize that if we hadn't come when we did, you might have been killed there in the cabin. Thank goodness you put that note in my pocket so we knew which cabin you'd gone to. If you hadn't done that, we'd still be looking for you and you might have either ended up overboard or dead."

The realization of the consequences hit home and tears began to well up in Selwyn's eyes. Michael sat on the bed and hugged Selwyn tenderly. A panting, out of breath Rob entered the cabin.

"I couldn't catch him, but I'm damn sure I know who it was."

"Who?" asked Michael.

"Brent! I know that there are other bald African-Americans on this ship, but I'm almost one hundred percent positive it was him that I saw."

"So what do we do now?" enquired Michael.

"You two stay put in your cabin. We'll be next door and if anything untoward happens in the night, you shout. In the meantime have security been alerted?"

"Yes, Doctor Smith contacted them."

"There is one redeeming factor and that is we don't dock anywhere tomorrow, so the perpetrator cannot get off the ship and escape. In the meantime, I'm going to take security to Brent's crew's quarters to see if he's there and to question him."

"Rob would you mind very much if you just told my Mum and the others why we haven't gone back to them?"

"Sure thing, Mike. Don't worry about a thing."

Rob left them in their cabin and went in search of Brent.

Chapter 18

"Mr. Clayton, I'm afraid he's not in his cabin. We know that he wasn't on duty tonight so he should either be in his cabin or in the crew's lounge, but he's in neither," said the head of security, who at this stage of the cruise was not Rob's most favorite person, having ignored Rob's earlier warnings about Gary.

"If he's not there in his quarters, do you think that he's fraternizing with the passengers?"

"That I can't say."

"Is he due to report for duty in the morning?"

"According to the roster, yes. He should be in the kitchen by 05:30 and finish his shift at 13:30. He won't be needed again until we dock in the Bahamas."

"So that means he'd be free tomorrow afternoon while the bodybuilding contest was taking place? My concern is that unless we find him, he poses a threat not only to the passengers, but to your ship and her reputation."

"Mr. Clayton, we'll do everything in our power to locate him."

"I sincerely hope so. I'm sure that you don't want another attempted murder charge linked to the *Caribbean Queen* and her crew, do you?"

"No sir. Leave it to us."

There was nothing more Rob could do, so he went and found the others in the disco, Myra included, and told then what had happened. Myra immediately left for Michael and Selwyn's cabin.

When she arrived there, she knocked quietly on the cabin door.

"Who's there?" asked Michael.

"Michael, darling, it's Mum."

He opened the door and Myra came in. Selwyn was asleep in his bed, blood soaked bandage around his head. Michael sat in one of the cabin easy chairs.

"How is he, love?"

"He'll be OK Mum, but will probably have a heavy head in the morning. The doctor said he didn't need stitches, but I think it's more the shock than anything else. If Rob and I hadn't gone when we did, he could have been dead by now."

"Do you know who did it?"

"Rob's with security now. He thinks it's the guy that worked with Selwyn in Derek's store," replied Michael.

"Oh dear. I know this is going to upset Derek. First Chris and now Selwyn."

"Mum, don't say anything to him in case it does upset him. Obviously he's bound to hear eventually, but if we can catch the guy first, before Derek gets to hear of the attack, he might not feel so bad."

"Perhaps you're right, my boy; but look after Selwyn, and if you need anything, call my cabin."

"Thanks Mum. You get yourself off to bed and I'll see you later."

Myra left and Michael switched off the main light in the cabin, leaving only a side lamp burning while he sat in the easy chair to watch over Selwyn.

In the early hours of the morning, both Josh and Rob returned to their cabin and quietly opened the connecting door to Michael's cabin. Selwyn was asleep in bed while Michael was also asleep, curled up in the easy chair. Rob tiptoed to the side of the bed and switched off the bedside lamp, then tiptoed out, closing the inter-leading door behind him.

Michael woke up with the sun streaming through the balcony sliding doors. He stretched and yawned, then saw that Selwyn was also in the process of waking up. He rose, crossed to the bed and leaning over Selwyn, kissed him gently on the lips.

"Hi, there, beautiful. How are you feeling?"

"Not to bad for an old drag queen."

"Hey, don't put yourself down; drag queen you might be, but old you're not. Can I get you anything?"

"Some water would be nice, thanks."

"How's the head feel?"

"Tender, but surprisingly I don't have a headache as I thought I would. Any news about my attacker?"

"I don't really know. I fell asleep in the chair last night. Hey, I left the side light on last night, but it's not on now. Did you wake in the night and put it off?"

"No, love. I was lights out, if you'll excuse the pun."

"Then someone was in the cabin. I wonder if it was Rob or Josh."

"Don't wake them now, but when they get up we can ask them. Are you going up to the pool deck for breakfast?"

"Maybe we should order room service seeing that you're not one hundred percent fit."

"Hey! I'm a tough cookie. Just let me have a shower and try to make myself presentable and we can both go up for breakfast."

"Are you sure you want to, because I'm happy to stay here with you."

"Do you think I want to miss all those hunky men at the competition this afternoon? Never! I'm getting up, injuries or not."

Selwyn tried to get out of bed and immediately felt dizzy. He sat for a moment and then stood with the help of Michael.

"Do you want to sit out on the balcony and get some fresh air?"

"Sure that might be nice," replied Selwyn, moving gradually to the balcony and sitting down, in his briefs.

Both young men sat out in the sea air, enjoying the sun's rays on their bodies and the gentle sea breeze as the ship sailed majestically towards the Bahamas.

"Anyone here?" called Rob, entering through the connecting door.

"Out here, Rob," replied Michael.

Rob and Josh went out onto the balcony.

"How's the patient today?" enquired Josh. "You actually don't look too bad. I expected to see you with half your head missing!"

"I feel as though half of it is missing, but as I said to Michael, I'm a tough cookie. P.I. assistants can't just lie down and die."

"That's what I like to hear," said Rob, giving him a pat on the back.

"Are you guys staying here today?" asked Josh.

"Josh, are you taking part in the competition this afternoon?" asked Selwyn.

"I've been persuaded by the man in my life, so yes."

"Good, then I'm getting up. This I can't miss. You supported me in the talent contest, so I'll support you in the *Mr. Caribbean Queen* contest."

"Thanks Selwyn, I appreciate that, and I take it you'll also be there Michael?"

"What a stupid question. We'll all be rooting for you, and if Chad's also entering, we'll root for both of you."

"Breakfast!" said Rob, firmly. "I'm hungry."

"Come on," said Selwyn getting up and going back into the cabin. "Let me just throw some shorts on this tired body and we can all go together.

They waited while Selwyn dressed, and then all four set off for the pool deck and breakfast.

Slowly, bodies began to appear on the pool deck vying for places to eat their breakfasts in the glorious sunshine. A couple of guys decided to take an early morning swim before having their breakfast, while others had been to the gym or done a couple of laps around the ship's jogging track. The pool deck was fast becoming a color palette of tanned bodies, red, blue, yellow, white and black Speedos, bright shirts and vests adding to the already open colorful umbrellas. People were fast booking places around the pool for once they had finished breakfast, they intended to tan and swim.

After breakfast, the four boys found themselves some sun loungers that were vacant, placed their towels on them and then settled down to take up as much sun as possible. Selwyn asked for an umbrella to shade his head from the sun, so Michael found one for him.

"Josh, do you have any idea who else might be entering this competition this afternoon?" asked Michael.

"Haven't a clue, but I'm just going to enjoy myself," he replied.

"Oh here comes Chad, maybe he knows," said Rob, eyeing the young man striding towards them.

"Hi guys, have you eaten?"

"Yes, we had breakfast up here by the pool," answered Selwyn.

"How are you feeling?"

"Fine thanks, Chad. No hangover head, thank goodness."

"Hey Chad, are you entering this afternoon?" asked Josh.

"Sure, are you?"

Josh nodded.

"Great, we can beat the pants off the others, between us," he laughed.

"You might, but I have my doubts about me," continued Josh, rubbing tanning oil onto his legs and stomach.

"Do you know what we have to do?"

"Apparently we have to strut our stuff in shorts and a T-shirt or vest, then it's bathing costumes. Oh, and they're going to ask us questions, so I heard."

"That doesn't seem too complicated," replied Chad.

While they were lying in the sun, absorbing the rays, one of the deck stewards brought Chad a drink. He looked bewildered at the steward and said that he hadn't ordered one.

"No sir, this is with the compliments of that gentleman over there," said the steward turning and pointing in the direction of the said gentleman.

Chad and the others in the group turned to see who the man was. Seated on a lounger on the other side of the pool was a tall, dark-haired man of about late twenties. He had a pleasant enough face and body along with an engaging smile.

"Not bad," muttered Rob, "but not my taste."

"Mine neither," echoed Josh.

Chad smiled and nodded his head to the young man as a sign of thanking him for the drink.

"Do you know him, Chad?" asked Michael, pulling down his sunglasses to peer over the top of them.

"Never seen him in my life," answered Chad.

"Well, it looks like you have another fan, an admirer," said Rob, still trying to work out who this man could be. "I don't think I've seen him before, but there are so many people on this ship, it's easy to miss one or two."

Chad continued to drink his beer that was brought to him, but caught the eye of the deck steward who brought it and called him.

"Tell me, do you know who that gentleman is?" asked Chad when the steward was near.

"Sorry sir, I can't say."

"Oh well thanks, anyway."

Occasionally, when Chad glanced in the direction of the young man, he noticed that he was being observed.

"He keeps looking this way," muttered Chad only loud enough for those close to him to hear. "Do you think I should go over and talk to him?"

"It's your choice, Chad, but I wouldn't, only because he's not my type, but also, you owe him nothing. You didn't ask him to buy you a drink."

"He might think I'm ill-mannered by not going and thanking him for the beer."

"Chad, you nodded and smiled. What more do you want to say to him, unless of course you're interested in him?"

Chad blushed at Rob's comment. He had spent almost a week of sexual abstinence without his partner and nothing had developed between himself and Rob or Josh, so to have a strange man buying him drinks and observing him so closely, this could be the moment he'd been waiting for on the ship.

"Maybe he fancies me," commented Chad, with a slight laugh coming from him.

"He obviously does," said Rob, also laughing.

"Well, you know I've been a good guy since I came on board, so maybe I must take my chances and go for the guy."

Rob immediately looked hurt and he and Josh glanced anxiously at each other. They had done nothing to invite Chad to their cabin and now some other man was trying to move in on the guy they both fancied.

Michael anticipated Rob's thoughts, and said, "I don't think you're that desperate Chad, and in any case, I think you're worthy of someone better. I obviously don't know the guy, but on looks, I would look elsewhere. Hey, buddy, if you really are desperate I'm sure that we can accommodate you, won't we Selwyn."

Selwyn giggled and became suddenly camp. "I'd love to please you; with that body of yours, I could play music on those abs just so long as you don't hit or touch my head, and I mean this one," he said, tapping his bandaged head.

"Selwyn, with an offer like that, I couldn't refuse," chuckled Chad, and with that a smile appeared on Rob's face.

Chad never received any more drinks from his admirer, but the young man didn't stop observing Chad, and when Chad did dive into the pool and then exited, the young man watched closely how Chad's wet Speedo clung to his torso, revealing the outline of his well-hung appendage.

The rest of the morning was taken up with swimming, sun tanning and having the odd few drinks followed by a light lunch of salads. Myra hadn't been seen all morning. Maybe, thought Michael, she was wheeling and dealing in order to be a judge of the *Mr. Caribbean Queen* competition. At 13:00, Myra appeared in a very summery outfit.

"Hi Mum. Where have you been? We haven't seen you all morning."

"No darling, I've been talking to the captain."

"About what, Mum, are you trying to get a date with him?"

"I've already told you he's too old for me. No, I was talking to him about the attack on Selwyn. He even offered to upgrade you boys and move you to a bigger suite, but I said I didn't think you'd want it."

A chorus blasted Myra. "How could you do that?" "Why didn't you ask them first before you made a decision?" "How can you think for us, Mum?" Questions were coming from every side and angle and poor Myra, only smiled as the verbal attack continued.

"I'm only teasing you," said Myra having managed to quieten down the boys to some extent. "I wasn't lying about talking to the captain, but I've got some other information for you. Your attacker has been apprehended."

Another avalanche of questions bombarded Myra. "Where? When? Who is he? Why didn't they tell us?" And so on.

"Boys listen. He was found at about 9:00 this morning, hiding in one of the lifeboats. We can only assume that he was hoping to stay hidden until we reached the Bahamas and then duck off the ship and escape. The captain phoned me in my cabin and told me. He said he'd tried Rob's cabin but there was no reply."

"But why would he phone you?" asked Michael.

"Darling, you forget I judged the talent contest with him and we got along very nicely thank you."

"Excuse me," said Michael a little facetiously. "So there might be something between you, even if he is too old for you, Mum."

"Where have they taken him, Myra?"

"He's apparently locked up somewhere near the captain's quarters."

"Michael, are you coming with me. I want to go and see him," said Rob getting up from his lounger and pulling on his shorts and shirt.

Michael did likewise and was about to head off to find the captain, when Selwyn said, "Do you think I should come along as well?"

"Why not," replied Rob. "You guys stay here and we'll be back in no time."

The three men hurried off to find the captain and on doing so, he explained how they had found the culprit. One of the crew had heard a sound come from the lifeboat; a sound of someone snoring. He had peered in and seen someone lying there sleeping, so he called security that came and arrested the person.

Captain Montgomery took the three young men to the cabin in which the attacker was situated. On entering, all three stared at the lone figure.

"Why Brent?" asked Selwyn.

Brent looked up, tired and haggard, and then he lowered his head.

"Brent, Selwyn never did anything to you. Neither did Chris, so why did you attack both of them?" enquired Rob.

Brent stared once more at the three, along with the captain, but said nothing.

"We've tried to get him to speak, Mr. Clayton, but he refuses."

"Captain, if I may have your permission to question him, I think I'll get him to talk."

Captain Montgomery looked at the giant of a man, his broad shoulders almost the size of two men standing side by side, and then said that Rob could ask Brent some questions.

Rob moved closer to Brent; threateningly close and towered over the man. Brent cowered and hung his head. Rob went up close to Brent's ear and whispered into it. The others couldn't make out what Rob was saying, but they could see terror etched across Brent's face.

"Brent," said Rob in a quiet, calm voice, "I have only one question to ask you: why did you attack Selwyn and instigate the attack on Chris?"

Brent looked intimidated by the large man at first, and then he opened his mouth and very quietly began to speak.

"It was because of Bobby."

"Did he put you up to it?"

"In a way, yes, but also in a way, no."

"Well, is it yes or no?"

"No."

"Then why?"

Brent hesitated and then when Rob glared at him, he began to explain.

"I was angry that Chris and Selwyn had been responsible for Bobby going to jail and I wanted revenge."

"But Brent, they weren't responsible for Bobby going to jail. Bobby was responsible for it himself. He was the one who stole. He was the one who was being fraudulent, not Chris and Selwyn."

"But it was because he was in jail that angered me."

"Why would that anger you to want to attack two harmless people?"

Again Brent hesitated, and again Rob's cold stare got him talking again.

"Bobby and I were close..."

"Obviously you were. You were probably also stealing from the store."

"No, I never stole. He was ..."

"Yes?"

Brent's head sunk down onto this chest.

"My lover."

"I beg your pardon?"

"Bobby and I were lovers."

"But Selwyn, you said he had a girlfriend, didn't you?"

"That's what I thought," replied Selwyn.

"That was his sister," said Brent, almost inaudibly.

"So you and he were lovers and you wanted to protect him or avenge his being incarcerated?"

Brent nodded his head.

"Captain that's all I wanted to hear. I'm not interested in how he got to hide in a lifeboat, or when he did it. Now it all makes sense, but will you have him formally arrested once we reach the Bahamas?" asked Rob.

"Yes Mr. Clayton, but in the meantime, he'll be kept under lock and key."

"Captain, thank you for your help in this matter," said Selwyn, shaking the captain's hand.

"Princess Selena, it was my pleasure and I'm glad that we could put to rest this awful incident for you. The least I can do is offer you an upgrade to one of our suites for the pain and inconvenience you've endured on our ship."

"Thank you captain, but I couldn't. You see if I didn't have my friends around me, I might have been killed by this man, so if I move to a suite, I'll be away from my friends and that wouldn't do."

"I fully understand and respect your decision. Maybe next time you sail with us you might take up my offer."

The three once again thanked Captain Montgomery and left his quarters.

"Damn it!" exploded Rob, "I thought he was going to say we could all have an upgrade to a suite."

"Rob, I prefer having you right next door, even with a connecting door," said Selwyn, and I wouldn't have been happy if we were not together. It's better this way, but I'm totally shocked at Brent's revelation. At no time did I ever think that Bobby was gay least of all that he and Brent were in a relationship."

"I think it's come as a shock to all of us, Selwyn," said Michael, "but it's over now. Now we can really relax and enjoy the last two days, what's left of them."

The three made their way back to the pool, excited to tell the others of what had happened, but on the way, Michael had one pertinent question to ask Rob.

"Rob, what did you whisper in his ear for him to appear fearful of you?"

A broad grin emerged across Rob's face.

"I told him I'd fuck him if he didn't speak and added that I wasn't small!"

Both Selwyn and Michael roared with laughter when they heard what Rob had said.

Back at the pool, everyone was so excited at the criminal being apprehended, but Selwyn had thought of Chris.

"Do you think that Chris and Derek know, Rob?"

"I don't know, but I'll go down and tell them. I'm sure that Derek will be more than pleased to hear the good news."

Sitting together out on their cabin balcony, Chris and Derek were more than pleased when Rob broke the news of Brent's arrest to them.

"You know if I'd known about their relationship, I might have done something differently to help them, especially if they were almost down and out financially," said Derek.

"Derek, I don't think helping them would have made any difference. I see them as being greedy; desiring everything they saw whether they could afford it or not. I really don't think helping them would have stopped them from stealing or being fraudulent," replied Rob, shaking his head in disagreement.

"How's Selwyn?" asked Chris.

"He's much better thanks Chris. In fact he's up by the pool waiting for the hunks to appear. Why don't you come up there with us? I think he'd like your company."

"Shall we go and watch the competition?" Chris asked Derek.

"What time is it being held, Rob?"

"I'm not sure but I think it's about 13:30 or thereabouts."

"Good idea, Chris, let's get out of this cabin and enjoy ourselves now that our nemesis has been caught." So Chris, Derek and Rob returned to the pool deck to await the afternoon's competition.

Chapter 19

"Ladies and gentlemen, could I have your attention please," came the voice over the microphone at the pool area. "There have been some rumors floating around regarding how today's competition is going to be judged. The contestants will be required to appear in casual beach wear, followed by bathing costumes and during this second leg of the competition, questions will be asked of the contestants. It is important to note that this is not, and I repeat, not, a bodybuilding competition. Now will all the budding entrants please come over to the Jacuzzi to give their details to our organizer."

A flurry of men surged forward to give their names.

"Some of those must really be joking if they're going to enter," remarked Michael, watching with interest this sudden surge.

There were men of all shapes, sizes and colors; young one and older ones; tall ones and short ones; some without a hope in hell of winning and others who could quite easily walk off with a Mr. Universe title should this be a bodybuilding competition. Both Chad and Josh went over to enter.

"What about you Rob?" asked Michael.

Rob laughed. "You're joking of course, what with all that competition over there, I wouldn't stand a chance."

"Give it a go," pleaded Selwyn.

Rob merely shook his head and replied, "I'll leave it to the youngsters."

Once their names were taken, if they didn't have beach wear with them, they could quickly get some.

The judges were introduced to the fans, waiting patiently for the fun to begin.

"Ladies and gentlemen, it is with much pleasure that we have with us today as our judges, Captain Montgomery, his son, Jonathan and as usual, our handy and handsome doctor, Doctor Smith."

"That's the guy who was eyeing out Chad," remarked Rob, pointing out the captain's son, Jonathan.

Even Chad looked a little bewildered and wondered what his chances were now going to be like, having not gone over to the young man and personally thank him for the drink. Well, it was too late to do anything about it now.

Twenty-six young men lined up one behind the other, wearing various forms of beachwear, and on the signal, paraded around the outer edge of the swimming pool so that all could see. As they walked around, the inevitable snide remarks were passed to those who really didn't look like winning, while words of encouragement went out to those with incredibly good physiques. Both Chad and Josh were among those who received compliments as they passed around the pool.

The majority had chosen to wear shorts and vests not only to show off their bodies, but also because it was extremely hot. Once they had done their round in their beachwear, they then paraded in their bathing costumes. This time the comments were even more of a personal nature. There was much whistling at sights that left most of the crowd breathless and boos to those who should have stayed in their cabins.

Myra was almost drooling at some of these young men.

"They never made men like this in my day," she recollected, "and it seems as though all the best looking ones are gay. That's actually a travesty."

"Not for us, Mum."

"I'm sure if I were twenty years younger, I could have converted many of these young things to becoming straight," continued Myra, still not accepting the amount of beauty around her.

Once the men had paraded around the pool, they were going to be called up one at a time to be questioned by the judges and that would be a chance to see each one individually.

As each contestant went before the judges, the audience responded either approvingly or otherwise. The crowd dealt the first contestant a heavy blow. He got booed and jeered. In fact Michael and Selwyn both said that they had felt sorry for him. He was a skinny, short man who had no physique to speak of, but had entered for the fun.

"If you became *Mr. Caribbean Queen* what contribution could you bring to gay communities around the world?" asked Captain Montgomery.

The poor man hesitated for some time while he pondered the question, and then said, "Could you repeat the question please."

There was an instantaneous booing to such an extent that Captain Montgomery was unable to repeat it, so the man was ushered away from the judging area. And so it went on.

The Mr. Universe look-alike from the team competition that took place on the poles over the pool came before the judges. Jonathan Montgomery posed the question, smiling sweetly at the hunk.

"Number eighteen, can you tell me what your views are on monogamous relationships among gays?"

Mr. Universe returned the smile with an equally broad smile, which obviously pleased Jonathan.

"I think that with the advent of HIV/Aids, we have to be ultra careful and having one person in your life is the ideal."

"Do you by any chance have one person in your life?" asked Jonathan.

"No!" came a chorus from his friends.

"Oh well, there's a hypocrite for you," commented Michael. "Because of that I wouldn't vote for him."

Josh appeared before the judges wearing a skimpy white Speedo. Josh was clever in choosing white, because it was a color that revealed and enhanced his package.

The doctor posed Josh's question.

"Can you tell me what would be your reaction if you found out that your partner was having an affair with someone else?"

"I'd tell him to share," replied Josh, much to everyone's delight.

"And if he refused to share, what then?"

"I'd ration him to two nights a week with his affair and the other four would have to be with me."

"What about the one extra day?"

"That would be for him to recover!"

Everyone enjoyed Josh's sense of humor. It just made a difference from the mundane, often hypocritical answers that most of the men gave.

Then it was Chad's turn to be interrogated. Standing tall and strong, muscles glistening in the sun, having been oiled with sun tanning oil before starting the parade, and with his over-sized package bulging heftily in his skimpy Speedo, he awaited his question.

The question came from Jonathan Montgomery, the man who'd bought Chad a drink.

"What would you do if a strange man bought you a drink?"

Chad smiled, knowing to what the young man was alluding.

"I'd smile and thank him," replied Chad.

"But if the stranger had ulterior motives?"

"He didn't say he had those when he bought the drink."

Jonathan smiled and stared at Chad.

"If you knew that his motive was to get you into bed with him, what would you do then?"

Again Chad smiled, keeping his cool.

"It would depend on what the other person was like. I wouldn't just jump into bed with a guy because he bought me a drink. Intimate sex is something special, and a drink is not."

The smile disappeared from Jonathan's face, but Chad kept smiling.

"Of course, if I could get to know the person a little better, perhaps we could make a plan."

The smile reappeared on Jonathan's face.

Chad was allowed to step down and another contestant took his place. After all the questioning, the judges huddled together to debate their choices. Again, as there were prizes at stake, they had to limit their choices, but the judges had a problem; there were four people whom they liked and only three prizes were being made available. Eventually, the captain stood up to speak.

"Ladies and gentlemen, we've seen a broad spectrum of healthy, virile young men today, men I can say I'm proud to have aboard my ship. It's not often we have the opportunity to accommodate so many men at one time, but I must say that it's been a pleasure having you."

"You haven't had me yet, Captain," shouted a voice from the crowd.

Everyone roared with laughter, including the captain.

"As I was saying, although this cruise is not yet over, I want to thank you all for your considered behavior aboard my ship. Although we have had some drama aboard, I'd also like to thank the involvement of certain people who have assisted us in apprehending certain disreputable persons, and on behalf of the crew, I would like to apologize to those men who suffered as a result of those people's behavior. You know who you are and I salute you. To all of you I say congratulations for a wonderful cruise, and I want it known that at no time have I, or will I, see the people aboard this ship as gays and straights as is so often the case. You are people; people who have loves and likes, people who are happy and sad, people who show concern for your fellow man and for that I praise you. Now, enough of that and let's get to the prize giving. Unfortunately, or fortunately, whichever way you wish to see it, we have four contestants vying for three places, so we have decided to give two third places. Tied for third place and each getting vouchers to the value of $250, are number five and number twenty-four."

The two young men went up to collect their prizes amidst cheers and whistles of agreement with the judges' choices.

"In second place is number twenty. Please come forward and receive your prize of $500."

Josh bounced forward, thrilled to have won a prize. As he shook hands with the captain, he couldn't resist but give the captain a kiss on the cheek. Immediately the captain blushed and went scarlet, much to the delight of everyone on the deck. Josh took his place next to the third placed guys and waited for the winner to be announced.

"After much deliberation between the judges, it was decided that number twenty-one is our winner because of his charm and physique. Please come up number twenty-one and get your prize of $1000."

Chad moved as though in a trance of disbelief towards the captain. He was pleased that he had won, but he wondered if Jonathan had anything to do with it in an effort to win Chad's affections. Chad shook hands with the captain and asked, "Would you also like a kiss from the winner?"

Captain Montgomery replied, "That's entirely at your discretion," so Chad leant forward and did as Josh had done. Once more the captain blushed, but everyone was beginning to think that perhaps he was enjoying this manly attention he was getting.

Chad was definitely a very popular winner and all, possibly with the exception of Mr. Universe look-alike, cheered, whistled and congratulated him. A sash with *Mr. Caribbean Queen* written on it was placed across his chest. People were patting his back as they congratulated him, and even a few patted his firm ass, much to Chad's delight. Jonathan came up to him after the prize giving as groups were dispersing.

"Congratulations. I think you answered your questions well, and we'll have to see what sort of a champion you are."

Chad thanked him for the wishes and then added, "And thank you for the drink. I really appreciated it."

Throughout their short conversation, Chad noticed how Jonathan eyed his body, searching from top to toe and hesitating somewhere in the region of Chad's midriff and slightly south to his engorged cock, but Chad never reacted.

Rob and Josh, together with the others, huddled around Chad to congratulate him, and in the process it appeared that Jonathan was slightly sidelined. There was much backslapping and the odd ass-slapping as well, but nothing that Chad took offence to. Jonathan eventually moved away and was last seen chatting to the Mr. Universe look-alike, perhaps with the intention of whipping him off to bed.

The gang went back to their loungers to continue sun tanning and swimming. Chad was still being inundated with compliments and good wishes. Men who had never spoken to him before were coming up to him to make contact, and perhaps there might even have been a few invitations to spend time with other people, but Chad wasn't saying.

Both Rob and Josh noticed the attention which Chad was receiving and maybe felt a little envious, but they were not about to show their envy.

"Do you think we still stand a chance?" asked Rob.

"You mean our possible three-some with Chad?" enquired Josh.

"It looks like we might be getting lower and lower down the chain with all these guys making advances to him."

"I wouldn't worry, Rob. We can always go and knock on his cabin door if we feel like it."

"We actually don't know what cabin he's in," replied Rob, sounding a little despondent.

Josh smiled broadly. "Never fear when Josh is near!"

"What do you mean?"

"I know what his cabin number is."

"How did you find out?"

"Don't worry how I have it, just say thank you, if you want to have a scene with him."

"Have you been to his cabin?"

"Nope!"

"Then how did you get it?"

"He gave it to me."

"When?"

"Do you remember when we first met up with him? When we parted company on the ship, he wrote it on a slip of paper and gave it to me. It's cabin 6275."

"And you never said anything?"

"Better still, Rob, I didn't do anything."

"What are you two so deeply in conversation about?" questioned Michael.

"Just discussing Chad," replied Rob, looking at his subject and admiring his well-toned torso. "We were just wondering if Chad was going to have a very busy last few nights aboard the ship, with all these men now wanting him."

"You're right. We'll probably not see him again until we disembark," answered Michael, "but good luck to him. Maybe he'll meet someone he likes and they can get together, then Myra would get excited because she'd be able to set up a wedding for them."

"Do you think Myra's enjoyed her cruise, Mike?"

"I think so Rob. In fact if you think about it, we've seen very little of her because she's been too busy chatting up the guys on board to really worry about us. But I'm glad that she came. I thought it was going to be one of those cruises where you're crammed together and under each other's feet, but this has been fun."

"At least you get the chance to get off the ship and explore other places," commented Josh.

"And meet interesting new people," added Rob.

"Like whom?" asked Josh.

"Well, no one person in particular, but you know what I mean."

"I'm beginning to wonder if he hasn't found himself a side-kick that he's taking home with him," joked Josh to Michael.

"The only things that I'm taking back home with me are my suitcase and you Josh."

"Well I'm very happy to hear that. With all this hunky meat around, it could be quite easy to find a leg or a rump that's better than mine," said Josh.

"There's absolutely nothing wrong with either your legs or your rump," replied Rob, giving Josh's ass, which was handily within reach, a light slap. "In fact, I think it's time that they got some exercise."

"You mean going to the gym," quipped Josh.

Rob glanced back at Josh and replied, "No I mean going back to the cabin!"

"Are you serious?" questioned Josh.

Rob got up, picked up his towel and turning to Josh, said, "Follow me and see."

Rob started walking away when Josh realized that Rob was serious about his intentions.

"Looks like it's your lucky day, Josh," said Michael with a twinkle in his eye.

Josh also got up and took his towel and headed off with Rob.

"Hey! Where are you two off to?" shouted a voice.

Rob and Josh stopped and turned. Chad came running up to them.

"Are you guys going?"

Rob and Josh glanced at each other.

"We're going back to our cabin… if you'd like to come with us?"

"Now?"

"Yes," continued Rob. "We thought with all this hot sun and oil, we needed to get rid of some of our pent up hormonal pressures."

"Were you serious about me going with you?" enquired Chad.

"Absolutely," replied Josh, "if you're interested."

Chad smiled and nodded. The three men turned and headed in the direction of the cabins and were soon ensconced in Rob and Josh's cabin, three naked, muscular bodies entwined as they sought to bring pleasure to each other.

Both Chad and Josh knelt on either side of Rob's prone body as he lay naked on the bed and their tongues licked up and down the length of Rob's throbbing cock; then while Chad attacked Rob's balls, sucking each into his warm mouth, Josh continued to lubricate Rob's thick shaft. Both young men were eager to please Rob and he in return couldn't wait to slip into both young men's tight asses.

Rob maneuvered Chad on the bed so that his new young friend was lying flat on his back while Rob raised Chad's legs over the older man's broad shoulders. As Rob aimed his thick, long cock at the pulsating entry to Chad's ass, Josh engulfed Chad's stiff cock in his mouth. Slowly Rob penetrated the warm chute, feeling a tightness wrap around his shaft.

"Aargh fuck!" groaned Rob as he sank further into Chad's depths, a warm sensation engulfing him.

He went deeper an deeper until his pelvis brushed up against Chad's ass, then he held his position allowing Chad to enjoy the feeling of having a thick, long, hard cock embedded in him. After a moment of both men enjoying the feeling, Rob began to slide his cock in and out of Chad's opening, while Josh continued to suck on Chad's cock which was leaking small quantities of pre-cum.

For about five minutes they continued like this, and then Rob pulled slowly out of Chad's tight ass and told Josh to move in. Josh positioned himself between Chad's muscular legs and, holding the stem of his massive cock, he slid effortlessly into the already loosened up ass. Chad sighed as Josh sank into him and then felt the gentle thrusts that Josh began giving. Rob watched fascinated as Josh drove his long cock deep into Chad and how the two young men seemed to be enjoying each other's love making. Josh leaned forward as he drove into Chad and kissed him firmly on the lips, allowing his tongue to search in Chad's mouth. Rob was tempted to join in, but chose to watch like a voyeur instead.

After watch his two young friends for a while, he lay on the bed next to

Chad.

"Josh, sit on my cock," said Rob, holding his long shaft in his hand to guide it into Josh's tight ass.

Josh pulled out of Chad, slipped a condom onto Rob's throbbing cock and slowly slid down his full length. Once Josh's ass touched Rob's balls, he began to ride his lover's hard cock. It was now Chad's turn to watch, but not for long.

"Chad, slip a condom on and slide in next to me."

"Huh?" questioned Chad.

"I want you to fuck Josh with me," continued Rob, pulling Josh towards him so that Josh was now lying across Rob's chest.

Chad could see how Josh's ass had now opened up more, allowing him to enter alongside Rob's cock. This was an experience that Chad had never experienced before. Slowly Chad began to slide his cock along Rob's stem, entering Josh's ass.

Josh gasped as Chad's cock began to enter him as he felt his opening being expanded by the two thick cocks. Soon he relaxed as he felt both men inside of him, slowly sliding together, creating a sensation which was driving all three crazy with lust.

With two cocks plugged deeply in him, it didn't take long for Josh's climax to erupt, spurting warm cum over Rob's stomach and chest. Nor did it take long for both Rob and Chad to fire their loads into Josh, but when all three men had exhausted their juices, they collapsed on the bed together, breathing heavily.

Chapter 20

At eight in the evening, three sweaty bodies lay in Rob and Josh's cabin, their breathing having returned to a state of normality from their earlier state of heightened ecstasy. Rob lay proudly in the center of the bed with *Mr. Caribbean Queen* and the runner-up on either side of him, his arms around each one's shoulders. In his estimation, he had the two hunkiest guys on the ship to himself and he felt proud and satisfied; in fact all three were feeling satisfied.

"Are we going to have something to eat?" asked Rob, looking from one to the other.

"I thought, perhaps, you'd had enough to eat already," came the snide comment from Josh.

The three laughed and cuddled a little closer to one another. Chad's hand stretched across Rob and soon the three were getting themselves aroused once more.

"Enough!" exclaimed Rob, leaping form the bed and leaving the two young men lying there. "I'm exhausted. I think we need some sustenance and then perhaps we could carry on later, if you feel up to it."

Josh and Chad grinned at each other. Obviously they were up to it.

"Have a shower here with us," invited Josh, "Then you can go and get changed for dinner, if you like."

They squeezed into the shower cubicle, bodies rubbing up together as a result of cramped space, then dried themselves and Chad went back to his cabin to get changed and said that he'd return to Rob's cabin to meet up with them.

The whole gang met for dinner, which was quite a festive occasion, with wine flowing between the beers and Myra's whiskey. Everyone was lighthearted and jovial, especially Rob, Josh and Chad.

"You three look very happy tonight," whispered Michael to them as they were enjoying their dinner and drinks.

Both Chad and Josh blushed slightly, but Rob smiled triumphantly.

"Let's just say, we make a good trio," replied Rob, winking back at Michael.

During the course of the dinner, Myra clinked her wine glass with a fork and said, "I want to propose a toast."

She stood up at their table a said, "I want to thank Michael and Selwyn for allowing me to come on their honeymoon with them. It's very seldom that the mother or mother-in-law accompanies the newly weds on their honeymoon. I think the only reason I was allowed was because they're not newly weds, but thank you. To the rest of you boys, I thank you for your friendship and for making my trip such an exciting and eventful one. Chad to you, I think I can honestly say you have been accepted into the family as it were, along with Rob and Josh who have already had their baptism of fire from me, many years ago. My only role left is to find someone for Chad…"

"You don't have to worry about that Myra," replied Chad, cutting short her speech.

"Boys I toast you and thank you with all my love and heart. To you boys!" said Myra, raising her glass

"To us," replied the boys in unison.

The dining room was a hive of activity with much laughter and heated conversations.

"Do you realize we've only got tonight and tomorrow and then this will all be over," said Selwyn, mulling over his thoughts on the trip.

"I think we've got to do something like this again," suggested Michael, "even if it's not for a honeymoon."

Everyone concurred, and some even suggested that as soon as they got back home they should start planning for the next cruise. While they were debating their next holiday, Chris and Derek came to their table.

"Where have you two been all this time?" enquired Selwyn.

Chris's eyes sparkled with delight when he answered, "Looking at the ceiling!"

"What on earth would anyone want to look at a ceiling for?" enquired Myra.

All the boys who understood Chris's comment, burst out laughing at Myra's innocence.

"What's the joke?" Asked Myra

"Myra," said Rob, trying to prevent himself from laughing too much, "when you have sex you're usually lying looking up at the ceiling, aren't you?"

"Oh dear," gushed Myra, joining in the laughter. "You see, I don't think of things like that."

"You're forgiven Mum. Don't you guys want to pull up a couple of chairs and join us?"

Chris and Derek found some chairs and joined them. A waiter appeared but they said that they had already eaten in one of the other restaurants, but wouldn't mind a drink, so the waiter duly took their order.

"We were just saying what a wonderful time we've had on this cruise and how much we were looking forward to organizing another one for our next holiday," said Selwyn as the two injured men sat together.

"You won't believe what happened tonight," said Chris, excitedly.

"You had sex!" shouted all the others.

"No! Derek has agreed to come to the disco with me."

Everyone applauded Derek's brave move.

"I thought it was time that I loosened up a little and enjoyed myself," replied Derek. "Not only that, I also thought it was time that I took more of an interest in Chris's activities and interests and not just think of myself and my business."

Again, they all applauded.

As they were sitting enjoying themselves, Michael made an observation that others in the restaurant also made.

"Is it my imagination, but we're not moving?"

They all looked around them and others were looking out of windows and questioning as to why the ship had come to a halt. Some left their tables and peered through the large windows, into the night, while others left the restaurant and headed up to the decks.

"What do you think the problem is?" enquired Selwyn.

"I don't know, but to me we are definitely not moving," replied Michael.

"I don't think we need worry," said Rob, taking a large slurp of his beer, having disposed of his wine. "Let's rather enjoy our dinner and each other's company."

Some of those who had gone up on deck returned excitedly to tell their friends and others that someone had fallen overboard.

"Probably some drunk," suggested Chris, "or someone trying to be clever by climbing on the railings."

"Maybe they fell from their balcony," said Josh, offering an alternative view.

Once it became known that someone had fallen overboard, the engines had been cut and the large liner slowed and was turning to see if they could locate the person. The rescue was being made all the more difficult as it was night and therefore difficult to see in the dark. Lights were being shone over the side of the ship into the sea, but nothing could be seen. After an hour of searching, it was called off and the ship continued on its route to the Bahamas.

After dinner, the group went into one of the lounges to relax for a while before either attacking the dance floor or going gambling. As they sat discussing the incident, Captain Montgomery approached the group and took Rob and Derek aside.

"I'm sorry to have to inform you, but the incident that occurred some while back involved a man falling overboard. That man was Brent. He was being taken from the cabin in which he had been kept to another, when he broke loose. The security guards gave chase and caught up to him as he was climbing onto one of the railings, intending to jump ship. They saw him jump and from the lights of the ship, saw him swept towards the aft of the ship and the propeller area. It's our opinion that under these circumstances, his chances of survival would be minimal as he would most probably have been sucked under the water and into the propellers. We have turned around and searched the area, but there is no sign of him or any other evidence of his existence. I thought I'd better tell you gentlemen as it was he who caused all the trouble on your trip. I'm sorry that justice couldn't have taken its place in a court of law, but then perhaps justice has been carried out."

"Thank you for informing us Captain. I'll tell the others. Are you going to inform those on board?"

"Not with the details, Mr. Clayton. An unfortunate accident happened, but I don't think we need to put a damper on everyone's spirits at this stage, do you?"

"You're right Captain. But, once again thanks for telling us."

Captain Montgomery left the group and probably headed back to the bridge, while Rob informed those of the group who hadn't overheard the captain's story. Naturally, they were shocked by the news, but on the other hand, relieved that they could now endure the last few nights of the cruise in peace. Also, it would probably mean there wouldn't be a drawn out court case that they would have to attend.

Soon they all felt the shudder as the ship once again got underway and this was like a signal for the festivities and partying to start. All eight, which included Derek, headed up to the disco to go dancing. When they arrived there the place was packed to capacity. The music was pumping loudly and the perspiration was flowing freely from sweaty, hot bodies. It didn't take long for the likes of Michael and Selwyn, Rob and Josh, and Chad and Myra to take to the dance floor, but Derek was a little hesitant. He was not used to crowded places like the disco, so he and Chris were like wall flowers.

After a while, Chad and Myra came off the dance floor and Myra, being the outgoing type, whisked Derek onto the floor, while Chris and Chad joined them.

The whole night was spent swapping partners and thoroughly enjoying themselves. By midnight, all were amazed at how much Derek had come out of his shell and was enjoying himself.

"I should do this more often," he was heard to shout above the noise of the music.

"Does that mean we'll go out more often," shouted Chris back to his lover.

Derek grinned and nodded his head.

The night and the sea continued to roll by and soon tired bodies were wandering off to quieter areas, such as lounges, for a nightcap, and cabins.

"Guys, Michael and I are off to bed. We'll see you in the morning," said a very tired Selwyn.

They were soon followed by Chris and Derek along with Myra. Chad, Rob and Josh continued enjoying themselves. Shirts had been stripped off and the sweat glistened in the disco lighting over their buffed bodies. By 01:00 a.m., they decided that it was now time to turn in. They made their way to the elevators and when they got in, Rob turned to Chad and asked, "Are you coming back to our place?"

"If you'd like me to, that would be great."

"What a question," said Josh grinning with delight.

They made their way to Rob's cabin and fell into bed together where very little sleep was had by them.

Chapter 21

Friday morning. Another bright, sunny day aboard the *Caribbean Queen* and Michael and Selwyn were standing on the balcony to their cabin, watching the sea go by on their way to the Bahamas. Next door, bodies were awaking and greeting each other. Soon the neighbors were up and also on their balcony. Michael peered around the dividing wall to their balconies and spotted Josh and Rob standing together.

"Hi there! How are you two?"

"We're wonderful," said Josh stretching upwards, expanding his chest as he did so.

Michael observed the developed chest and admired it. "Did you two have a good night's sleep?"

Both chuckled and as they did so, a third body emerged from the interior of the cabin.

"Oh Hi, Chad," said Michael, on seeing him. "I take it that the reason you two are chuckling is that you obviously didn't have much sleep then?"

"You're right there," replied Rob, "In fact we might go so far as to say, we still haven't gone to sleep."

The three hunky guys stood together with Rob in the middle, also watching the calm sea glide by. Rob, Josh and Chad, seemed to be bonding more and more. It seemed that their friendship was developing more strongly and that there seemed to be an attachment between them, but what was going to happen when they got back to land, no-one knew, but while they were at sea, the three had decided to enjoy each other's company.

Selwyn peered around the dividing balcony wall and saw the three neighbors all standing in their briefs, which excited him.

"Hi Selwyn," said Josh. "How are things?"

Selwyn was tempted to say that his temperature was rising at the sight of three hunky men in their underwear, but instead he stammered that he was well. Embarrassed by his own predicament, Selwyn went back into his cabin.

"Michael, do you think that Rob and Josh are having an affair with Chad?"

"Who knows? But perhaps they are. Maybe they really like threesomes."

"In my mind, I'm trying to work out … well you know…?"

"What?"

"Who's doing what … you know…!"

"Selwyn, in all the years I've known you, I've never known you to be at a loss for words. Are you trying to ask me who is screwing whom?"

"Yes!" exclaimed a relieved Selwyn.

"I don't know and it's no business of ours. They're our friends and what they do is their business, and so long as they are happy, then I think we should respect their decisions."

"You're right, Michael, I'm sorry, It's just that I was wondering about Rob and Josh. Do you think that Chad pushed his way into their relationship?"

"I really don't know, and you know what, it doesn't matter. As I've said, if Rob and Josh are enjoying Chad's company, then good for them. They have to deal with the permutations, not us."

Selwyn sat puzzling in is mind how they were having sex together, and Michael could see this deep concentration taking place.

"Selwyn, I know what you're thinking, so if you really are desperate to know, then why don't you ask Rob when you get back to work."

Selwyn once again looked embarrassed as though he had been caught out doing something illegal.

"It's actually not so much who's doing what to whom, but how do they sustain their relationship?"

"To be perfectly honest with you, I think it would take enormous discipline and trust. I'm sure that there has to be other factors that perhaps we haven't even thought about. Perhaps to us it seems strange, but then think about it, there are groups of people in many places around the world where they have more than one wife, so it might be just the same in a gay relationship."

"Like where?" enquired Selwyn.

"Here in America we have people who are permitted to take more than one wife. How do they divide their love equally between their partners? I don't know, but obviously they do, somehow. I also know that there are tribes in Africa where the men are allowed more than one wife, and there's also the Middle East."

"Do you think you could have a three-way relationship?"

Michael thought about Selwyn's question.

"I don't really know." Then he smiled. "Having one of you is bad enough, can you imagine the trouble I would have if there were two of you?"

Selwyn grunted with disgust at the insult.

"Love, if I really think about it, I can only think that I would take on the extra person for sexual gratification, but I suppose I might grow to love the other person as much as my original partner. I've only known one other couple who took in a third person to join their relationship."

"And who was that?"

"I forget their names, but I do remember there was age differences, which might have made it easier, if that's at all possible."

"When you say age differences, what do you mean?"

"Well the original couple was forty-five and thirty, when they started their relationship, then they met a young guy in his early twenties who they both liked. He moved in with them and each had his own bedroom, so some nights 'A' would sleep with 'B' and then on others, 'B' would sleep with 'C'. Occasionally all three would shack up together and that's how they lived for as long as I knew about them, which was five years, then they moved off to another city."

"But, do you really think that constitutes a relationship?"

"Who am I to judge? I still say, that if Rob, Josh and Chad are happy the way they've set up their affair, if it's an affair, then good luck to them. The real issue is to see what they do on land; whether they're all going to move in together."

"You know, Michael, I don't know why we're going on about this because we've done it before. We've had a scene with another person but it never impacted on our relationship; it was pure lust and at the time we enjoyed it, so what's the big issue?"

"I don't know," laughed Michael, "but you were the one who brought it up originally."

Meanwhile, unbeknown to the two boys, through the connecting cabin door, Josh, Rob and Chad lay side by side on the bed discussing very much the same topic.

"I don't know about you two, but you've both made me a very happy man," said Rob taking a hand of each man on either side of him and giving them a squeeze.

"Where to we go from here?" asked Josh.

"I don't know," replied Rob, "but I would like this to go on. I like both of you guys very much and Chad, although Josh and I are together and very happy that way, I wouldn't like to lose you. If I had a wish, it would for the three of us to live together."

Josh and Chad eyed each other. Perhaps Josh might have felt a little insecure because he was already in a steady relationship with Rob, and now Rob wanted to bring in a third party. It seemed fine for the three of them to have sex together, but sharing a relationship was something that jarred in Josh's mind. Sure, he loved Rob and he found Chad incredibly sexy, but how would that impact on their lives?

Chad, on the other hand had recently come out of a broken relationship so might be seen as being on the rebound. He too found both men sexy and he liked being with them. He felt as though he might be very happy to spend his life with both of them; after all, both he and Josh had similar interests, one being an architect while the other was an interior designer, and he enjoyed Rob's company very much.

"What do you guys feel about us carrying this on when we get back home?"

asked Rob.

"I think we need to think hard about this, Rob. I really like both of you, but you don't think that three in a relationship is a crowd, and I don't mean to be offensive to either of you?"

"Maybe Josh's right, Rob. I don't think that this is something to rush into," replied Chad. "As much as I like the idea, I think we need to sit down and discuss this properly."

"Well isn't that what we're doing now?" queried Rob.

His two younger companions looked at each other. It would seem that Rob had a determined desire to have both young men with him, but they were not sure how it would work.

"What worries me," said Josh "is that this has been great. The time that we have spent together has been incredibly wonderful; that I cannot deny, but I'm worried about how this will continue on land. Here we're three horny guys who get off on each other because we've got nothing else to do. This is the sort of thing you do on holiday, but when we get home, it's down to mundane everyday functions, it's no longer holiday time, and I'm just not sure how we're going to survive with each other."

"Perhaps, Josh, you're seeing a relationship much as a heterosexual marriage where there are two distinct roles: that of a man and a woman. But, I don't see ours like that. When you are in bed with someone, you might take on a particular role, but I don't believe that that's your label for life. What I'm trying to say to you is that, although I might enjoy slipping into Chad, he might do likewise with you or vice versa. In other words, tonight you might be the dominant partner, but tomorrow you're not. I don't think we should compartmentalize our relationships. I just think that if our emotions and feelings are strong enough, we can handle any situation."

Both young men gave this a great deal of thought, then Chad spoke up.

"Rob, I appreciate your feelings, but I also appreciate Josh's. When you two came onto this ship you were in a relationship together and I was on my own. You befriended me and took me into your circle of friends, which I'm grateful for. For some reason you both found me attractive, and I must confess, my feeling towards you both was mutual. I couldn't have asked for two more hunky guys to enjoy myself with. I don't want to come between you two guys. I don't want it to appear as though choices have to be made like between Josh and me."

"I'm not making choices," replied Rob. "I want both of you."

"Rob, I think that when we get back home, to begin with at any rate, I should stay at my place and you two go back to your lives, but we can still meet and have fun together. I mean, it's not unusual for couples to get together with a third person for some fun, without there being an impasse situation being caused."

A slight smile filtered onto Josh's face. He was happy with the decision of Chad's, so much so that he rolled across the bed and Rob, and hugged Chad.

"I'd like that, Chad," said Josh, "but we stay the best of friends."

Rob seemed a little disappointed in the decision, but he respected it.

"OK," said the burly man, "but don't think either of you are getting away with this. When I want you both, I expect you to be there, understand!"

Josh and Chad glanced at each other and grinned.

"Yes, master!" they echoed together.

The stand-off had been broken and all three hugged and kissed until they found themselves in the same situation that they had been in all night long.

It was only at lunchtime that the three boys surfaced and left their cabin; all three glowing happily.

The long, low resonant drone of the ship's hooter sounded and passengers rushed to the railings to see Nassau and what it had in store for them. On the wharf-side, a band played merry music, while on board passengers were lining up to disembark and visit the island, the gang included.

"How long are we here for?" asked Selwyn.

"Not long, babes. I think we sail again at around 19:00, so we'd best make the most of our visit."

They all set off together, taking a horse-drawn carriage to visit old Nassau. They squeezed themselves into the carriage, happily laughing and shouting to passers-by as they wound their way through the streets, then they landed up at Fort Fincastle, where they enjoyed a fantastic view. After returning to the main commercial area, it was Selwyn and Myra's turn to delight in shopping. The others tagged along behind as Myra and Selwyn came into their own, much to the delight of all.

As it was a short stay in the Bahamas, and because it was to be their last night on board, added to which was the Captain's Farewell dinner, they decided to return to the ship early in order to get ready for the evening.

It was to be a formal occasion, so all were preening and sharpening up their appearances in readiness for meeting with the captain. They met for a pre-dinner drink first and then, en mass, the gang descended on the dining room. When they arrived, the captain and some of his senior members of staff were waiting at the entrance, where they were greeted and shook hands with Captain Montgomery.

"As this is such a formal occasion, Captain, I won't kiss you tonight," said Selwyn, smiling and glowing.

Captain Montgomery, laughingly said to Selwyn, "As you're not here as Princess Selena, we'll forgo the kiss."

As they were ushered in, it was to their surprise that they were taken to the captain's table.

"Are you sure we're at the right table?" asked Myra of a steward.

"Yes ma'am. You are all guests of the captain tonight."

And so Selwyn, Michael, Myra, Rob, Josh, Chad, Chris and Derek, found themselves the focus of attention, but it was only natural that Myra landed up seated next to the captain.

"Tough luck, Mum," said Michael, seeing where they were placed.

"Why, Michael?" replied his mother.

"Knowing how you don't like older men!"

"It's quite all right, my boy, because I have the hunkiest young men on this ship sitting with me."

The group applauded Myra's observation, and soon they were joined by Captain Montgomery, his son Jonathan and two of his senior staff.

Dinner was a treat; a gourmet's delight, and throughout, the wine flowed and so did the conversations. Jonathan kept an eye on Chad all night, and both Chad and Rob became aware of this, but as they were not seated next to each other, it became difficult to communicate to each other. Everyone was in a festive mood and with the addition of the alcohol, it wasn't long before the volume had increased and people were laughing out loud and cracking jokes; the formality of the occasion seemed to have faded.

Chad became uneasy with Jonathan's staring and smiling because he was aware that both Josh and Rob were watching and although he was being polite at the table, given the choice, he wouldn't want to spend his last night with Jonathan.

When it came time for coffee and biscuits at the end of the meal, people were drifting off to other venues so seats became vacant. As soon as Chad saw an opening at their table next to Josh, he moved.

"Josh, talk to me," said Chad in hushed tones. "I've been eyed all night and I'm not interested."

"Yes, Rob and I noticed. In fact I think had the captain not been here, Rob was ready to tell Jonathan to just where to go."

Just then Captain Montgomery came over to where Chad was sitting.

"Excuse me young man," he said, addressing Chad, "but my son wondered whether you'd consider going to the disco with him tonight after dinner?"

Chad looked shocked. This young man was getting his father to do his work for him. Of course he knew it would be rude of him to reject the captain's request and this made it even more repulsive, because Jonathan would have known that he couldn't refuse.

"Captain," said Josh, butting in, "Jonathan's welcome to join us because we're all going to the disco after dinner."

"That's wonderful. Thank you for the invitation. I'll tell him."

Captain Montgomery walked over to Jonathan and from his son's expression, it was clear that the young man was not a happy chappy.

"I owe you big time, Josh, thanks."

Rob moved over to where Josh and Chad were seated.

"What's going on?" he asked.

They told him of Jonathan's request and that he'd got daddy to do his bidding for him, which riled Rob, and made him even more protective of Chad.

"I don't care what either of you say, you're staying with us tonight Chad, and wherever you go, one of us will be right behind you."

With dinner over, they all made their way up to the disco, Jonathan included. Between Rob and Josh, they were going to try their hardest to prevent Jonathan from getting Chad, but they also knew that they couldn't prevent him all night, "in case he goes to daddy!" said Rob.

Myra, looking like elegance personified, had taken a liking to the Mr. Universe look-alike and was swiveling her hips in time to the music and making sure that he never left the dance floor. One never knows, but perhaps her motive was to tire him out so he'd collapse from exhaustion and she could get him back to her cabin!

At some stage during the evening, it had to happen; Jonathan managed to grab a dance with Chad. To watch him, was embarrassing to say the least. Jonathan's style of dancing, if it can be called that, was to rub himself up and down against Chad's body in a seductive way. Naturally, Chad tried his best to break free on every occasion, until Rob took matters into his own hands and cut in, saying he wanted the next dance.

At 02:00 in the morning, Myra was seen, arm in arm with Mr. Universe look-alike, heading off somewhere, followed soon afterwards by Selwyn and Michael.

"Guys, we're off to bed. We've had enough for tonight," said Michael, putting an arm around Selwyn's shoulders in a protective manner and escorting him back to their cabin.

Probably an hour later, Rob, Josh and Chad left for Rob's cabin, probably to stay awake until the ship docked, doing things that big boys do with each other!

As for Jonathan, he was last seen heading towards the rock climbing wall with Chris, where the door to the toilets behind the wall opened and the two disappeared inside.

Chapter 22

"All good things in life must come to an end," said Michael as he awoke to the sounds of Miami harbor's hustle and bustle. The *Caribbean Queen* had docked in Miami at 07:00 and he and Selwyn were busy packing their suitcases and preparing to disembark. Next door, they heard peels of laughter coming from Rob, Josh and Chad. The telephone in the cabin rang.

"Hello," said Selwyn, picking up the receiver.

"Hello darling. Are you and Michael up and packed yet?"

"Yes, Myra, are you?"

"Not quite. I thought I'd pack last night, but unfortunately I never got round to doing so, so I'm busy packing now."

"Did you enjoy yourself last night?" enquired Selwyn.

"Darling, I had the most wonderful time. Tony and I came back to my cabin after the disco."

"Who?"

"Tony. Sorry darling, Mr. Universe look-alike to you and Michael."

"Myra, you didn't!" exclaimed Selwyn.

"She didn't do what, Selwyn?" asked Michael, overhearing only half the conversation.

Selwyn placed his hand over the mouthpiece of the phone and turned, horrified to Michael.

"Your mother took Mr. Universe look-alike back to her cabin last night," whispered Selwyn.

"She did what? Give me that phone."

Michael snatched the phone from Selwyn and started speaking to his mother.

"Mum, what's this I hear about you and that hunk?"

"Don't worry your pretty little heart, I'm quite all right."

"Mum, I'm not concerned whether you're OK or not. That man's gay. You haven't been trying to convert him have you?"

"Of course not, darling. In actual fact, Tony, or your Mr. Universe, happens to be bi-sexual."

"Oh no!" sighed Michael. "Mum, you didn't!"

"I did and why not, son? If you can do it, then why can't I. Sex is not a restriction for the youth only, you know."

"Mum, we're going to go up to the departure deck when we're ready. We'll wait for you there."

"Fine. I'll see you both soon. Bye."

Michael replaced the handset and stared in disbelief.

"I don't believe it, Selwyn; my mother's just had sex with Mr. Universe."

Selwyn roared gleefully and applauded. "Good for the old girl. She's obviously still got it."

"Selwyn this is not funny," reprimanded Michael. "This is serious. I think it's disgusting that my mother is having sex with a younger man."

"Oh, hypocrite, and it's OK for you to have sex with a younger guy?"

"You're not younger than me."

"No, but you've been with other guys who were younger than you. So, sweetie, if it's good enough for you, then it's good enough for your mother, so don't say another word about it."

Michael was somewhat surprised at how Selwyn was defending his mother, but what his partner said was true, so Michael shut up and never said another word about his mother's night of passion.

Once their luggage was packed, it was placed outside their cabin, ready to be collected, and then they made their way to the departure deck. After hanging around there for at least half an hour, Rob, Josh and Chad arrived.

"We heard you guys laughing heartily this morning," said Selwyn.

"We sat up all night," replied Rob, "talking and laughing. I hope we didn't keep you guys awake."

"We were like babies – fast asleep," said Selwyn.

"We thought the noise coming from our cabin might wake you."

Michael grinned at Rob. "Were you at it again?"

"I have to make every opportunity count, Mike. When you've got two handsome men in your company, you can't say we'll wait for a rainy day."

"So what's going to happen with you guys?" asked Michael, taking Rob to one side.

"Mike, I'm nuts about the two of them, but Josh and I are going back to our place. We're definitely keeping in touch with Chad; in fact he's coming to stay with us this weekend. We're going to play it by ear, and if fate means that we should be together, then we might move in together."

"How does Josh feel about this?"

"He digs Chad. They actually get on very well together and if I'm out of town on a case, I know that the two of them will get together. At least I'll know that the two men that I really fancy are safe together while I'm away."

A beaming Myra soon arrived with Mr. Universe look-alike carrying one of her bags. Rob, Josh and Chad stared in disbelief, while Selwyn and Michael grinned, knowing the story behind Myra and her beau.

"What's going on here, Mike?" muttered Rob.

Michael wasn't about to discuss Myra's exploits, so he merely said, "I think she asked him to help her with her luggage."

They said their goodbyes to those remaining on board for yet another cruise; waved to friends they had made during their voyage and then walked from the ship back onto terra firma. Myra said a sad farewell to Captain Montgomery, who, she thought, wasn't as old as he might be.

Once they reached the wharf-side, they hailed a cab and set off back to Miami Airport where they were catching their flight back home.

Having obtained their boarding cards for the flight, they went and sat having a drink in the airport terminal. While they were sitting there, they noticed Jonathan approaching. He walked up to Chris, who was in deep conversation with Derek and Selwyn and said, "Could I have a word with you please, Chris?"

Derek and Selwyn both looked up on hearing the voice.

"Sure," replied Chris, rising and walking a little way away from the group. Jonathan handed Chris a piece of paper on which was written his telephone number.

"If you'd like to, give me a call Chris; I'd like to make contact with you again."

Jonathan turned and started to head away, when he turned to Chris and said, "Oh by the way, thank you for last night."

Chris blushed, Derek stared at Chris and Selwyn merely shut up and didn't say a word. He knew to what Jonathan was referring.

The flight to New York was called and they all went to board their plane. On the journey, Selwyn slept, resting his head on Michael's shoulder, probably dreaming of their Caribbean honeymoon, while Rob, Josh and Chad, sat in heated discussion about their plans for the coming weekend. Chris and Derek sat solemnly silent. As for Myra, she was in dreamland, probably with her Mr. Universe look-alike, maybe even dreaming of her gay match-making services she would open and offer, but irrespective of what their thoughts might be, they all seemed content and happy, in their own peculiar ways, and were probably all thinking about their next cruise together.

About the Author

Lew Bull, who lives in Johannesburg, South Africa, has been published in a number of anthologies including, among others, *Ultimate Gay Erotica 2007* and *2008, Treasure Trail, Fast Balls, Travelrotica and Travelrotica Vol. 2, Don't Ask, Don't Tie Me Up, Cruise Lines* and *My First Time Vol. 5*.

Although he is involved in education, and has a Doctorate in this field, it is writing and traveling that brings him most pleasure.

Lew Bull is also the author of ***Power Buddies, Wet, Wild and Willing,*** and ***The Bonds of Friendship***. Available at your local bookstore, Amazon.com or TheNazcaPlainsCorp.com.

www.ingramcontent.com/pod-product-compliance
Lightning Source LLC
Chambersburg PA
CBHW071213260626
47162CB00004B/1276